P9-CQW-426

PURE
DEAD
FROZEN

Debi Gliori

ALFRED A. KNOPF ✦ NEW YORK

THIS IS A BORZOI BOOK PUBLISHED BY ALFRED A. KNOPF

This is a work of fiction. Names, characters, places, and incidents either are the product of the author's imagination or are used fictitiously. Any resemblance to actual persons, living or dead, events, or locales is entirely coincidental.

Text and illustrations copyright © 2006 by Debi Gliori
Jacket illustration copyright © 2007 by Jimmy Pickering

All rights reserved.

Published in the United States by Alfred A. Knopf, an imprint of Random House Children's Books, a division of Random House, Inc., New York.
Originally published in Great Britain by Doubleday in 2006 under title: *Deep Fear*.

KNOPF, BORZOI BOOKS, and the colophon are registered trademarks of Random House, Inc.

www.randomhouse.com/kids

Educators and librarians, for a variety of teaching tools, visit us at
www.randomhouse.com/teachers

Library of Congress Cataloging-in-Publication Data
Gliori, Debi.
Pure dead frozen / Debi Gliori. — 1st ed.
p. cm.
SUMMARY: The Strega-Borgias make one last stand to defend their home against invaders who seek the Chronostone—and one little baby who may not be what he appears.
ISBN 978-0-375-83317-5 (trade) — ISBN 978-0-375-93317-2 (lib. bdg.)
[1. Babies—Fiction. 2. Goblins—Fiction. 3. Changelings—Fiction.
4. Magic—Fiction. 5. Witches—Fiction. 6. Castles—Fiction.
7. Family life—Scotland—Fiction. 8. Scotland—Fiction.] I. Title.
PZ7.G4889Ptt 2007
[Fic]—dc22
2006035565

Printed in the United States of America
August 2007
10 9 8 7 6 5 4 3 2 1
First American Edition

This one's for my family, with all my love.

*Thank you—a thousand, million Nantoes
for putting up with seven years of*

1. Me, writing: Why couldn't I have chosen a "proper job"?
2. Supper being frequently (a) late and (b) inadequate
   (though delicious, even if I say so myself).
3. Weekends, weeks, months—years, actually—hijacked by the
   Strega-Borgias and their outrageous demands.
4. Promises (as yet unfulfilled) of Yes, yes, we'll stay at the Ritz
   (and I'm not talking little crinkly-edged biscuits for cheese,
   either), and Yes, there will be a red carpet, and Yes, yes, I
   promise I'll introduce you to all the glitterati.
5. Summer holidays waiting for what passes for Mummy's
   Brain to return from StregaSchloss and resume being a
   parent rather than a writer.
6. The Munchies, the Drys (aka the Blocks), the Frets, the
   Weeps, and the Grimms.
7. Inappropriate outbursts, wild hysteria, and dreadful puns
   accompanied by unladylike snorts of mirth at my own jokes.
8. The sneaking suspicion that your lives might have been
   filtered, inflated, polished, tweaked, and finally served up as
   fiction.

Contents

Dramatis Personae

THE FAMILY

TITUS STREGA-BORGIA—thirteen-year-old hero
PANDORA STREGA-BORGIA—eleven-year-old heroine
DAMP STREGA-BORGIA—their two-year-old sister
LITTLE NO-NAME—the newborn Baby Borgia
SIGNOR LUCIANO AND SIGNORA BACI STREGA-BORGIA—parents of the above
STREGA-NONNA—great-great-great-great-great-great-grandmother
(cryogenically preserved) of Titus, Pandora, Damp, and Little No-Name
DON LUCIFER DI S'EMBOWELLI BORGIA—evil half brother to Luciano
APOLLONIUS "THE GREEK" BORGIA—ancestor and portal portager

THE GOOD HELP THAT WAS HARD TO FIND

MRS. FLORA MCLACHLAN—nanny to Titus, Pandora, Damp, and Little No-Name
LATCH—StregaSchloss butler
MISS ARAMINTA FRASER—backup nanny to Damp and Little No-Name
LUDO GRABBIT—estate lawyer and tutor to the reluctant assassin

THE BEASTS

TARANTELLA—spider with attitude
SAB, FFUP, NESTOR, AND KNOT—mythical dungeon beasts
TOCK—highly domesticated crocodile
THE SLEEPER—Scottish unreconstructed-male mythical beast
ORYNX—salamander and Hadean refugee
VESPER—Damp's bat familiar

THE IMMORTALS

ISAGOTH—demonic defense minister
S'TAN—First Minister of the Hadean Executive and television chef
DEATH—as himself
THE CHEF—divine being from the Other Side

In the Land of the Snoke Ween

"I don't know about this," the dragon complained. "Are you absolutely positive that we're in the Snow Queen's neighborhood? It's just that it's sooo *cold*. I mean, why would anyone want to live here? Can't we just turn back? It must be nearly time for tea.... Someone'll notice we've gone...."

The little girl sighed and folded her arms in a fashion that indicated that her mind was made up, even if her companion was having second, third, or even fourth thoughts. The dragon continued, undeterred.

"You know, I think you've magicked us into the middle of a *National Geographic* special Antarctic issue rather than between the pages of one of your fairy tales...." The dragon slumped and added, "Don't get me wrong, Small. I mean, you're a brilliant sorceress, but next time could you choose a warmer fairy tale? Like 'The Princess and the Pea' with extra quilts, or . . . um . . . er . . ."

Tapping one foot impatiently, Damp sighed even louder, forcing air down her nostrils like a disgruntled duchess who'd just been mistaken for a commoner.

"Okay . . . okay . . ." Ffup threw up her forelegs in surrender. "Don't *snort* like that, girl. You might . . . uh, accidentally . . . *you* know."

"Make hot hot burny by nax dident?"

"Yeah. And since right now we're tiptoeing across a snow-bridge slung between two crevasses, more flames would be a very bad idea. Heck, *any* flames would be catastrophic."

The little girl's eyes widened as the meaning of the dragon's words sank in, and she slipped her hand into Ffup's paw for safety. Underfoot, a glassy blade of pale blue ice stretched ahead, its glazed surface pitted in places by rockfalls and avalanches from the surrounding mountains. This was a hostile place, scoured by vicious winds that made eyes water and plucked at clothes and skin with determined tugs; a bleak place with no trees, no grass, and little color; a land of ice and stone and sky that stretched all around.

This land was nothing like Damp had imagined it, back then. However, back then, Damp had been pink and warm, fresh from her bath, wrapped in flannel pajamas and curled up in bed in the nursery, her father's voice as warm as the flames that flickered and danced in the hearth. Back then, the land of ice and snow was just a story. Back then.

"My feet hurt," the dragon moaned, the rhythmic *scrunch, crunch* of her footsteps coming to an abrupt halt as she turned round to peer behind her, trying to gauge how far they'd traveled. "It's this horrible snow," she explained. "It sort of gathers in freezing clumps in between my paw pads, until eventually I'm walking on massive snowballs. It's making it hard to keep my balance. Harder, in fact."

Wordlessly, Damp tugged Ffup behind her like a gigantic pull-along toy, ignoring the dragon's litany of complaint and forging ahead, seemingly unaware of the weight of wet snow caking her own body from the waist down or of the dizzying drop on either side of the snowbridge.

"*And* it's soooooo cold," Ffup whined. "My nostrils are icing up, you know. Pretty soon I'll have to stop and try to clear them, though without using my nasal flamethrowers, I have no idea how I'm supposed to de-ice. . . ."

Overhead, the highest mountain suddenly turned gold, reflecting the setting sun, which gilded its lethally steep western face. This brief exposure was enough to thaw a glistening finger of water ice, which started trickling down the mountain, trailing small chips and flakes of loose rock behind it. As these fragments fell, they began to snowball, gathering layers of soft snow about themselves, rolling silently toward the two figures, one large, one small, carefully picking their way across the snowbridge to the relative safety of the glacier beyond.

"Can you hear a rumbling sound?" Ffup stopped, her golden eyes widening with the first prickle of fear.

"Nearly time for supper." Damp smiled up at the dragon

and reached out a mittened hand to pat the scales of the giant beast's belly. "Shush, tummy. Not home yet."

Now there was a faint vibration in the air, as if the blue of the sky fairly hummed and trembled above them. The insignificant rockfall had become an altogether more serious affair, the patter of tumbling pebbles triggering a vast slab of snow into shearing off a rock face, and it was this that vibrated and rumbled as it plummeted toward the tiny figures on the edge of the glacier.

"That was *not* me or my tummy," Ffup snapped, stung by this implied criticism of her digestive excesses. "Why *is* it that you humans immediately assume that any bad smells, loud parps, or distant rumblings are always the product of the nearest beast gut? You lot are perfectly capable of producing some window-rattling, eye-watering little numbers yourselves. And don't go all huffy on me either. . . ." Ffup dug Damp in the ribs with a playful talon, oblivious to the vast wave of snow towering above her back. "*You*, if I recall, were still wearing nighttime diapers until as recently as last nighhh—"

Spinning round, Ffup registered the oncoming death wall of blurred white, and in the same instant scooped Damp up between her forepaws, her wings snapping open to bear them both into the air, straining and heaving against the heavy suck of snow churning beneath her belly.

A cloud of spindrift boiled up, hiding both mountain and glacier from their sight as they flew up for what felt like forever, gaining height, heading out of the deadly white snow chopping beneath them, devouring the bridge, obliterating their footprints, and turning Damp's vision of the kingdom of the Snow Queen into something far more lethal than Hans Christian Andersen had conjured from words alone. Then the sun vanished behind a ridge, and all at once the snow turned to blue. Beneath them lay a field of darkness, its features completely transformed by the avalanche. The tumbling slabs of snow slowed and juddered to a halt, a vast puff of powdered ice settling on the ground like a shawl. Now silence blanketed the glacier, and overhead the first cold stars began to appear in the sky. In the distance, a far-off cowbell chimed, and from a long way below came the sound of laughter echoing across the ice.

Damp shuddered, blinked, and laid her head against Ffup's neck. Beneath them, hundreds of yards below, the glacier shivered and cracked open. The distant laughter stopped, as if a switch had been thrown.

"Gerda?" came a thin cry from far below. Then the bell. Insistent now, closer and louder, a vibrant summons at odds with the frozen world under Damp and the dragon.

"Gerda?" again, but this time tinged with something close to despair.

"Make it stop," Ffup whispered. "I hate this bit. Snow, ice, Gerda, Kay, the Snow Queen, all that eternity stuff . . . eughhh. I just don't understand why humans feel they're obliged to wallow in such sad stories."

"Not sad," said Damp firmly. "This story's got a nappy ending—"

"*Damp?*"

Damp's shoulders slumped. Uh-oh, she thought. Big sister alert. Not *now*. Not when I'm just getting the hang of this. Go *'way*, Pandora.

"Damp! For God's sake. I've been going purple in the face from calling and calling and *calling* you. Eughhh, *children*. I'm *never* going to have any when I'm older."

The sound of approaching footsteps galvanized Ffup into action. "Okay, okay. Let's go, let's get outta here. C'mon." The dragon plucked Damp off her neck and flapped toward a huge white door that had appeared in the sky ahead of them. The door resembled a detached sail etched against the deep blue of the sky, luffing and flapping as if a strong wind were hitting it side-on. Ffup clung to one edge with her talons and began to poke Damp through the undulating whiteness into whatever lay beyond.

"*Go,*" she insisted. "Out. Back. *Home*. You may be the sorceress, but I'm your rear guard. You have to go first."

"Damp. You *know* you're not supposed to play up here on your own. The attic's out of bounds to tots."

At this, Damp's bottom lip popped out mutinously, but a stiff shove from Ffup reminded her that if she ever hoped to use her abilities as a baby magus to return to this kingdom of ice and snow, she had to cover her tracks. Scrabbling through the white door-sail, she fell heavily onto the floor of Strega-Schloss's biggest room—a massive attic running the entire length of Damp's ancestral home. Ffup tumbled down behind her in a cloud of dust, her wings sending a rusty birdcage rolling across the attic floor until it came to rest against a slumped and silent set of bagpipes.

The attic trapdoor began to open just as the white door to their ice kingdom began to shrink. When Damp's big sister, Pandora, climbed into the attic, the much-diminished white door fluttered down to the floor before squeezing itself between the well-worn pages of the picture book from which it had come.

"*Look* at you," Pandora groaned, catching sight of her little sister and clapping a hand to her forehead. "What a *mess*. You're *soaking wet*. What on earth have you two been up to?"

Ffup peered intently at her talons, turning her paws this way and that, as if wondering whether a manicure might be in order.

"Ffup?" Pandora marched across the attic and halted in front of the dragon. Although she only came up to the giant beast's nipples, she radiated such fierce determination that Ffup quailed before her, blinking rapidly and breathing through her mouth in frantic puffs.

"Stop avoiding eye contact," Pandora snapped. "*Look* at me."

"Gosh," the dragon squeaked, "and don't you look *nice*. What's changed? Hair? Nope, don't tell me. You've taken your glasses off?"

"I don't *wear* glasses, as you well know."

"Well, *some*thing's different," Ffup insisted, edging toward the trapdoor, her golden eyes swiveling wildly as she tried to avoid being skewered by Pandora's steely glare. "Oh, please stop it. I *hate* it when you look at me like that. It makes me feel all hot . . . and squirmy and . . . and . . . like I might need to go to the bathroom. Soon. You know, I'll wet the floor if you keep on looking at me like that. Really, I will."

7

"Oh, for heaven's *sake*," Pandora snorted. "I came up here to tell you it's teatime, not to torture you. However, that doesn't change the fact that neither of you is supposed to *be* up here in the attic. Damp, you're too young, and Ffup, you"—the dragon flinched and attempted a winning smile—"are too heavy."

"HEAVY? Are you saying that I'm *fat*?" Ffup's voice rose an octave, leavened by outrage. "I'm *so* not fat," she continued, her voice wobbling with indignation. "*I* am 'with dragon,' actually. There are two of me standing in front of you, in case you hadn't noticed."

"I could hardly fail to notice," Pandora retorted. "Even Mum isn't as baby-obsessed as you are, and *that's* saying something."

"Your mother is expecting her fourth child, which is, you must admit, a bit of a nonevent, seeing as how she's done it all before, and before and before, whereas *I'm* only on my sec—"

"Whatever," Pandora muttered. "Anyway, the point I'm trying to make is that the attic was, is, and always will be out of bounds to smalls and beasts. Besides"—Pandora smiled as she pointed toward the open trapdoor—"it's teatime, and Dad's making pizzas. . . ."

Ffup's expression softened, and her eyes developed a faraway look. Pandora turned to leave, adding over her shoulder, "And if you get a move on, you'll be able to select your own toppings."

A loud rumbling, rolling twang echoed round the attic, causing Damp to frown and stare at her own midriff. Ffup cleared her throat and scooped the little girl up in her forepaws.

"*That,* my small mountaineer, was no avalanche," the dragon whispered, poking Damp's tummy and grinning. "*That* was a rumble a dragon might be proud of."

From far off came the distant ringing of the dinner gong.

"Hungry," muttered Damp, stating the blindingly obvious.

Oh, Baby

"Eughhh, wee hairy fish," moaned Titus, turning to the fridge for comfort as his father, Luciano Strega-Borgia, arranged—in Titus's opinion—a gruesome surfeit of anchovies across the top of a pizza as big as a pillowcase.

"Cara mia?" Luciano turned to his wife, Baci, his eyebrows raised in query.

Expertly assessing the pizza for anchovy coverage, Baci decided to ignore her son's preferences fishwise.

"Perhaps just a few more?" she murmured, laying aside her notes and abandoning a halfhearted attempt to revise what little she remembered of Invocations, Exorcisms, and Assorted Summonings (Intermediate Level II) from the approved syllabus of the Institute for Advanced Witchcraft. "So boring, all this studying." She yawned, smiling

sleepily at Luciano. "Still, if I can scrape a pass in InvExoAss-Sum II, then re-sit my written paper on Hunch, Prescience, and Sibylline Awareness, the Examination Board might allow me to skip Practical Demonology on account of"—she patted her pregnant tummy, which responded with a lusty kick— "Little No-Name, and *then* I could rejoin the third year halfway through the second term."

"Who's going to look after the baby if you go back to college?" Titus demanded, slamming the fridge door shut. Not waiting for an answer, he slouched across the kitchen to the pantry, muttering, "Why is there *never* any food in this house? When is supper going to be ready? I'm *ravenous*. What time is it, anyway? Where is everybody?"

Mercifully, the pantry door closed behind him, rendering his remaining comments inaudible. Baci and Luciano did a synchronized eye-roll.

"Teenagers," came a voice from the direction of the kitchen china cupboard. "Lordy, how they *do* go on and on," it continued. "And *I* should know. I've just fed *my* daughters, and listen to them. . . ."

"Muuum. This fly's *off*, you know. It's, like, *totally* rancid. You know I hate flies. I *told* you I hate flies."

"Why is there *never* anything decent to eat in this web? I'm *starving*."

"When is it proper suppertime? This pathetic pile of sun-dried gnats is just a wee snack, right? What *is* for supper, anyway?"

As if pursued by Furies, a huge tarantula sprang out of a

willow-pattern teapot on the cupboard and dropped to the floor on a hastily spun length of spider silk.

"Give me strength," she moaned, limping across the flagstones toward Baci. "What on earth possessed me to bring these vile children into the world? When I think back to how easy my life used to be before they arrived . . ." Tarantella, the harassed spider mother, wearily began to ascend the leg of the kitchen table, gaining the tablecloth just as a posse of assorted vast mythical beasts and a crocodile crashed through the door from the kitchen garden, followed by a baby dragon, who in turn was followed by an unspeakable stench.

"It's freezing out there." Tock shivered, his crocodile's teeth rattling like dice in a cup. "Any chance of anything to eat? I'm famished."

"Join the queue," muttered Tarantella, arranging herself comfortably on top of a pomegranate withering in the fruit bowl. "Take your place behind the teenage man-child and my daughters—"

"Anyone seen Ffup?" interrupted Sab, his leathery griffin's hide covered in goose bumps as he headed for the range and unfolded his huge wings to dry over the stovetop. Baci reached up to pat her pet griffin and gave an involuntary squeak. She took a deep breath and rubbed her stomach, her expression inwardly focused.

In the fruit bowl, Tarantella paused in mid-groom to stare at Baci with many calculating eyes. The tarantula's gaze swiveled to take in the kitchen clock, then dropped back to resume combing her furry abdomen.

"Ffup?" Luciano frowned, his nostrils wrinkling as an unpleasant smell rolled across the kitchen. "I thought she was with you."

"Yeahhh, so did we," mumbled Knot, the Strega-Borgias' pet yeti, sidling across the kitchen to slump against the range next to Sab. In the warmth of the stove, his fur began to give off a faint odor of rotting vegetation.

"The reason I ask," Sab continued, now mouth-breathing to avoid inhaling the ripe perfume of Knot's pelt, which was matted and clotted with the evidence that the yeti still hadn't worked out how to transfer his dinner from bowl to mouth without mishap. "The reason I *ask*," Sab repeated, upping the volume, "is because Ffup's baby is in dire need of a diaper change."

Silence greeted this statement as everybody suddenly found several pressing matters urgently requiring their undivided attention.

Sab drummed his talons on the lids of the burners and sighed. It was no coincidence that Ffup disappeared every time Nestor needed a clean diaper. The baby dragon had a knack for suddenly turning from a milk-scented infant into something that smelled infinitely less pleasant; witness Baci's pained expression as the first waft of Nestor's diaper floated within range of her nose. For a brief moment she even closed her eyes, apparently overwhelmed by the baby dragon's offending reek. Tarantella frowned, staring hard at Baci, and once again checked the time. She smiled and nodded, as if confirming something that, for the moment, she had decided to keep to herself. Oblivious to Tarantella, Sab sighed deeply. Obviously diapers weren't Baci's thing. Hence the fact that as well as a butler, the Strega-Borgias employed *two* live-in nannies: one upstairs recuperating from a near-drowning incident, and the other . . .

"Oh *dear*. Nestor? Was that you?"

Nestor froze in place, caught licking a chair leg where an overlooked lump of Damp's breakfast porridge had stuck several days before. The baby dragon's tail drooped, his entire expression radiating regret.

"Oh, Nestor, poppet. We had an agreement, no?"

A young woman stood in the doorway to the kitchen garden, balancing on one leg while she removed a sparkly pink Wellington boot and placed it beside its identical twin. She shook out a mane of golden hair and beamed at the assembled family and beasts.

"What a whiffy, huh?" she continued, striding toward the baby dragon and scooping him up in her arms as if he weighed no more than a bag of sugar. She peered into the offending diaper and groaned. "Come on, my darling. Let's get this nasty thing off your bottom and give it a decent burial. . . ."

Nestor submitted to this indignity, hanging in the young woman's arms like an understuffed draft stop while she gathered together a selection of dragonish toiletries and bore the baby beast off to the downstairs cloakroom.

Immediately the kitchen began to smell better.

"What was their agreement?" Luciano wondered out loud, drizzling the top of the pizza with olive oil.

"What, Nestor and Minty?" Baci said, shifting uncomfortably in her seat. "Being a fully qualified nanny, Minty made a star chart to encourage Nestor with toilet training and other things. As I understand it, if he can get through a whole day with no dirty dia—" Baci broke off in mid-sentence and gasped.

Tarantella glanced at the kitchen clock and pursed her mouth-parts. "I'd say they've been coming every two minutes," she said cheerily. "You *might* just make it in time, if *he* can be persuaded to drop his precious pizza and drive you to the hospital—"

"Knot—for Pete's *sake*," Luciano roared. "Would you go and toast your bottom somewhere else? How am I supposed to get this into the oven with you in the way?"

Unabashed, the yeti began to drool at the sight of what Luciano held in his hands. "Ooooh, yessss," he slobbered. "Pitzer. Pits? Or is it patzi?" he hazarded. "My favorite. And with those wee hairy fishies as well. *Yum*meee."

"On the other hand," Tarantella muttered, "we could all squeeze up at one end of the kitchen table to give you space to get on with having your baby while we have supper...."

"LUCIANNNNNOOO!" Baci wailed.

The pizza crashed to the floor as Luciano spun round to face his wife.

"Baci?" he quavered. "Is it the baby? Now?"

"Get...the...car," Baci muttered through clenched teeth, levering herself to her feet with some difficulty.

"KEYS!" shrieked Luciano. "Where the hell...?"

"This *is* exciting," said Tarantella, clambering to the top of a candlestick to get a better view. "I've never seen a live birth before—eggs are more my kind of thing."

"Darling," Baci groaned, "those are the keys to the lawn mower. . . ."

"AUGHHHHHHHH!" roared Luciano, one foot embedded in the raw dough of his abandoned pizza, the other desperately seeking purchase on the floor, which was now slippery with olive oil and scattered anchovies. "What bloody idiot spilled food all over the floo—?"

"Now, *dears*," came a voice from the door to the hall, "why don't you let Latch drive you both to the hospital? He's bringing the car round to the front just now. Signora, dear, I've taken the liberty of packing your suitcase; there's a clean nightie, your chamomile pillow, a bottle of lavender water, some mint tea bags, a wee pot of honey, and that beautiful book of flower paintings from beside your bed. . . ."

As one, all heads turned to gaze in astonishment at the frail figure of Flora McLachlan silhouetted in the kitchen doorway. She stood before them, her silvery hair unpinned and tied with a black velvet ribbon in a long plait down her back. She looked smaller than they remembered, perhaps diminished by the horrors of the previous summer, when she had so nearly drowned. Mrs. McLachlan, so much more than simply the children's nanny—the family regarded her as a combination of best friend, sister, guardian angel, and the wisest and most loving person they had ever known. Her eyes shone very brightly as she gazed back at the family. In the silence, Titus poked his head round the pantry door and stared at Mrs. McLachlan as if she had recently arrived from Betelgeuse.

"Don't gawp, Titus, dear," she said softly. "We don't all need to see that you had three bowls of Miserablios and all of the Selkirk bannock for breakfast. . . ."

Titus's mouth snapped shut and he blushed crimson.

"What a fat *pig*," muttered Pandora, appearing in the shadows behind Mrs. McLachlan. "I wondered where the bannock had gone. Typical. He always eats the best stuff and leaves the grot for us. *I* had to have brown bread for *my* breakf—"

"That's enough, Pandora *dear*," said Mrs. McLachlan firmly, grasping Baci's arm and leading her toward the hall.

Baci turned round in the kitchen doorway and addressed her husband somewhat brusquely: "Luciano?"

"Cara mia?"

"Are you coming or not?"

"Personally, I'd've eaten him *years* ago," muttered Tarantella, pulling out a tiny lipstick from an abdominal cache and carefully applying it to her mouthparts. *"Husbands,"* she continued. "Waste of good lipstick. Talking of which, check out this new shade of lippy . . ."

"Somebody, please, shut that spider up," Titus demanded, to no avail.

". . . I got it as a pre-Christmas present from a delicious chap I ran into last week." Tarantella ran a small black tongue over her glistening mouthparts and arranged her features into an approximation of a faintly regretful smile. "In his honor, I'm only going to use it on special occasions—"

"Shut up, shut up, shut up," Titus begged, rocking backward and forward in time to his words.

"Now, what was it called again?" Tarantella murmured to

herself as Luciano ran out of the kitchen and disappeared down the hall after Mrs. McLachlan and Baci. Unperturbed, the tarantula peered at the base of her lipstick with her multiple eyes. She emitted a deep sigh of happiness when she finally focused on the tiny label stuck to the lipstick's cap. Looking up, she made sure that she had Titus's full attention before saying, "Of *course*. How *could* I have forgotten? How singularly appropriate. It's called Boy Bait."

When Hell Freezes Over

For the first time ever in demonic history, an overnight snowfall had turned the mountains of Hades white. Blizzards crept stealthily over its blighted landscape, its swamps and sewage plants froze solid, and ice feathered windows in the silent slums of its capital cities. As dawn broke, Hades' demon citizens awoke to a world they barely recognized as their own. Moments later, phones began to ring in furnace rooms across the land.

"How many times do I have to tell you? This Is Not My Fault. Right, okay, keep your fur on, I'll try again...." The duty demon rolled his eyes and put down the phone. With little enthusiasm, he crossed the furnace room to lay another fifty lashes across the back of the laboring troll who was endeavoring to stoke boiler

no. 666. The duty demon returned to his seat and picked up the phone again.

"Right. *There.* Happy now? . . . You're *still* freezing? . . . No, I won't. . . . Don't be a complete cretin. Bigger whips would only kill the troll. . . . No—that doesn't mean I'm some kind of namby-pamby troll sympathizer either. . . . There's no need to take that tone, I'm only doing my job. Yeah. I hope yours shrivels up and falls off too. . . . Knobs on, yup. Uh-huh. . . . Drop dead, pal—" And with this cordial farewell, the duty demon slammed down the phone.

However, the caller had been right about one thing. It *was* freezing. The troll's efforts at firing up boiler no. 666 weren't making a blind bit of difference to the ambient temperature, despite the fact that no. 666 looked as if it was about to melt into a pool of molten pig iron. To his continuing dismay, the demon could see his breath forming in misty clouds in front of his face. This was all so *wrong,* he thought. What was going on? Hell wasn't supposed to freeze over. It hadn't been designed to cope with ice or snow. Its infrastructure wasn't built to withstand so much as a light breeze, never mind the polar winds now whipping round the demon's ankles and blowing glowing furnace ash straight down the troll's boxer shorts. Hell's citizens weren't designed to cope with life in a Big Freezy. The demon looked down at his own inadequate clothing—a thong, a black leather string vest, and a pair of flip-flops—and wondered how he was expected to make it back home without freezing to death. Even the thought of the walk back to his apartment brought him out in odd little shivery pimples.

Minutes later, shivering uncontrollably, he huddled against the boiler, trying to tune out the howls of agony now coming from the smoldering troll, who had, he assumed, generously set himself alight in a doomed attempt to provide his master with more warmth. With little hope of success, the demon phoned first for a taxi home (line busy), a rented car (ditto), a chauffeur-driven limousine (no answer whatsoever); then, in utter desperation, he phoned the Hadean Bus Company in the hope of finding a bus that might take him in the general direction of home before his toes froze solid and snapped off one by one. On the other end, a mechanized voice informed him that due to unprecedented snowfall, all services were canceled until further notice.

*Snow*fall? The demon's brows plunged toward his nose, and his eyes squeezed shut as if to expunge such a hideous notion. It *never* snowed in Hades. That was unthinkable. And yet, as he opened his eyes again . . . there they were, little white flaky things dropping out of the sky, drifting in through the doorway and sizzling on the hot troll by the furnace. The demon swore loudly. This was simply not on. It was outrageous. Someone had to tell S'tan what was happening. Someone had to alert Him to the fact that His domain was on the verge of collapse. Someone—the demon swallowed—someone brave enough to endure the fiery blast of His rage when He was informed that He had a problem with His furnaces. The demon bit down on a squeak of terror. Whoever was *insane* enough to face down the ire of S'tan, His Imperial Inflammableness; S'tan, the First Minister of the Hadean Executive . . . whoever was brave *and* insane enough to do *that* would stand about the same chance of survival as . . . say . . . a snowflake in Hell.

"Kinda sums it all up," the demon mumbled to himself, keying in the number that hopefully, after many labyrinthine twists, turns, menus, options, and multiple choices, would finally allow him access to the inner sanctum of the Lord of Misrule, S'tan Himself. Perhaps it was an electrical fault, the demon thought, staring at the icicles that were forming on the ceiling of the furnace room. Or maybe the other furnace-stoking slaves were on a go-slow. As he half listened to the dial tone, a heretical thought passed through his mind—surely it couldn't be that the fabled powers of his Loathsome Leader, his S'tainless S'teeliness S'tan, the Arch-Fiend, were failing? The duty demon groaned out loud. How could he even *think* such a thought? S'tan was invincible, all-powerful. He wasn't going to fail. . . . His powers weren't dimming like some kind of cheap battery—

"Welcome to Below, region of eternal Punishment, everlasting Torture, and unending Despair," the phone interrupted. The demon's shoulders slumped. A recorded message. Gosh, what *fun*.

"For barbecue with added fork-and-skewer involvement, press one," the phone continued, its merry, upbeat tone at odds with the menu it was detailing. *"For lies, lies, and more damned lies, press two. Ha-ha—only kidding. Press three . . . Or is* that *a lie?"*

The demon sighed. The only thing to do was hang on with gritted teeth until the recording reached the "speak to a real person rather than a machine" option. That was, if there *was* such an option. This *was* Hades, after all.

"For fraud, bouncy checks, and armed robbery, press six. For Deadly Sins, press seven. For . . ."

Using a none-too-pristine fingernail, the demon picked his teeth and waited.

"For using a cell phone in a manner designed to alert anyone within a half-mile radius to the boring minutiae of your tedious life, press eight."

On the point of hurling the phone against the glowing metal belly of the furnace, the demon was astonished to hear:

"Operator services, how may I be of assistance?"

"Um, yes," babbled the demon, caught unawares. "Put me, uh, through to the Pit, would you?"

"Would that be the Deep Pit, the Even Deeper Pit, or the Abysmally Profound Pit?" the voice demanded.

"Uh . . . the Deep Pit would be great," the demon guessed, confused by the range of options, pitwise.

There was a click, a hum, and then the return of the ringing tone. The demon closed his eyes and was on the verge of hanging up when a voice spoke in his ear.

"THIS IS ONE'S ANSWERING MACHINE," the voice announced, its superior tone instantly identifying it as belonging to S'tan Himself. Before the duty demon could draw breath, S'tan, or rather S'tan's answering machine, continued: "ONE IS FAR TOO BUSY TO COME TO THE PHONE RIGHT NOW, SO WHY DON'T YOU JUST LEAVE YOUR PATHETIC LITTLE BLEATINGS—OOPS, I MEAN, LEAVE YOUR *MESSAGE* AFTER THE TONE."

Then came an extended pause, during which the demon

could distinctly hear the sound of heavy breathing, followed by S'tan's voice, the volume lowered as if He were talking to some unseen person:

"WHO GIVES A FAT FIG WHAT MESSAGES THEY LEAVE? YOU DON'T REALLY THINK ONE HAS TIME TO LISTEN TO ALL THEIR TEDIOUS WHINGEINGS, DO YOU? WHATEVER DO YOU TAKE ONE FOR? ONE IS A CELEBRITY, NOT AN AGONY AUNT. NOW CALL ME A CAB—ONE HAS A FLIGHT TO CATCH. . . ."

There was the sound of a distant door slamming and a hiss of static. Then came several electronic beeps and whooshes, a short silence, then a click followed by a woman's soft voice enunciating:

"*You're through to the* Totally Toast *studio at Bee-Bee-See, dot coh, dot You-Kay. No one is available to take your call right now, so leave us a message or send a fax after the tone.*" And then came the unmistakable sound of someone, probably S'tan, blowing a loud and mocking raspberry.

A Boo at Bedtime

Night fell over StregaSchloss, making the house look as if it were floating in the surrounding shadows, like an ocean liner far out at sea. Lit windows punctuated the vast darkness, and overhead the silent stars went by. A bitter wind shook branches of the wisteria against the darkened nursery window, where they tapped on the glass, flailing and tossing. In the warmth of the Ancestors' Room, snug behind curtains of moth-eaten damask, Minty looked up from a recipe book. Was that a cry? Had Damp woken up? The young nanny was halfway down the corridor to the nursery before she remembered that Damp didn't sleep there anymore.

The nursery was covered in dust sheets, all its furniture huddled in the center of the room, the carpets and rugs rolled and stacked in a corner while the room was in the process of being redecorated to within an inch of its life. Well ... perhaps not quite *that* far, Minty amended, recalling how Signora Strega-Borgia's sudden enthusiasm for redecorating had vanished almost entirely upon the discovery of just how many coats of paint would be required to cover up five decades of smoke from log fires kindled in the nursery fireplace.

"But I've painted it *twice*," Baci complained, standing, brush in hand, in the middle of the empty room, gazing in defeat at her newly painted walls—walls that, despite her best efforts, seemed determined to remain the exact shade of yellow of a crocodile's tooth, crossed with a color best described as that of a pipe smoker's lung. Shortly thereafter, Baci had abandoned the entire project of preparing the nursery for the soon-to-arrive youngest Strega-Borgia, turning her maternal energies instead toward the bushes in her rose garden, spraying, mulching, and tenderly swaddling their thorny stems in what appeared to be miles of horticultural fleece.

Damp's new bedroom looked down on her mother's shrouded rose garden, its wrapped roses ghostly against the deep and velvety darkness. A pale light shone through a gap in the bedroom's distressed silk curtains, their linings tattered beyond repair. Like so many battered relics at StregaSchloss, these curtains were kept solely for their sentimental value: a long-dead relative had embroidered every silken inch with pale pink rosebuds, thus ensuring the fabric's immortality. Possibly this was the same relative who had hand-painted the wallpaper in this room with her eccentric version of *toile de*

Jouy: hundreds of perfectly rendered nymphs and satyrs, some gamboling round Damp's walls, others pausing above Damp's fireplace to wind daisies around the horns of a singularly depressed-looking Minotaur, the whole originally painted in a particularly aggressive shade of pink, which thankfully had faded with each passing summer. Snug in her first proper bed, Damp slept on her back with her arms above her head, the slow rise and fall of her chest barely visible beneath the pillowy cloud of her goosedown quilt.

Minty watched her sleep, sure now that the cry she had heard earlier could not have come from this child. Slightly puzzled, she stroked Damp's forehead, dropped a kiss into one little hand that lay unfurled on the pillow, and then, remembering that she'd put bread into the oven to bake, checked her watch. The loaves would be ready in a few minutes, and then there was that recipe she'd just found for pear-and-marzipan cake, which had looked so intriguing that she'd decided to bake it right away. . . . Head full of matters culinary, the young nanny failed to notice that she was being secretly observed by three pairs of eyes, all six of which followed her progress around the room as she pulled curtains tightly shut, picked up discarded clothes, turned Russian dolls till they all faced out, and at last left the door to the corridor ajar and disappeared downstairs.

"Feee-yooo," said a small bat, unfolding his wings and drifting down from the ornate plaster rose in the center of the bedroom ceiling. "I thought our cover had been blown for sure," he added, landing with a thump on Damp's pillow.

"It hath to be thed that Mith Minty ithn't very obthervant," remarked a baby salamander, uncoiling himself from inside an empty candleholder on Damp's bedside table. Damp wriggled round onto her tummy and ducked down to drag a heavy book out from under her bed. With a grunt of effort, she hauled it onto her pillow and opened it at random.

"Oh, come *on*, Orynx," complained the bat. "Couldya hurry it up with the ill-yoomin asians? I can't see my wings in fronta my face."

Orynx slitted his turquoise eyes at the bat and gave a dismissive sniff. "You, thir, are a complete petht," he stated. "You're never thatithfied. You're a *bat*, thilly. You don't need a thalamander to provide you with illuminationth. You're thuppothed to be able to *thee* in the dark."

Vesper, the bat, clapped one wing dramatically against his forehead and sighed. "Lordy, lordy," he said. "If you aren't the most ornery crittur I have ever had the misfortune to bunk down with—"

"You two, shoosh," Damp said, looking up from her book with a faintly harassed expression. "I'm trying to contrinsate. What d'you think? 'Three Bears' or back to 'Snoke Ween'? I've got my Wellies on, so I'm all ready."

As they all bent over Damp's picture book, trying to decide where her magic might take them to, a gust of wind rattled the windowpanes, and downstairs they heard a door slam shut. This was followed by Nestor's wail echoing up from the dungeons—"Want Mumma . . . want my *mumma*"— reminding Damp that she too was temporarily mumma-less.

"Poor Mama," said Damp in a very small voice. "She's gone to hostiple with Dada—"

"YES!" Vesper's voice assumed a tone of enforced jollity. "Isn't that just *great*! We're all so *excited*, aren't we, team? Soon there'll be a new baby! Won't *that* be fun—?"

"Yeah, great," muttered another voice, adding, "Damp. What *are* you doing still awake? It's sooo late." And now Pandora's shadow stretched across the room, joined to its owner at the toes. The shadow shrank as Pandora came toward the bed.

Uh-oh, thought Damp, hope she doesn't notice what I'm wear—

"And why have you got your *Wellies* on? In *bed*? Just what exactly is going on?"

Right, thought Damp, gritting her teeth. Distractor. I'm sure I can still remember how to do this. *Not* that I want to, but still . . .

"And what's that awful sme—? Oh, *Damp*."

"Waaaaaaah," Damp said, slightly appalled at herself, but carrying on with diaper-filling nonetheless. "WAAAHHHH," she roared, hamming it up, eyes squinched shut, fists clenched, and mouth wide open for maximum volume. "WANT MAMA. NOT GO TO HOSTIPLE. WANT MAMA NOT NEW BAYYYBEEEE. . . ." Taking a deep breath, she opened one eye to see how this was going down. Excellent distractor. Pandora was gazing at her with the kind of horrified expression she might have used if she'd found an eyeball in her soup. Vesper and Orynx, on the other hand, were staring at her with wide-eyed admiration.

As Pandora hauled her bathroomward, Damp's last glimpse of her co-conspirators was of Vesper giving her the double bat-thumbs up and Orynx glowing with pride on her behalf.

Overlooked entirely in Damp's deliberately staged drama was the picture book. It lay open on the pillow, its pages turning very slowly as if blown in a draft. Seeing this, Vesper shivered and huddled closer to Orynx. Images flicked past—illustrations of three bears, a wolf, a golden goose; then the pages would halt and the whole process begin in reverse—a golden goose, a wolf, and three bears—almost as if something unseen was riffling through the pages, searching for a particular one.

"That's weird," Vesper whispered. "Whaddya think's making them do that?"

"I think thomething wicked thith way comth." Orynx sniffed, frowned, and sniffed again. "I can thmell it."

"Well, don't look at *me*," Vesper protested. "He who smelt it dealt it. The smeller's the feller—"

"For heaventh thake," the tiny salamander groaned. "I'm not accuthing you. I'm *telling* you. I thmell thomething obnoxioth. Thtinky. Offenthive—"

"Yeah, yeah. I catch your drift," Vesper snapped. "Cut to the chase, buster. What? Whaddya smell?"

"Thulfur," the salamander whispered, adding, "the thent of demonth."

The picture book fell open on a familiar scene from children's fiction: in the distance, a child in a red cloak with a wolf tiptoeing exaggeratedly behind her through a dark forest; in the foreground, a cottage—a face, probably a grandmother's face, just visible through the upstairs window. Or was that so?

Orynx blinked, uncertain if he'd seen something else out of the corner of his eye. For a moment there . . . but surely not? That *was* a child, and the wolf *was* reassuringly hairy, but the grandmother . . . Oh dear, no . . . Orynx's eyes snapped shut. Grandmothers are simply not supposed to have red eyes and feral grins. Nor, he thought, are their chests meant to be covered in fur. And that *wolf*. It only had two teeth, long yellow curving ones, like a gigantic rat. Orynx steeled himself to take a final look to confirm what he'd seen and immediately wished he hadn't. The grandmother had vanished from the window of the cottage—only it wasn't a cottage now, it was a rotting, collapsing gingerbread house, covered in mold like a furry bruise, buzzing with blowflies and writhing with pale, blind worms. The child had disappeared entirely, but the wolf wore a hooded cape and carried a scythe under one arm. It was picking its way delicately through briars and thorns as if its burning red shoes weren't causing it any pain at all.

Orynx found himself unable to drag his eyes away, although every cell in his body was shrieking *"RUN!"* and his mind was demanding that he put as much distance as possible between himself and the unfolding horror of the picture book lying sprawled wide across Damp's pillow.

Then came footsteps, and a woman's voice in the corridor outside.

"Och, my wee pet, whatever are you doing out of bed? And Vesper, would you stop flapping around me like that? Calm down. Pandora, dear, you should have come and found me. You don't have to do that. Diapers are my job. Here, let me take her."

The sound of Mrs. McLachlan's voice was enough to break the hold of whatever dark energy had forced Orynx into being an unwilling viewer. As the salamander fled for what he hoped was the book-free darkness under Damp's bed, the picture book continued to scroll through a nightmarish smorgasbord of the darkest episodes in children's literature, each grotesque tableau trying to outdo the one that had gone before until the very pages of the book began to disintegrate under the savage assault.

Orynx quivered under the bed, unable to raise as much as a candle's worth of luminescence, each breath an effortful wheeze as he tried to master his terror. It hadn't been the barbarity of the illustrations that had frightened him, it had been what they represented. Orynx had more knowledge, more personal experience than anyone at StregaSchloss of the depths to which demons could sink. Born into slavery in Hades, the salamander's first memories were such a tangle of pain, horror, loss, and despair that it was a wonder he could draw breath. Orphaned, and regularly beaten, Orynx was pressed into service as a demon's cigarette lighter from the moment he first raised a flame in anger. Isagoth, his master, had paid little or no attention to the well-publicized dangers of smoking, reckoning that since the darkness of his deeds was a source of pride, he might as well have lungs to match. At first, like all his kin, Orynx would respond with fiery ire to the lightest squeeze, bursting into flames at the merest pressure; then, as time and usage took their toll and his spirit began to weaken, so too did his fire. A squash, a shake, a vicious tweak: soon Isagoth would have had to resort to desperate measures to kindle Orynx's wrath. Had his master not mislaid him, the little salamander would have had his fragile skull slammed against tables, floors, and walls in an effort to batter him into ignition.

Although he was still only a baby, Orynx had seen his entire family and everyone he'd ever known used, abused, and ultimately thrown away. Orphaned, abandoned, homeless— throughout that time, every breath Orynx took was tainted with the filthy stench of demonic corruption, the sulfurous imprint of Hades. And now here, curling under the bed like a beckoning claw, coiling and twisting in the darkness where Orynx trembled and wept, was the proof that evil was once more trying to find a way into the heart of StregaSchloss.

Enter the Reluctant Assassin

Titus had headphones clamped over his ears, had his back to the door, and was too involved in the rigors of treadmilling to hear his sister come into the room. He'd just decided that music really helped him get through the awful bits, a discovery that he intended to share with his father just as soon as he came home—but that didn't seem likely to happen anytime soon, given that it was now seven p.m. and Dad had been gone for about two hours.... Gosh. Probably right in the middle of having the baby— Nope. Let's *not* go there. Titus upped his pace a little in an attempt to distract himself from thoughts of just what, exactly, his parents might be doing at that precise moment. He pressed the keypad on the treadmill again, increas-

ing both the speed *and* the slope, and within seconds found that yes, music did help—gasp, wheeze—but . . . what really helped . . . more . . . phew . . . pfffffff . . . than anything . . . was to . . . to . . . *STOP*. Ow. Oh, *owww*.

God . . . oh, how that *hurt*. Legs on fire. Muscles made of one hundred percent wibble-wobble jelly. Why am I *doing* this? he wondered, opening his eyes to gaze in loathing at the digital display in front of him.

DISTANCE TRAVELED, it informed him: 0.2 KM. Roughly the same distance, Titus calculated bleakly, as a trip downstairs to the fridge . . . and back. Except, he thought, cheering up slightly, round trips to the fridge had guaranteed calorific rewards, coupled with the added advantage of possible Minty sightings. Titus conjured up a mental image of Minty's golden hair, her lavender-blue eyes, her—

"Titus?" Pandora's voice broke into his reverie, dragging him back from a blissful daydream of the beautiful Minty offering him a rosebud-tipped, white-iced cupcake from a plateful of several still warm from the oven. *Take another,* she seemed to be saying, but Titus wasn't sure, as he gazed at her lips and wondered if he'd read them correctl—

"TITUS!"

Titus flinched and spun round. "*What?* God, Pandora, d'you have to sneak up on me and bawl in my ear like that?"

"Whatever do you mean?" Pandora's eyes widened in mock outrage. "I did nothing of the sort. I've been standing here for . . . forever, waving and calling your name while you, you dope, have been standing there wearing little more than headphones and an inane smile. I mean, for heaven's sake, Titus—

you look like a complete idiot, smiling at the treadmill as if you've only just discovered how beautiful it is. . . . Ugh," she continued, holding out her hands, palm upward, and gazing in disgust at first one, then the other, "I just so can't *bear* the thought that I've got the same awful flawed DNA as you. I keep hoping I'll wake up one day and discover it was all just a terrible dream—"

"Yeah. Right. I can imagine. Then you'd roll over on the straw and find that your snout was rammed up against the dear little curly-wurly tail of your identical twin sist—"

"Ah. That's better. Insult For The Day. Now I *know* it's you. For a moment there, I thought that the real you had been replaced by one of the Titus clones in the freezer—but no, it's really you, isn't it?"

Titus gave a heartfelt groan and half fell, half leapt off the treadmill. "Ow—my *legs*. What a *beast*. I don't know how Dad stands it. Come to think of it, I don't know why he even bothers." Titus gazed around the room—previously the Chinese Bedroom—in reluctant admiration. The P'ing Dynasty furniture had been removed to the attic, and in its place stood several shiny machines, all of which appeared to have been designed with the express purpose of parting portly adults from their limbs and their money simultaneously. There was a leg-exercising machine, a bottom-exercising machine, a thing like a medieval rack that promised to do something nasty but highly worthwhile to one's abdomen, and a couple of machines to tear one's arms off if the other machines hadn't proved vicious enough. In the fireplace was an exercise bike, and blocking the window recess was the machine Titus had attempted: the treadmill.

Dotted around the carpet was the workmanlike assortment of wrenches, hammers, screwdrivers, and assembly instructions that had occupied Luciano's every waking moment for the previous weeks. Little by little and bit by bit, he had built his home gymnasium from the carpet up, much to the puzzlement of his children, who had rarely seen their father use a screwdriver or—heaven forbid—exercise his muscles in the pursuit of anything other than sculling a boat out into the middle of Lochnagargoyle, all the better to admire the sunset. However, what Luciano had omitted to tell his children was that, concealed beneath the leather bench of the machine that resembled a medieval rack, there was a gun safe, where he had secreted a recently purchased double-barreled shotgun and a selection of ammunition sufficient to rid Argyll of its entire deer population—plus a brace of gamekeepers, should Luciano's aim prove to be as appalling as he suspected it might be. Pacifist, peacenik, and lifetime supporter of Amnesty International, Luciano sincerely hoped never to have to resort to removing the gun from its secret cache. Even holding it filled him with feelings of dread: he loathed its stink of gun oil, detested its cold weight in his arms, and reeled at the weapon's potential for harm, for ruining lives and destroying hopes in one brief, blinding blast. Notwithstanding all that, he had gone ahead and bought it, along with its required ammunition; bought it from a terribly well-spoken chap who had managed to confer a bizarre air of respectability to the whole sordid business of purchasing a weapon built to turn flesh and bone into so much lifeless pulp.

"Think of it as a necessary evil," the family lawyer had instructed him, seeing Luciano's face blanch at the prospect of ever using his new and loathsome purchase. "All right, then. Think of it as self-defense. What else are you going to do? Reason with the murderers who are coming to destroy not only you, but your family as well?"

Luciano had glared across the desk at Ludo Grabbit. The lawyer's craggy features were arranged into an expression that somehow managed to convey true empathy allied with extreme frustration.

"Luciano"—the lawyer shook his head—"you're not thinking straight. Listen to me: your half brother is not a decent chap. He's a killer. Always has been, always will be. Are you going to pretend otherwise, right up to the point where he's holding a gun to your head? Or Baci's? Or . . ."

He didn't need to go any further. Luciano placed both his shaking hands on the leather of the desktop and took a deep breath.

"Right. I get the message, Ludo. What you're saying is that it's kill or be killed, yes? I keep this new gun hidden until my half brother, Lucifer, breaks down my door one night, and then I'm allowed to run downstairs in my dressing gown and shoot him dead, yes? This is legal, yes?"

"Luciano, if you used your gun right now you'd be more of a danger to your family than to Lucifer. You need shooting lessons if you want to avoid blowing your own toes off, or, God forbid, accidentally maiming a member of your fam—"

"RIGHT!" Luciano stood up so fast his chair tipped over onto the floor. "You don't have to spell it out. Now you're saying I need to be *taught* how to be a killer. Tricky, don't you think?" He spun on his heel and began to pace the perimeter of Ludo's office, massaging his temples and half shutting his eyes as he measured out first one circuit of the room, then another, his mind describing another orbit completely. "I mean," he muttered to the book-lined wall on the other side of the room, "it's not as if I can just place an ad in the *Herald Dispatch,* can I? Imagine: *Tutor urgently required for learner assassin. References essential. The ideal candidate must have a flair for homicide, be able to spot the vendetta-obsessed mafioso lurking in the middle of a crowd, and be quick on the draw and even quicker to whip his weapon out of sight and pretend to be a postman when the occasion demands. . . ."*

"Luciano . . ." The lawyer's face was wreathed in smiles as he shook his head slowly from side to side.

"Hours and salary negotiable," Luciano continued, stopping mid-pace to slump with a groan onto a button-back leather sofa. "Oh, for heaven's sake—I wouldn't even know where to *begin.*"

"But you have begun already, dear boy," Ludo said. "You've told me. Or rather, I've told you what you need, and now I'm telling you that I can provide the tuition."

"You?" Luciano's eyes opened wide and he stopped massaging his forehead.

"I know, I know. You've got me earmarked as a bit of a tweedy old duffer." Ludo peered across at Luciano, adjusting his half-moon spectacles and raising his eyebrows as if to say, *Haven't you?*

Luciano had the grace to blush as the lawyer blithely continued, "No matter. Suffice it to say I'm not quite such a dry old stick as most people think. One did have a previous life before hanging out one's shingle here in Auchenlochtermuchty, you know. Some day I might even be persuaded to tell you about what I *used* to do for a living. For now, though, you need to learn how to fire a shotgun, and I am going to teach you."

"But . . . but . . . ," Luciano bleated as Ludo bulldozed onward, his eyes twinkling wickedly.

"Shouldn't be too difficult for you to learn. You don't need to be good, you just need to be lethal. And let's hope you never have to use what I'm about to teach you. . . ." *And pigs might fly,* he added silently, a wave of sympathy for Luciano's predicament temporarily derailing his upbeat semi-bullying approach to the whole ghastly mess. *Poor Luciano,* he thought sadly. *The man has simply no idea what he's up against.*

And so began Luciano's education in the use of firearms. He was a reluctant pupil, but an obedient one, and in the space of a few lessons was able to load, shoot, reload, and shoot again without nipping his fingers, dropping ammunition on his feet, or hurling his gun to the floor and stomping off in a tantrum. However, achieving a degree of accuracy in hitting a given target was going to take more time, and Luciano was beginning to suspect that time was running out. With this in mind, he embarked on a program of weight training in the hope of turning himself into less of a pathetic and weedy specimen of Italian manhood. Perhaps if he became fitter, sprouted some muscles, and scowled a lot, he might stand a better chance of defending his family from whatever it was that Ludo wasn't telling him about.

So Luciano set about building a home gymnasium, thus sparing himself the humiliation of going to a public gym to work out in the company of the bruisers, he-men, and muscle-bound gargoyles of Argyll. In answer to Titus's, Pandora's, and Baci's understandable queries about his newfound obsession with exercise, Luciano lied through his teeth.

"Doctor's orders," he claimed, gasping out this utter fiction to Baci as she watched him heave and gasp under the weight of dumbbells that, to her, looked as if they were every bit as heavy as a pair of small bungalows with matching lean-to carports. A while later, when Luciano had moved on to the horrors of the exercise bike, his two older children came into the newly refurbished Chinese Bedroom and stood watching for a moment.

"But why are you doing this?" Pandora demanded, raking her father with the kind of withering glance that only a loving daughter can bestow. "I mean, it's not as if you needed to lose any weight. Unlike lard-chops over there."

"Hark," Titus said. "I hear the merry squealing of little curly-tail! Bless. How happy her short life must be. There she stands, all unknowing, innocent as to the tragic fate that awaits her. The cleaver, the sawdusty abattoir floor. The *(whisper)* sausages, the bacon, the spareribs, the salamis—"

"Dad." Pandora ignored Titus entirely, positioning herself between her beetroot-red, panting parent and her palely malevolent brother. "Dad, you're not hiding anything from us, are you?"

It was fortunate for Luciano that he was already bright red, or Pandora would have immediately spotted the guilty pink flush sweeping across his face.

"You're . . . you're not *ill*, are you?" Giving voice to this terrifying possibility, Pandora's voice was barely audible over the whine of the exercise bike's whirring pedals.

Don't, Titus begged silently. *Don't, don't, don't.*

"I mean, you would tell us if you had something awful, like . . . like ca—"

"STOP IT!" Titus roared. "Just shut *up*, would you? Dad, make her stop, for God's sake. She's always doing this. I can't stand it. Her mouth. It's just—it's—"

"Come on. Both of you. Enough. Calm down." Luciano was trying to disentangle his feet from the toe clips on his exercise bike. Unfortunately, he could only manage to release himself from one, and trapped embarrassingly by the other, he was engaged in a doomed attempt to shake himself free. Trying to pretend he wasn't making a complete idiot of himself, he carried on as if nothing was happening. "The doctor, um . . . he said . . . Ah, damn this stupid thing."

"I thought you had Dr. Holgram."

"Yes, Pandora, I *do* go to Dr. Holgram," Luciano snapped. Now he had partially dismounted from the bike's saddle, but with one foot still trapped, he was forced to hop on the spot as he tried and failed to release the offending toe clip.

"Well, Dr. Holgram's female, not male. You said *he* said—"

"DAMMIT, PANDORA!" roared Luciano, toppling sideways and crashing into the disused fireplace, the bike slowly tipping over and falling on top of him. "Who *cares* if he's a she or whatever? Whose *business* is it if I've decided to improve my fitness? Why do you and your mother always subject me to the Spanish Inquisition if I do anything out of the ordinary? Why won't you just go away and leave me in *peace*?"

All of which, of course, convinced Pandora that her father wasn't telling the truth.

"Titus?" Pandora was sitting on the exercise bike, which, several days later, was still missing one of its toe clips and looking rather the worse for wear after its brief encounter with the iron grate of the disused fireplace. She took a deep breath. "It's just, oh, um, Titus, I know I'm probably being an idiot, but it's so unlike Dad to pay any attention to what he looks ... I mean, how he ... it's, like, he's *Dad*. He's always been, like ... like ..."

Titus glared at her. Slowly he raised his eyebrows. "Like?" He shrugged. "Like *what*? He's like Dad always is. Nothing's changed, as far as I can see. So what if he's going through a keep-fit phase? Better that than turning into a couch potato."

"Yeah, Titus. I guess you're right." Although she agreed with Titus's assessment, Pandora's voice lacked conviction. "Dad's just getting older. Perhaps he's having a midlife crisis thing. Probably something to do with growing bald. ... It's just, oh, he's my *dad*. It's ..."

Mine too, Titus thought, wondering if he'd be forgiven for gagging his sister and locking her in the dungeons. Just for a year or so. Nothing too permanent . . .

"It's just that I know him backwards. I know what he's saying, and I hear what he's not saying too. And, Titus, I'm positive there's something huge going on that he's not telling us about."

"Pan, give up, would you? This may come as a surprise to you, but Dad's an adult. Don't you think that adults are allowed to keep some things hidden from their kids? If he wants to tell us, he'll do so. Myself, I think you're reading way too much into his health kick. You wait: Dad's inner slob will reassert itself and will mount a spirited defense against his inner athlete. Soon he'll be bench-pressing nothing heavier than a pan of pasta, running nothing more taxing than a bath, and exercising only the major muscle groups in his mouth. Give him another month and you'll see. . . ."

Titus might as well have saved his breath. Closing in on StregaSchloss were several entities that were determined another month was a luxury none of the Strega-Borgias would live to enjoy.

Hello, Baby

The nearest hospital to StregaSchloss was housed in a tiny prewar building surrounded by beautifully maintained lawns and gardens. The actual hospital consisted of two microscopic wards—one for men and one for what the Ward Sister referred to as "my ladies"—an administration office squeezed into a broom cupboard, and a maintenance and cleaning department sharing space with an outside toilet. When Baci and Luciano's car drew up in the darkened parking lot, at first they were convinced that Latch had mistakenly driven them into someone's private garden.

"This *can't* be it." Luciano peered blindly into the blackness beyond the car windows. "Are you sure?"

"I'm absolutely positive." Latch turned round to face his employers. Baci's eyes were closed and her breathing was ragged, and

Luciano had the eyes-out-on-stalks appearance of someone teetering on the edge of hysteria. Just as Latch climbed out of the driver's seat and came round to open the rear doors, reassuring them that this was indeed the West Argyll Cottage Hospital, a beam of light cut through the darkness and a woman's voice greeted them.

"You'll be the Siggy-Borshters, I assume. Your staff phoned to let me know you were on your way. . . ."

On the point of correcting this woman's hideous mangling of his surname, Luciano managed to stop himself in time. He also suppressed the involuntary squeak that had risen from his throat at the sight of the flashlight-bearing gorgon glaring across the parking lot. As wide as she was tall, Sister Passterre stood on the doorstep of her hospital like a condensed Doric column, sweeping the beam of her flashlight along the path leading up from the parking lot, her face set in the kind of expression more commonly found on a pit bull. Sister Belinda Passterre (known to her ladies as the Blister Plaster) was a woman not to be trifled with. Her most stubborn patients became strangely compliant and putty-like under her care, preferring to subject themselves to a thousand humiliations rather than incur her wrath. Such was her reputation that the most arrogant of consultants quailed before her, regressing in an instant to the stammering, quivering medical students they had once been, many years before.

However, Baci didn't turn to putty and nor did she quail. Instead, with an apologetic smile for Luciano, she turned round, climbed back into the family car, and slammed the door shut. Seconds later, Luciano, Latch, and Sister Passterre heard the distinctive wail of a newborn.

Secretly watching this drama unfold from the vantage point of Ward One's bathroom was a middle-aged man with both legs encased in plaster. He watched intently, hidden in the darkness, through a window that stood slightly ajar, all the better to remove any trace of the small black cigar he was enjoying while the gorgon Passterre was otherwise occupied with matters obstetric. Some weeks previously, this man had been admitted to the hospital following an accident that had washed his broken body onto the shores of Lochnagargoyle. When he recovered consciousness, the nonappearance of any concerned relatives phoning on his behalf and his apparent ignorance of who he was, how he'd broken both his legs, or where he'd come from had led the medical staff to diagnose him as an amnesiac. This misdiagnosis was one that the man with the broken legs was keen to encourage. For one thing, he wasn't a man—he was a demon—and for another, as his broken legs had mended, so too had his memory.

Now, fully recovered, he knew that his name was Isagoth, and he also knew that he was in deep trouble. He'd been thinking about this, thinking dark and increasingly more desperate thoughts, when the Volvo had pulled up outside the hospital and events had taken a decidedly dramatic turn. To his astonishment, Isagoth discovered that he recognized the driver of the car: it was none other than dear Mr. Butler, the one he'd brainwiped several months ago and left for dead on the front steps of that ridiculous house—what was it called? Strega-something? How curious. *Ssso, Mr. Butler,* Isagoth thought, staring out of the window at Latch. *What brings you to this little hospital? Visiting?* Then the rear door of the Volvo had opened to disgorge a hugely pregnant woman and a thin, hysterical man.

Yesssss, Isagoth hissed. He recognized them too. They were the employers. Not only of Mr. Butler, but also of that *creature,* that Flora McLachlan woman, that infernal, interfering . . . Smoke hissed from between his teeth and coiled upward to wreathe his head in thin gray wisps. If that *woman* hadn't got in his way, he'd not be in such trouble now. No . . . Isagoth sighed; now he'd be home in Hades, back in S'tan's good books, not hiding out here in this backwoods hellhole, too terrified to let S'tan know that he, Isagoth, onetime Defense Minister of Hades, had been outwitted by a mere Scottish nanny. . . .

However, he reminded himself, all was not lost. A smile straight out of a horror film hovered around his mouth as he saw what fate had delivered straight into his hands. Cigar trembling in his grip, the demon Isagoth could hardly believe his luck. There, out in the parking lot, wailing its outrage at being born on the backseat of a middle-aged Volvo sports wagon, was Isagoth's ticket back home to Hades. What was more, he realized, hugging himself with glee, was that with a newborn baby as leverage, he'd be able to upgrade his ticket to first class. Out in the parking lot, lights were going on, white-jacketed hospital personnel were appearing, a porter was trundling a wheelchair across the tarmac, and no one was paying any attention to the patient with the broken legs who was hobbling down the corridor as fast as his crutches could carry him in search of a telephone.

"Baci, *cara mia* . . ." Luciano was barely able to speak, so blown away was he by the speed with which he'd become a dad for the fourth time. It was as much as he could do to stop himself bursting into tears at the sight of his wife being assisted into a wheelchair and gently rolled across the parking lot, their tiny newborn child wrapped in her arms.

"Mr. Borshter?" The Ward Sister stepped across his path, her deepening frown indicating exactly how affronted she felt by the Strega-Borgias' decision to have their baby in the parking lot. "I'm going to have to insist that you take a seat in the waiting room, Mr. Borshter. Just while we get your wife and baby checked out. If everything appears to be . . . *normal*"— here she gave the sort of sniff that implied that this was a possibility that she very much doubted, *normal* not being an adjective she would ever apply to unscheduled deliveries in parking lots—"then you'll be allowed to see your wife tonight for ten minutes before going home. That is, *you* going home, and *she* staying put." She held up one scrubbed red hand to forestall any objections from Luciano and raised her eyebrows in a highly challenging manner, as if to say, *Go on, punk, make my day. I dare you to raise an objection.*

Luciano wisely kept quiet, consoling himself with something

that, in his innocence, he didn't realize was a complete fiction: his certainty that no harm would befall his wife or baby as long as they were in the care of Sister Passterre. Meekly, he followed her through the front door of the hospital, blissfully unaware that anything more malign than a stray bacterium could be lurking in the shadows within.

Lightly Toasted

The phone rang in the great hall at StregaSchloss, its urgent shrilling causing everyone within range to run to answer its summons. Thus Titus, Pandora, Minty, Mrs. McLachlan, Knot, Sab, and Tock were all in time to witness Ffup playing butler.

"Hellurrrr," she murmured throatily, her normally harsh dragonish tones muted down to a husky purr. "Strrrega-Borrrgia rrresidence. Ffup here. How may I be of assistan—?"

At which point Minty briskly plucked the receiver out of Ffup's paws and hissed, "*You* may be of assistance by going downstairs to the dungeons and reading *your* baby a bedtime story." Then she turned her back on the gaping dragon, changed her tone completely, and said, "So sorry. Bit of a

mix-up there. You're through to the Strega-Borgias. Can I help?"

Pandora glanced up at the landing, where Mrs. McLachlan stood smiling down at Ffup's indignant splutters and snorts of flame as Minty shooed her dungeonward to her neglected baby, Nestor. Considering that the first time Minty had clapped eyes on Ffup, the young woman had fainted dead away, it was remarkable that she now felt brave enough to push the huge beast around, Pandora thought. As well as being brave, Minty was also tactful, always deferring to Mrs. McLachlan, consulting the older nanny over every decision regarding what had been, until recently, Mrs. McLachlan's sole responsibility. Now the two nannies effectively job-shared—a state of affairs that suited everyone perfectly, allowing Mrs. McLachlan to recoup her strength after what everyone referred to as her "accident" in Lochnagargoyle. This accident had been a weird near-drowning occasioned by Mrs. McLachlan's throwing herself into the loch on purpose and, even more weirdly, not washing *back* upon the loch shore until almost two months later. Far easier, Pandora thought, to refer to the whole thing as an "accident" and mentally file it under "Forget." *One day,* she vowed, *one day when Mrs. McLachlan is one hundred percent better, I'm going to ask her what really happened, but not now.*

Downstairs, Ffup had finally given in and was dragging herself at a snail's pace across the great hall, taking as long as possible to reach the dungeons in the hope of not having to read "The Little Mermaid" to Nestor for the tenth time, and also in case the telephone caller had any news about whether Baci's baby was a girl or a boy.

"No, I'm sorry. The Signor and Signora have gone to the hospital tonight. . . ." Minty turned round and made a shooing gesture at Ffup. *Go on,* the young nanny mouthed silently; then, turning her back on the dragon: "Yes. We're just waiting to hear about the baby. Mmmm. Very exciting time, yes. Absolutely. May I tell them who called?" There was a pause while Minty raked in the drawer of the telephone table, trying to find a pen or pencil with which to take down the caller's details. "Hang on a second . . . ," she muttered, hauling out a selection of dried-up old felt-tips, a nibless fountain pen, and several pencils with such impossibly hard leads that they didn't so much write as *carve.*

Titus, seeing an opportunity, seized it. "Look, here, hey . . . um, use this," he said, vaulting downstairs and holding out his mobile phone to Minty. Her puzzled frown told Titus that she, along with his entire family, was a stranger to twenty-first-century technology. Probably prefer a goose quill dipped in ink, Titus thought gloomily, calling up the voice-recorder menu on his phone and passing it over to Minty.

Understanding dawned. Her face brightened, and nodding to show Titus that she was now with the program, she repeated with exaggerated care what the caller was telling her.

"Loo-doh Grab-it. Most unusual name."

This, Titus decided, was a bit steep, coming from someone who rejoiced in the name Minty.

"Signor Strega-Borgia has your number? Great. I'll let him know that you called. . . . Yes. Even if he doesn't come home till late? . . . No. Not a problem—I'll leave him a note. Tomorrow, late morning? . . . Yes. Consider it done. . . . You too. Good night."

Ffup's wings slumped as she reached the door to the kitchen. There was to be no last-minute reprieve, then. No avoiding having to read "The Little Mermaid" to Nestor. Again. Silently praying that the new Baby Borgia would arrive in the next few minutes, Ffup continued her glacially slow progress toward the dungeons, where, had she but known it, Nestor was already fast asleep, taloned thumb in mouth, having given up waiting for his mummy nearly an hour before.

Inside the cramped broom cupboard that served as the hospital administration center, the demon Isagoth was encountering some technical difficulties in getting through to his boss, S'tan. Unlike humans, who were required to sacrifice goats and initiate weird rituals involving candles, pentagrams, and incense, when demons wanted to talk to His Horned Horribleness, S'tan, First Minister of the Hadean Executive, all they did was pick up a phone.

That, at least, was the theory. In practice, all calls to Hades were screened, and thus all demons had to work their way laboriously through a score of labyrinthine menus before even being allowed to speak with a fellow fiend. Even then, there was no guarantee that a phone call would ever reach its intended destination. Especially if, like Isagoth, one had the kind of pukka accent marking one out as a member of the Demonic Elite, namely, a minister in the Hadean Executive enjoying all the bungs, freebies, and privileges that such a position entailed.

By contrast, on the other end of the line was an underpaid demon who'd just been forced to walk to work through the foot-high snowdrifts, black ice, and severe blizzards that were currently paralyzing Hades' entire transport network. Frozen to the marrow, the demon was in no mood to be pushed around by some git like Isagoth, who, it seemed, was lucky enough to have been posted somewhere that wasn't Hades, even if it *was* Scotland in winter. Out of spite, the demon shivering in the Hadean call center decided to be as awkward as possible, thus sharing some of the misery of his life with the overprivileged Isagoth.

"Whaaaat?" he bawled. "Can't hear yer. You're breaking up, mate. Wossermarra? You on a train or sumfin'?"

Unable to raise his voice to anything above a whispered hiss for fear of being overheard by the dreaded Blister Plaster, Isagoth tried again: "I need you to put me through to the Internal Offices of His Imperial Inflammableness."

Silence greeted this request—a silence that Isagoth didn't realize was entirely due to the demon in the call center's removing his headset, dropping it into a filing cabinet, and going off to make himself a cup of hot vitriol. All unknowing, Isagoth tried to appeal to the drone's better nature.

"Pleeeassssse," he hissed from inside the filing cabinet.

"This is really urgent. It is a matter concerning the stone. I must speak to His S'tainless S'teeliness at once. The very future of Hades depends on it. . . ."

Silence rolled down the phone to where Isagoth hunched over Sister Passterre's desk, idly rifling through her handbag, wondering if there was anything edible, smokable, or even valuable in its depths. So far he'd found nothing of note save for a passport, two pounds fifty in change, an underripe banana, and half a low-calorie oat-and-prune energy bar. Isagoth devoured the banana and had just sunk his front teeth into the unappetizing prune confection when he distinctly heard the demon on the other end mutter something about an overpaid plonker who'd had the nerve to phone up and demand to speak to the Boss. At this, Isagoth's blood pressure soared and a red mist appeared before his eyes. To add injury to insult, in the background he could distinctly hear the demon loudly suggesting exactly where his caller could stick his telephone, and at this, Isagoth blew a fuse.

"Listen up, lard-for-brains," he snarled. "When I said I wanted to speak to the Boss, I didn't mean I wanted to speak to a stunted goblin with out-of-date cottage cheese between its ears—"

"I BEG YOUR—" a voice broke in, but Isagoth was not for begging.

Eyeballs bulging, spitting oat flakes and flecks of prune across the desk, he hissed, "You, pal, can do as you're told for once. Get off your overstuffed rear end and put me through to the Boss—"

"YOU'RE THROUGH TO HIM," a voice informed him. "IT IS I. HIMSELF. OR, AS YOU WOULD HAVE IT— HOW WAS IT YOU PUT IT? SO QUAINT, SUCH AN ELEGANT TURN OF PHRASE. . . . AH, YES, 'THE STUNTED GOBLIN WITH OUT-OF-DATE STILTON BETWEEN ITS EARS—' "

"Cottage cheese," Isagoth corrected him before he could stop himself.

"INDEED. COTTAGE CHEESE. YOU, SCUM, ARE GO-ING TO LOOK LIKE YOU'RE *MADE* OF THE STUFF BY THE TIME I'VE FINISHED WITH YOU. ISAGOTH, ISN'T IT?"

Isagoth's knees, under their plaster casing, turned to jelly. It was *S'tan* on the other end. At some point that ghastly little guppy at the call center must have put his call straight through. . . . Oh, Hell's teeth, Isagoth thought. This was *disastrous.*

"I ca-ca-can explain, Your Abysmal Aggressiveness."

"THAT I VERY MUCH DOUBT. TELL ME, USING ONE SYLLABLE ONLY, DO YOU HAVE MY STONE?"

This was not going at all well, Isagoth thought. He'd hoped to be the bearer of good news along the lines of *Returning soonest with Your stone plus newborn baby soul,* rather than the kind of bad news that usually preceded the death of the bearer—viz. *Regret have failed utterly in mission to rescue Your precious stone and am returning for execution.*

"LET ME JUST REFRESH YOUR MEMORY," S'tan continued. "I'M TALKING ABOUT MY STONE. MY

CHRONOSTONE, *COMPRENDEZ?* WITHOUT WHICH I AM DECIDEDLY LESS EVIL THAN I WAS. THE LESSER OF TWO EVILS, YOU MIGHT SAY. WHEN I CHARGED YOU WITH THE TASK OF RECOVER- ING MY STONE, I DID NOT ANTICIPATE FAILURE ON YOUR PART. I NEED THE STONE TO RESTORE DOMINION OVER THE FORCES OF LIGHT THAT SEEK TO OVERTHROW HADES. NOW. ONCE MORE, WITH FEELING. DO YOU HAVE MY STONE, MIN- ISTER?"

Isagoth's bowels turned to water. "Ye-e-e-s," he managed, and then good sense got the better of him and he qualified this with, "Well, no. I mean, I know roughly where it is, Your stone, but I haven't got it. At least not personally."

There was a long pause at the other end, during which Is- agoth wondered if his translation into cottage cheese would be swift and painless. Somehow he very much doubted it. No. Of one thing he was absolutely one hundred percent certain: S'tan didn't do mercy. After all, Isagoth reminded himself, S'tan was the Devil, the Arch-Fiend, the Earl of Earwax and Prince of the Pit. Mercy? Sadly not. However, what S'tan *did* do was a nice line in terror, punishment, retribution, and re- venge. Isagoth could plead till he was blue in the face, explain how his mission to find S'tan's missing stone had been thwarted by the actions of one woman acting on her own— one tiny middle-aged woman called Flora McLachlan—but somehow Isagoth knew that no matter what excuses he of- fered, S'tan would be deeply unimpressed. Nor, he realized, was there any point in telling S'tan that His stone could be found amongst a million other stones on the shore of an island that had never been charted on any map in existence; Isagoth sensed that S'tan would be somewhat underwhelmed by that snippet of information as well.

The only hope to which Isagoth could cling was that without His stone, S'tan's power would be so diminished that He'd barely be able to turn pale with rage, let alone turn His failed servant into a particularly pointless cheese. Chewing with a mouth turned dry by fear, Isagoth wished that he'd chosen something a little more easily swallowed than an oat-and-prune energy bar for his last meal on Earth.

"STILL THERE, HMM?" S'tan sounded . . . it was weird, but S'tan sounded cheery, almost playful.

With a considerable effort, Isagoth swallowed. There, ughhh. "Yes, Your Gruesomeness?"

"YOU'RE AN IDIOT, D'YOU KNOW THAT? A COMPLETE FAILURE. HADES IS FREEZING OVER BECAUSE YOU HAVEN'T BROUGHT MY STONE BACK. MY KINGDOM, THANKS TO YOU, IS CURRENTLY FATHOMS DEEP IN SNOW; IT'S BLOWING A BLIZZARD; THERE'S A WIND SO SHARP IT COULD SLICE BREAD . . . TALKING OF WHICH"—S'tan gave a little un-S'tan-ish giggle—"I'M IN A TELEVISION STUDIO RECORDING MY COOKERY SHOW, *TOTALLY TOAST,* SO FRANKLY, I'M NOT TOO FUSSED ABOUT WHAT'S GOING ON BACK HOME BECAUSE I'M NOT SUFFERING IN PERSON"—another merry S'tanic snicker—

"WHICH IS WHY I'M NOT EVISCERATING YOU, YOU MORONIC LUMP. NO. THAT PLEASURE CAN WAIT. IN FACT, IT CAN BE POSTPONED INDEFINITELY IF—"

If? Isagoth seized upon that small word as if it were a life preserver. "Anything," he babbled. "I am Yours to command. Just say the word—"

"AND THE WORD IS *SHADDUP*," S'tan snapped. "ZIP YOUR LYING LIPS. PUT A CLOVEN SOCK IN IT. I HAVE A JOB FOR YOU. A MISSION. A CHANCE, IF YOU DON'T MESS UP, TO REDEEM YOURSELF IN MY SIGHT. A GUARANTEED PARDON IF YOU ARE SUC-CESSFUL. I NEED YOU TO DESTROY SOMEONE FOR ME. AM I CLEAR?"

"As crystal, Your Vileness."

"NOW, WHEN I SAY 'DESTROY,' I DON'T MEAN 'DE-STROY' AS IN 'DROP A BOMB ON TOP OF.' NOR DO I MEAN 'DESTROY' AS IN 'EXECUTE.' NO GUNS, KNIVES, OR DYNAMITE, UNDERSTOOD?"

"Perhaps You mean more of a mental and spiritual destruc-tion, Your Nastiness?"

"PRECISELY. DELIGHTED TO HEAR YOU BACK ON FORM, MINISTER. I MEAN BREAK HIM, CRUSH HIS SPIRIT, DESTROY EVERYTHING THIS MAN BELIEVES IN, YES? BUT LEAVE *HIM* STANDING. MY CLIENT WAS VERY CLEAR ON THAT POINT. HE SPECIFI-CALLY DEMANDED THAT HIS HALF BROTHER WAS TO BE LEFT ALIVE. ALIVE, BUT SO PSYCHOLOGI-

CALLY DAMAGED THAT HE'D WISH HE WERE DEAD. THAT'S THE BRIEF."

Isagoth stared across the tiny room, his mind spinning with vicious possibilities.

"SHOULDN'T BE TOO DIFFICULT," S'tan continued. "ONE WOULD DO IT ONESELF, BUT ONE IS BUSY WITH CAREER MATTERS REQUIRING ONE'S CONTINUED PRESENCE IN LONDON AND THE VICTIM IS IN SCOTLAND, SO . . ."

"Leave it to me, Your Vindictiveness," Isagoth breathed. "Consider it done. Whoever he is, he'll wish he'd never been born. . . . Er . . . Boss? Who is it?" Not trusting his ability to remember names, Isagoth grabbed the first thing he could find in the darkness and scrawled the name of Luciano Strega-Borgia in waterproof, super-permanent indelible pink laundry marker across the back of his hand. As he wrote Luciano's name, he realized that he knew *exactly* who this prospective victim was. Luciano Strega-Borgia. The man in the parking lot with the no-longer-pregnant wife. Mr. Butler's boss. And— Isagoth closed his eyes and swayed slightly—Luciano Strega-Borgia was also the boss of that infernal, pestilential nanny thing, that Flora McLachlan who'd got him in such deep water in the first place. . . .

It wasn't until S'tan hung up that Isagoth remembered about the baby. In the heat of the moment he'd forgotten to mention that he'd found a newborn soul, ripe for the taking. Since souls were regarded as a superior form of currency in Hades—the demonic equivalent of, say, gold doubloons—it was to Isagoth's considerable advantage that he'd stumbled across such a one. He had a sneaking suspicion that the baby might have some intrinsic value here on Earth as well. Therefore, he vowed, no matter how inconvenient it might be to kidnap it, that was precisely what he intended to do.

Their Baby's Deepest Fear

The hospital ward was tropically hot, its thermostat set at a perfect temperature for raising orchids, nursing the old and frail, and overheating any visitors unwise enough to arrive dressed in anything more substantial than a bikini. Consequently, the tribe of Strega-Borgias and staff gathered around Baci's bedside, all of them swathed in layers to insulate them against the freezing winter weather, were in imminent danger of melting. Furthermore, being adolescents, Titus and Pandora flatly refused to remove any outdoor clothing at all, and thus they stood, pink and perspiring, looking down at their new baby brother with expressions several smiles short of delight.

Seeing this, Baci bit her bottom lip and tried hard not to cry, but Damp had no such qualms.

She wriggled free from Mrs. McLachlan's grasp, hurtled across the ward, sprang onto Baci's bed, and burst into loud and inconsolable sobs. Titus and Pandora traded been-there-done-that looks and then resumed their identical expressions of faint boredom. Damp wailed all the more, attracting slitty-eyed glares from Sister Passterre, who was counting scalpels with an air of barely concealed anticipation. In vain did Luciano try to appease the wailing toddler; Damp was beyond appeasement, consolation, comfort, or even bribery.

"... and because you're being so *big* and *grown-up*"—— Luciano rolled his eyes, acknowledging to his wife that he was indeed lying through his teeth about Damp's behavior— "Mumma and Dada have bought you a *lovely* new tricycle."

"*That* old trick," muttered Titus, walking away from the crowded bedside to gaze out of the window. Outside, in pajamas and dressing gown, was a man walking with the aid of two crutches. Despite the cold, he was determinedly crossing the frosty lawn, trying to catch the attention of two lumpy figures shrouded in thick coats, the photo IDs dangling round their necks marking them out as hospital employees leaving at the end of their shift. Behind Titus, Damp eloquently declined her father's generous offer.

"NO LIKEIT. No WANTIT tie-sickle."

And Titus was instantly transported back in time, all the way back to an August morning, eleven years ago, when—

They'd promised him a tricycle, but instead they showed him a shawl-wrapped thing lying in his old rocking cradle. He'd looked out of curiosity and saw, under a puff of jet-black hair, a pair of navy blue eyes glaring up at him, surrounded by a pink crumpled thing that he hesitated to call a face.

"Here's your little sister, Pandora, darling."

So . . . that's what it was. He'd turned away, but a banshee wail made him turn back. A hole had opened in the middle of the crumpled pinkness and deafening noises were coming from it. Titus watched with interest as his parents ran around like headless chickens.

"Shouldn't you feed her?"

"She's just been fed."

"Well . . . shall I change her?"

Into what? wondered Titus, alone and overlooked.

"Oh, I can't bear to hear her cry like that. . . ."

"Well, do something, then."

"I don't know what to do. We've tried everything."

"I know what," said Titus, sensing a chance to become less lonely and overlooked. "Let's take it back to the hostiple."

As he returned to the present, Titus could still recall the look on their faces. Pandora's arrival had been a turning point in his life, a milestone after which nothing had ever been the same. Sleety rain blatted against the windows, drawing Titus's attention to the world beyond the hospital. Outside, the man on crutches had managed to blag a cigarette from one of the off-duty staff. Now he was hunched over, trying to light it, both his crutches abandoned on the lawn, a strange bright pink mark, or tattoo, on his left hand. He straightened up, took several unaided and apparently pain-free steps toward the hospital like a miracle cure in action, and then, spotting Titus staring at him, he spun round, loped back across the lawn, seized his discarded crutches, and turned to face the window. Despite the heat in the ward, Titus was instantly frozen to the core. The man smiled slowly—a vile parody of a smile: a leer, a sneer, more of a snarl, really—and then . . .

"*AoWW!* My *eye!*" Titus yelped, jerking backward from the window, both hands flying up to his face in a belated attempt to protect himself. A white-hot needle of pain flared in one eye, as if a sharp point had been plunged straight into his eyeball. Tears streamed through his fingers as the outraged organ tried in vain to eject what ailed it. Blinded on one side, Titus couldn't even open his unaffected eye, because every blink was automatically and agonizingly duplicated by the injured one.

Several lifetimes scrolled by, or perhaps it was more a matter of several seconds, but for Titus, time lost all meaning. The icy burn in his eye was spreading across his skull, filling his ears with an avalanche of static hiss, stilling his tongue and catching at the back of his throat before finally seizing his heart, driving a spike through its frantically beating muscle and lodging itself as a splinter of ice deep within its innermost chamber. At which point the pain stopped.

Outside the window, the demon Isagoth gave Titus the thumbs-up and exhaled a gray plume of smoke. Titus frowned and turned away, a snowy amnesia descending on his thoughts and blanketing his memory in icy whiteness. Across the ward, Mrs. McLachlan had poured oil on troubled waters and now had both the new baby *and* Damp on her lap for an introductory chat.

"No, pet. Let's *not* pull the new baby's fingers off—he might need them later on. . . . Yes, *and* his eyes too. Useful things, eyes. Titus, dear, you look as if you've seen a ghost. . . ."

Unaccountably, the new baby opened his navy blue eyes and began to scream in a manner that made further conversation impossible. Moments later, not to be outdone, Damp joined in, and shortly thereafter Sister Passterre reluctantly left her scalpels and came over to Baci's bed to declare that visiting time was over.

As the last visitor trooped gratefully out of the ward into the fresh air, a wintry sunshine dappled the ceiling above the new Baby Borgia's cot. The baby peered out at the world through dark blue eyes and tried to make sense of all the newness bombarding him from every angle. Sister Passterre's huge shape loomed, boomed, breathed hotly, and withdrew, roaring loudly to itself. Occasionally an efficient hand would haul the new baby's legs into the air and a sudden coolness would envelop its bottom. Slippery stuff would be slopped all about; then would come a scrunching, scrumpling sound, whereupon the baby's bottom would be once more encased in papery, padded warmth.

It was all so *new*, and mainly it was all fairly pleasant, but best by far was being wrapped in Baci's arms, where the new baby would surrender to the familiar beat of his mother's heart, surrender to her unique smell, surrender utterly to her particular brand of fumble-fingered, deeply devoted, soft and tender mothering. . . .

The new baby slipped into a deep, deep sleep . . .

. . . was gently placed back in his cot . . .

. . . and woke abruptly into sheer hell.

Ungentle hands seized him like so much dirty laundry, a hand clamped over his tiny mouth, and he was jolted, bounced, and thrown about as something hard and huge and horrifying bore the helpless Baby Borgia away from everything and everyone that loved him.

A cloud had slid across the sun by the time Baci returned from her shower, and the ward was decidedly cooler, as if a door or window had been left open. The baby lay on its back, its green eyes watching where Baci stood nearby, furtively popping a champagne truffle into her mouth before jamming the box back into her locker and clambering back into bed. Stretching across to stroke the baby's cheek, Baci frowned. The baby's green eyes blinked back at her, and moments ticked past. Then a metallic clatter announced the arrival of morning coffee, and a distant telephone rang twice. Baci blinked and shook her head. *Obviously,* she thought, *I'm overtired. The baby's eyes have always been green. Honestly, whatever was I thinking?* Then, turning her attention to the approaching trolley, Baci wondered if there would be a little something to soak up the bitterness of the hospital's scaldingly hot and mouth-shrivelingly stewed coffee. And if not, she decided, absentmindedly stroking the baby's head, somewhere in her locker Mrs. McLachlan had tucked a small box of homemade lavender shortbread, which would more than compensate for any shortfall in the hospital's biscuit rations.

Forcing itself not to flinch or sink its needle-sharp teeth into Baci's hand, the changeling submitted to the petting. Never before had its raw skin been caressed. Never before had it known kindness. Raised in the nurseries of Hades, it had experience of being handled with only a kind of detached efficiency. Now here it was, encountering something utterly alien: a mother's loving caress. Baci's hands were warm, smooth, and gentle. Relaxing under her touch, the changeling baby closed its eyes and was asleep within seconds, dreaming, as it always did, of blood-red flames blossoming in the darkness like dangerous flowers.

Blow Your House Down

As had been his habit since taking Luciano on as an apprentice gunslinger, Ludo Grabbit brought his ancient Land Rover to a shuddering, rattling halt on the rose quartz drive outside Strega-Schloss at eleven o'clock precisely. The house was silent, its windows blank, the surrounding gardens glittering under a rime of frost. However, the steps leading up to the front door had been de-iced with salt, and Latch's face at the open door was shining with happiness.

"The new baby?" Ludo murmured, preceding Latch across the hall toward the kitchen.

"A grand wee laddie for the Signor and Signora. Tucked up safe in hospital with his mammy." Latch smiled, adding, "We're expecting them both home this afternoon."

"Great stuff," Ludo said, pushing through into the kitchen and beaming at the assembled company. "I believe congratulations are in order?"

"Yes," said Titus flatly, his voice devoid of both color and enthusiasm. "We're very pleased."

I don't think *so,* Ludo decided. *I don't think you're pleased at all, young sir. What's up with this chap? Jealous? Surely not.* Ludo pressed on, "And where's the happy paterfamilias?"

"The *what?*"

"Oh, come *on,* Titus," Pandora interrupted. "Stop being like this." She turned to Ludo and said, "Ignore my brother. He'll improve once he's eaten something. Just think kindly of us all: you only have to endure this for one day in every seven; *we* have to put up with Mr. Grumple-Snurk every day of our lives...."

"Yeah, right," mumbled Titus, the return of the nagging pain in his injured eye causing him not to rise to the bait. "If you mean Dad, he's upstairs, working out."

Pandora rolled her eyes and groaned. "They're not called dumbbells for nothing, you know. I just *so* don't get it, all that huffing and puffing...."

Perhaps it's to stop a wolf from blowing your house down, Ludo thought, smiling at the children and standing aside as Minty came into the kitchen from the garden, a breath of freezing air rolling in behind her. Damp stamped in behind her, her voice raised in determined inquiry.

"Why is newbaby coming home? Why not leave it in hostiple with Aunty Naytil?"

Minty wisely ignored this, merely assisting Damp out of

her fleecy jacket, unwinding her scarf, and tucking both mittens into a pocket.

"Not wantit anyhow. Not like *boys*."

"Thanks," muttered Titus, shooting Damp a look out of his uninjured eye that ought to have freeze-dried all her internal organs. Minty tried to hide a smile by turning away to set the kettle on to boil, and thus found herself face to face with Ludo.

Months later, on honeymoon in the far northwest of Scotland, both Minty and Ludo agreed that they had fallen in love in that instant, in front of the unaware Strega-Borgia children in the kitchen at StregaSchloss. Ludo felt the floor tilt under his feet, and was assailed by such a feeling of vertigo that he grabbed the towel rail of the range for support. He closed his eyes briefly, utterly at a loss to explain what had just happened to him. Minty's hand holding the kettle trembled so violently that water slopped out of the spout and fell, hissing loudly, onto the stovetop. Ludo's eyes opened, and without hesitation he reached out to take the wildly shaking kettle from Minty's grasp. Smiling, he looked at her, really looked, marveling as he did at the blueness of her eyes, just as Minty came to the realization that Ludo's face was exactly the face that she wanted to wake up to every morning for the rest of her life.

"Yeah, Damp," Titus snarled, blissfully unaware of the momentous events unfolding over by the range, being more concerned with exacting revenge for his youngest sister's blanket condemnation of all things boyish. "When *you* came along, both Pan and I took one look in your cot and went, 'Eeeyew. *Babies*. Not like it, babies.' Fat lot of difference *that* made. They didn't take *you* back to hostiple either, no matter how many times we begged them to."

Damp was saved from further unpalatable truths by the arrival in the kitchen of Luciano, fresh from exercising, aglow with sweaty virtue and in need of coffee, a second breakfast, and a more effective form of deodorant. Pandora took one look at her soggy father and rolled her eyes so hard that for a moment she resembled an extra from *Night of the Living Dead*. Damp clamored to be picked up for a hug, but once in her father's arms, she batted him away, wrinkling her nose and informing everyone within earshot, "Dada smells horbil. Go 'way, stinky, yuck."

Stung, Luciano deposited his younger daughter on a nearby chair and turned his attention to Ludo.

"You'll have heard our good news, then?"

Ludo blinked several times, dragging his gaze away from Minty; this, he found to his dismay, appeared to require an unimaginable effort. "Er, ah . . . um," he managed, and stopped to take a deep breath and try again. Fortunately, his training as a lawyer enabled him to talk fluently about one thing while thinking about something else entirely, and he pulled himself together, remembering the real reason he was here. "Delighted. Congratulations. You must be absolutely cock-a-hoop, old chap." As he spoke, his mind was spinning off, down darker pathways. Despite the dizzying nearness of the young woman at his side, despite the faintest scent of lilies that she carried with her like an invisible bouquet, despite the fact that if he was stupid enough to let her slip out of his life, he would never be able to forgive himself . . . despite all of these, Ludo's first responsibility was toward Luciano and his family. Today there would be no shooting lessons for Luciano, because Ludo had come to StregaSchloss to inform Luciano that time had run out.

A known Italian associate of Luciano's evil half brother, Don Lucifer, had been arrested in Bologna and charged with murder. Upon arrival in the police station, young Fabbrizio had taken one look at his future cellmates and had decided at that instant to repent and turn his back on a life of crime. One word in his jailer's ear and he was escorted to a sound-proofed cell and invited to spill the beans regarding the activities of his previous employer. Fabbrizio had recorded everything he knew about Don Lucifer di S'Embowelli Borgia onto a tape, a copy of which now nestled in the pocket of Ludo's tweed jacket. This was the reason for the lawyer's appearance at StregaSchloss that morning. Unaware that Ludo was the bearer of some very bad news indeed, Luciano smiled widely and crossed to the range to make coffee for his guest.

"We're *all* thrilled about our new baby," Luciano lied, blatantly ignoring Titus's fisheyed expression, Pandora's deep, meaningful sighs denoting terminal boredom, and Damp's Beethoven-browed, bottom-lip-puckered pout. Spooning coffee beans into a grinder, Luciano continued, "I'm bringing Baci and Little No-Name back this afternoon, and rather than having a huge celebration now, we were thinking about holding a small party in about a fortnight's time. I would hope that you'd be able to join us. . . ." The rest of his words were drowned out by the clatter and whine of the coffee grinder.

Ludo waited, keeping a tight leash on his urge to grab Luciano by the arm and scream, "For God's sake, man. You don't have time for parties, you don't even have time for coffee. You need to take your family, *all* of them, away from here, out of Argyll—maybe even the U.K.—and get yourselves into hiding before your half brother's hired assassins arrive on your doorstep."

Instead, Ludo forced himself to smile and wait as Luciano spooned ground coffee into the bottom half of an ancient espresso maker, wait and smile while he replaced the top half and screwed it down tight, smile and wait as Luciano placed it on the burner, took milk out of the fridge, found the cups in the china cupboard. . . . It felt like whole lifetimes had slid by before Ludo finally found himself alone with Luciano, upstairs in the study. Moving a pile of manuals, correspondence, and assembly instructions for exercise equipment to one side, Luciano offered Ludo a battered wing chair and perched himself on a stool before taking a deep gulp from his cup and extolling the coffee's virtues.

"Delicious. You can really taste the dark-roast beans," he muttered dreamily before Ludo broke into his reverie with the news he'd been dreading.

The only tape player Luciano could find at short notice

belonged to Damp, its cheery pink and sparkly exterior singularly inappropriate for the ghastly content of the tape currently spooling inside it. Fabbrizio's voice was faint and whiny, but both Ludo and Luciano could make out most of what he was saying.

"... si. *A pact. Don Lucifer made an agreement with Il Diavolo to destroy his half brother.*"

"Il Diavolo? Is this another gangster?" Luciano whispered, almost to himself. Fabbrizio's voice continued, the subject matter under discussion bringing Luciano out in a cold sweat.

"*The only name I ever hear Don Lucifer call this Diavolo was Stan. I do not know this Stan, but I do know that he is . . . pfff . . . very powerful. Like a gigantic octopus,* si? Capisce? *He has his tentacles dipped into every little pond and pool. There is nothing and nowhere that this Stan doesn't know about. I do not meet this Stan, for which I am very grateful.*"

Luciano's eyes were closed, almost as if he thought he could blind himself to what was going on—as if by denying the evidence of his eyes he could avoid the whole ghastly mess. Fabbrizio's voice whined on.

"*No. Stan was going to take care of this. Of all of them.* Si. *The wife and kids too*—" Here he broke off to give a mirthless snicker, as if the Strega-Borgias' lives were of no consequence, an amusing bit of target practice. "*Yeah. No one left standing. No one left alive to breed, to continue that branch of the* famiglia *Borgia. The end of the line. Who was going to do the job? All these questions,* signore. *I do not know—not Stan himself. No. No way.*"

That would be stupido. *Il Diavolo wouldn't risk getting personally involved. No, that's not how we do things. Stan would get one of his minions to do the dirty: a consigliere, a capo, a hired killer, some guy who's already in place in the area—*"

Ludo stopped the tape, his eyebrows raised, his hand hovering on top of the pink tape player as if he were about to ask a child whether another wee sing-along before lights-out would be a good idea.

" 'In place in the area.' " Luciano's voice quavered. "But . . . but . . ."

"Yes," Ludo murmured. "He's here already. Presumably he knows exactly where you are. Where Baci and—"

Luciano was on his feet. Moments later, the Volvo spun off across the drive, scattering rose quartz in all directions. Latch stood in the great hall, duster in hand, his puzzled expression reflected in the breastplate of a suit of armor he'd been polishing when Luciano had bolted past. Now Mr. Grabbit was running downstairs, taking the steps three at a time, obviously in a tearing hurry as well. Watching this reflected in the suit of armor, Latch saw the lawyer stop at the foot of the stairs, take a deep breath, and, as if he'd come to a decision, clear his throat and speak:

"Latch. Could we have a word? In private?"

"Right away," Latch replied, poking his duster into the suit of armor's codpiece and turning round to face the lawyer. "Might I suggest the Discouraging Room, Mr. Grabbit? That way we can be assured of absolute privacy."

This was no exaggeration. So depressing and meanly

proportioned was this room that the whole of the present generation of the family had never once set foot over its threshold. Not once, not even out of curiosity. Consequently, it was freezing cold, smelled of mold, and lived up to its name admirably. Following Ludo inside, Latch pulled the door closed behind them.

That Ring Thing

Ffup knocked respectfully on Mrs. McLachlan's bedroom door and, without waiting for an invitation, barged straight inside, in her haste allowing the door to slam behind her. Sitting at her dressing table, pinning up her long silver hair, Mrs. McLachlan sighed. In over six hundred years, Ffup's grasp of the rudiments of etiquette had not improved one whit. The dragon *still* behaved like an untamable teenager, despite being a parent herself. Wondering what had brought her upstairs, Mrs. McLachlan poked a final pin into her hair and turned to face her visitor. Clearly nervous, Ffup clasped and unclasped her front paws, her golden eyes fixed on the floor and little puffs of steam coming from both nostrils.

"Er," she began, "it's great to see you're back on your, um . . . We're so delighted that you're

feeling, er . . . I was wondering if now would be a good time, ah—" She broke off, embarrassed, as her stomach gave a loud roar of complaint, its digestive chorus running to several verses, each one longer and more embarrassingly loud than the one before.

What had the dragon had for breakfast? wondered Mrs. McLachlan. Or did her ridiculous diet forbid breakfast, along with every single food substance known to man or beast— with the sole exceptions of grapes and strawberries, neither of which were in plentiful supply this far into a Scottish winter? Ffup had, in fact, breakfasted well. She'd sneaked out of the house with a twelve-pack of tuna, three tins of anchovies, two jars of salmon in aspic, and a defrosted packet of fish sticks, taking this fishy feast down to the lochside to share with her husband-to-be, the gigantic sea serpent the Sleeper. When the loch waters had parted to reveal the huge head of her beloved, they also unfortunately exposed the undulating form of a smaller, perfectly formed, dainty *female* sea serpent, her coils coyly intertwined with those of Ffup's so-called fiancé.

Ffup's initial reaction had been to hurl tins of tuna at her faithless Sleeper, but as three tins sank without trace several hundred yards shy of their target, the betrayed and weeping dragon decided not to waste any more food on such a scumbag. Stomping off into the privacy of a vast rhododendron bush, Ffup indulged in a spot of comfort eating, wolfing down every last flake of fish, drop of oil, and blob of aspic in between floods of tears and howls of outrage. By the time the last fish stick had slid flabbily down her throat, she had come to a decision. The engagement was off. The wedding was canceled. She'd phone the florist, the caterers, the dressmaker, the printer, the coach hire company, the minister, the marquee people, the chandlers, and the firework display designers, and at the same time cancel her subscriptions to *Bridal Beast, Dragon Damsels,* and *Weight Wibblers Anonymous* . . . tomorrow. First of all, and most important, she had to go through the time-honored tradition of removing her engagement ring and flinging it back in the face of the . . . the faithless, lying, two-timing, slimy toad who . . . who had broken her poor innocent little dragon heart.

But before *that,* she had to find her engagement ring. Four months ago, when the Sleeper had slid the colossal diamond onto her talon, Ffup had been ecstatic. So ecstatic that, in all the girly froth of showing off her new engagement ring to her admiring family, she hadn't noticed Mrs. McLachlan drawing back from the ring with a gasp of horror. For Mrs. McLachlan had recognized the stone in Ffup's ring. She alone had realized that it was no diamond, no matter how brightly it seemed to glitter. She knew that the stone was older than a mere prehistoric lump of compressed carbon, older than Time itself. Unfortunately, she also knew that the stone was a prize that certain Hades-spawned entities would stop at nothing to acquire. When Ffup's talon had turned a hideous corpse-gray beneath the ring's embrace, Mrs. McLachlan had seized the opportunity to protect those she loved. On the pretext of allowing Ffup's talon time to recover, she had taken the ring, removed the stone from it, and thrown both herself and the stone into Lochnagargoyle in the hope of putting it beyond the reach of the Dark Side.

Poor Ffup had been devastated—losing both nanny *and* engagement ring had been hard for the dragon to bear—and she had turned to the contents of the pantry for comfort. Now, with Flora safely returned to StregaSchloss and no longer so frail after her near-drowning in the loch, Ffup had been waiting for a suitable moment to find out if her ring had also survived its immersion. Since Mrs. McLachlan had been the last person to lay hands on it, asking her appeared to be the logical first step toward its recovery. Hence Ffup's presence in her bedroom, an event whose significance was not lost on the nanny.

"Ffup, dear—you'll have come about your engagement ring? Och, I'm terribly sorry, pet, but I must confess that, yes, I do know where it is, but alas, I cannot find it for you."

Ffup frowned mightily. This was *not* the response she'd expected from the perpetually organized Mrs. McLachlan. Ffup had confidently assumed that the nanny would immediately turn to her wardrobe and, from a drawer labeled *R*, tucked in amongst an assortment of rose petals, rickrack, recorders, ropes, razors, reels, revolvers, reticules, retorts, and remedies, would retrieve Ffup's ring, wrapped in tissue paper for safekeeping.

"Huhnnn?" The dragon's jaw dropped.

"Ffup, pet lamb, that stone, the enormous diamond in your engagement ring . . . it's not what you think it is—"

"WHATTTT ?" Ffup couldn't believe what she was hearing. "Don't tell me it's not even a *real* diamond? Like, he was faking that as *well*?" A bolt of flame shot out of her mouth before she could clamp her lips together.

"Try to calm down, dear." Mrs. McLachlan reached out to pat the dragon's wildly flapping paws. "You're setting my lampshade on fire."

Ffup looked up to the ceiling, where the silk shade was blazing merrily. "Sorry. But . . . but . . . my *ring*. What d'you mean, it's not what I think? What *is* it, then? And, for that matter, *where* is it? If you know where it is, why can't you find it?"

"Och, pet . . . so many questions. It's on an island. I hid it there amongst other stones just like it, and—"

"You *lost* it?" Ffup shook her massive head from side to side, trying to make sense of this, trying to reconcile her image of Mrs. McLachlan, the perfectly organized nanny, with her new picture of Mrs. McLachlan, the totally disorganized space cadet who'd effectively flung a needle into a haystack. Deliberately. Dazed and confused, Ffup could only repeatedly bleat, "You *lost* it?"

"Sort of, dear, but not *exactly*. I was trying to protect you from it. You see, Ffup, dear, it's not really a diamond engagement ring, your ring. It's a . . ." The nanny faltered. She wanted to say it was a liability, a poisoned chalice, a magical artifact so powerful that it destroyed everything and anyone with whom it came into contact . . . but that would have only been part of the truth. Whatever she said, she had to discourage Ffup from trying to find it. Ever. Wrongly assuming that the dragon wanted her engagement ring back in order to wear it, Mrs. McLachlan unknowingly said the one thing guaranteed to whet Ffup's revenge-fueled appetite.

"You see, pet, the stone in your ring acts like a magnet, attracting only unhappiness to itself and to whoever might seek to possess it." So intent was she on alerting Ffup to the dangers of the ring that she failed to notice the odd smile playing around the dragon's mouth. "You're far better off without it, dear," Mrs. McLachlan continued, thinking to herself that this truism could have been applied to everyone who had ever been in contact with the stone.

Before Ffup had become its temporary owner, the stone had been locked away in the custody of the Etheric Library; before that, it had hung unnoticed for hundreds of years in the chandelier in the great hall of StregaSchloss. Now the chandelier was history—smashed to atoms—and the Etheric Librarian was missing, presumed dead. In a desperate attempt to put the stone out of harm's way, she, Flora McLachlan, had tried to hide it on the mythical island that lay on the outermost rim of Death's realm. Tried . . . and failed. True, the stone was hidden, safe from any casual search, but a determined or desperate seeker would eventually find some way of sifting through the millions of pebbles on the island's fringe and thus uncover the stone. Backbreaking as this would undoubtedly be, the stone was well worth the effort; some would go so far as to say that finding the stone was worth far more than mere human lives.

The stone was like nothing else on Earth. It was immeasurably ancient; had, in fact, always been in existence. It predated the planets but contained no carbon itself, which meant it was un-carbon-datable. It appeared to be made of nothing that could be analyzed or attributed to one of the elements in the periodic table. Furthermore, the stone's mere proximity made human clocks and compasses run awry, as it appeared to transmit an untraceable signal that jammed radio waves and caused mobile phones to hiss like enraged serpents. Interesting as these properties were, they were not the source of the stone's fascination for mortals, angels, and demons alike. The stone's allure lay in its being more than a lapidary anomaly, for what it represented was raw power in its most elemental form. Raw power of an order utterly beyond the grasp of human intelligence. Raw power that made the combined outputs from every single one of Earth's power stations look, by comparison, like a last gasp from a dying glowworm.

The stone was like a vast battery of the type that a planet could use to run its central heating—exactly the kind of battery that could be used, by those who knew how, to power a spell, multiply the effect of an incantation a thousandfold, or tip the wobbly balance between the powers of light and darkness and forever throw a shadow of evil around the world—

"So . . . let me get this straight—it's like a magnet for deep poo?" Ffup interrupted Mrs. McLachlan's meditations on the true nature of the stone. The dragon's mind was conjuring up several scenarios, all of which involved bucketloads of deep poo happening in the general vicinity of her about-to-be ex-fiancé, the faithless, lying, two-timing—

"Ffup, dear. The *carpet*."

Ffup snapped back to the present, where she found she'd

accidentally set fire to a corner of Mrs. McLachlan's rug. Horrified, she apologized profusely, smothering the flames with her tail and vowing to herself that this simply *had* to stop. She had to get a grip. At this rate, if she continued to wallow in such vengeful fantasies, she ran the risk of burning Strega-Schloss to the ground. If Mrs. McLachlan wouldn't help her find the ring, Ffup had a pretty good idea who else might.

Play to Death

The weak winter daylight that had shone over Argyll was fading rapidly as a curtain of gray clouds drew over the west coast of Scotland. Weather forecasters upgraded vague prophecies of wintry showers to far more serious predictions of severe blizzards, with major disruption to traffic across the entire western seaboard of Britain. Within half an hour, supermarkets the length of the U.K. had run out of bread, potatoes, pasta, and rice—the panicked citizens presumably intent on burying themselves up to their collective necks in white carbohydrates to mirror the whiteness piling up outside their windows. Airports shut down, flights were diverted to Holland, and a dimly remembered form of Second World War siege mentality seized the nation.

Watching the meadow disappearing beneath a mantle of snow, Pandora wondered if Titus might feel in the mood for a game of Monopoly for real money. In the past, they had played game after game, their tournaments spanning several weeks and causing them to rack up enormous debts to each other. They had both vowed to honor these debts, to pay them off in hard cash in a not-too-distant future when they were both not only older but richer as well. Titus's habit of offering Pandora seemingly generous terms of repayment—terms like double or quits—had resulted in Pandora's owing her brother the dizzying sum of twenty-eight thousand, nine hundred and forty-six pounds. All to be repaid in twenty-pound notes, except for the last forty-six pounds, which she swore she'd repay in single pennies. Four thousand, six hundred of them, to be precise. Pandora used her index finger to write on the steamed-up library window, calculating that at 3.4 grams per penny, her repayment would weigh in at more than twice Titus's own body weight. Heaving a huge sigh, Pandora erased all evidence of her calculations from the window with her fist. A far better plan would be for her to *win* the game. With Dad gone to the hospital to pick up Mum and the new baby, and hours to go before they returned, Pandora had time to kill. There was something deeply satisfying about being snug and warm, tucked up inside, playing pointless board games with your brother while the world turned white outside the windows. If Titus was willing to play another game of Monopoly, she could either erase the debt completely or increase it by a factor of one hundred percent to an eye-watering fifty-seven thousand, eight hundred and ninety-two pounds. It was a tough call, Pandora thought, leaving the window seat to huddle next to the fire, wondering if the Monopoly had been put away in the game room after her last disastrous attempt to wipe out the comparatively paltry debt of fourteen thousand, four hundred and seventy-three pounds. She'd been so ridiculously sure of winning last time, each throw of the dice transporting her little metal boot round a series of highly profitable circuits of the Monopoly board, her hoard of paper money piling in front of her in a most satisfactory fashion. Dizzy with amassing such wealth, she once, fatally, omitted her ritual of crossing fingers and kissing the dice three times for luck, and *that* was when she landed slap-bang on Titus's hotel on Park Lane. Next turn, despite multiple kisses and fingers crossed so tightly they hurt, she'd thrown snake eyes (a two) and capped her previous misfortune by landing on Titus's other hotel on Mayfair. That had wiped her out completely, doubled her debt to her brother, and made her almost radioactive with fury.

Maybe *not* Monopoly, then.

Pandora turned the handle and pushed open the door to StregaSchloss's game room. A scuttling sound gave away the whereabouts of the tincture squaddies, a battalion of hundreds of tiny warriors in kilts who had taken up residence on the billiard table after their arrival at StregaSchloss the previous year. None of them stood any taller than Pandora's thumb, and all were the result of the accidental spillage of a vial of dragon's-tooth tincture that Baci had brought back from the Institute for Advanced Witchcraft during the Christmas holidays. Baci had been vaguely intending to conduct an experiment with the tincture in the comfort of her own kitchen, but had completely forgotten about it until Titus had removed it from the back of the fridge in the hope that it might be not only edible but delicious. Fortunately, he was never given the opportunity to find out, since dragon's-tooth tincture was renowned in magical circles for being the single most effective method for creating an instant army. Once decanted, Baci's forgotten tincture mutated from a puddle of coffee-colored liquid into a seething mass of tiny limbs, which gradually unraveled, dusted themselves off, stood up, and announced themselves to be soldiers of the Fifth Dragon's-Tooth Engineers.

The vial of tincture had smashed across StregaSchloss's stone kitchen floor the previous winter, and now, holed up for the best part of a year upstairs in the game room, the tiny warriors had made the best of their bizarre billet and had put some of the Strega-Borgias' hoard of games to good use. Thus, the green baize of the billiard table became a parade ground; single playing cards folded in half were used as two-man tents; Scrabble tiles were employed as shields; and pickup sticks sharpened to lethal points made highly effective spears with which to catch dinner. To Tarantella the tarantula's disgust, she found herself now in direct competition with the wee warriors for StregaSchloss's limited fresh fly supply; fortunately, it hadn't occurred to the teeny tribesmen to try and hunt the spider, otherwise Tarantella might have found herself speared on a pickup stick, spit-roasted, and dished up in slices for high tea.

From the billiard table, the tincture squaddies kept a covert watch on Pandora as she hunted for a suitable game that might allow her to win her fortune back. Aware that she was under observation, Pandora wondered out loud if the tiny warriors were in good health. On several occasions over the previous year, both she and Titus had served as battlefield surgeons to injured members of the bonsai battalion—splinting broken legs with matches; administering minute crumbs of aspirin for sprains, migraines, and mystery fevers; once, unforgettably, performing an emergency amputation when an unfortunate warrior had his foot crushed under a falling mahjong tile. And yet, despite Titus's and Pandora's obviously kind intentions toward the tiny warriors, the appearance of any humans in the game room always caused a mass squaddie exodus, and hours could pass before they would reappear to negotiate favors from their giant benefactors. Today, with the temperature in the game room hovering around zero, the squaddies were caught out in the wide-open spaces of the billiard table, where they had been vigorously drilling, marching, and exercising, presumably in an attempt to stop themselves from freezing to death. When Pandora turned away to the glass-fronted cabinet where hundreds of games were haphazardly stacked, she could see masses of tiny kilted men reflected in its doors. Had there not been ripples of movement among their ranks, the squaddies might have been mistaken for model soldiers laid out prior to an adult war game. Plucking a battered Cluedon't set from a tottering pile, Pandora turned round to lay it down on the table in front of a group of suddenly statue-still warriors.

"Don't panic," she muttered. "I just need to check if all the bits are in the box. . . ."

"Er, yes." One of the tincture squaddies stepped forward, wringing his hands in apology. "I regret to have to tell you that the flask of botulinum toxin and the dodgy hair dryer have gone."

"And Sergeant Macdui took the concrete overshoes with him," added another squaddie, his long face arranged in such a sorrowful expression that Pandora wondered if a comforting hug would be in order. On reflection, she decided not, realizing she might do more harm than good by accidentally squashing the sad little squaddie. With the poison, the electrocuting hair dryer, and the Mafia shoes gone, it was becoming obvious that Cluedon't wasn't going to provide the perfect solution to her current financial crisis. The casual placing of the lethal hair dryer in the bathroom or the unobserved decanting of the toxin in the kitchen had been two of her favorite methods to dispatch Titus's pieces in previous games, with the concrete overshoes in the ornamental pond as backup if all else failed. Since these murder weapons were missing, there was little point in continuing. In front of her, the tincture squaddie shuffled his bare feet and coughed.

"Your Vast Giganticness," he began respectfully, bowing several times before continuing. "As you know, we soldiers of the Fifth Dragon's-Tooth Engineers have been camped here for almost twelve months. . . ." He paused, allowing Pandora to agree that yes, this was so. "And very nice it has been too, Your Epic Enormousity," the little squaddie hastily assured her, in case she thought he wasn't eternally grateful for the benefits of life in the game room of StregaSchloss. "Very nice indeed. Warm, cozy, comfortable, safe . . ." Here he emitted a sigh that sounded like the dying wheeze from a pair of ruined bellows. "Problem is, Your Humungous Mountainosity, we're not built for comfort. We're warriors, fighting men, gladiators." Here he flexed his diminutive biceps and took a deep breath. "We're growing soft, Your Immense Colossalness. With no enemies to kill, no battles to fight, and no *danger* in our lives, we've lost our reason for existence. Our days have become about as perilous as a game of tiddlywinks, and while you'd think that would make us happy, I have to tell you that all it's doing is making us fat and miserable. We used to be a lean, mean fighting machine, but these days we've become a bunch of flabby couch potatoes. We've lost our edge, begging your pardon, Your Titanic Magnificence. But it's been very nice. Really . . ." Behind him, the tincture squaddies nodded in agreement. From somewhere in their massed ranks came a ghastly scream, followed by a little thud.

Pandora gasped, "What on earth . . . ?"

"Pay no heed, Your Monumental Mightiness. I imagine that was poor Corporal Braeriach. I'm afraid he must have lost the bet. If I'm not mistaken, I think he was going to use the box jellyfish from Cluedon't."

"Pardon?" Pandora frowned. "What bet? What is going on?"

The tincture squaddie put his finger to his lips and motioned Pandora to follow him over to the window, out of earshot of the rank and file. Framed by a wintry view of the meadow and Lochnagargoyle, he whispered so quietly that Pandora had to practically invite him to crawl into her ear to make himself heard.

"My men are losing the will to live, Your Towering Immeasurability. They gamble from dawn to dusk, but lacking money with which to gamble properly, they use their lives as currency instead. It's . . . ochhh—" Here he appeared to struggle to explain himself. Then, inspiration dawning: "They play a form of Russian roulette. Only we're not Russians, we're Celts. And it's not roulette we're playing, it's Cluedon't. So, in short, we play Celtic Cluedon't, and losers lose all."

Pandora was aghast. "WHAT?" she squeaked. "But . . . but that's *sick*! You play to the death? Urrrghhh. That's *horrible*. No game is worth *that*."

"But *war* is a game, Your Whopping Extensiveness," the tincture squaddie interrupted, his face arranged in a sad little smile. "A game we play for the highest stakes, but a game nonetheless." Seeing Pandora's face, he continued, "Imagine: one day you see your opponents as your worst-ever enemies. You are determined to destroy them—their wives and children; their homes, lands, and oceans—as they are determined to destroy yours. Time passes and now you're trading with them, marrying their children with yours, and fighting alongside them against another, newer enemy. If you think about it, Your Gargantuan Jumboness, warfare and games have the same objective in mind—the purpose of both is to win. Once you have won, you shake hands, draw up treaties, execute a few scapegoats, and then your leaders sit down together and drink a toast to the health of your nations. If *that's* not a game, I'll eat my shield."

Pandora shook her head. For once, she had nothing to say. She loathed war; to her it seemed like a vast adult conspiracy designed to propel a nation's teenagers out of their beds and off to foreign lands from where, all too frequently, they would return in plastic bags. She gazed at the little warrior in dismay: war was too visceral, too bloody, and far too dangerous to be likened to a *game*.

Seeing the girl's obvious distress, the squaddie leaned in close to her ear again. "I don't mean to say that war is for *fun*, Your Himalayan Hugeosity. My men regard going to war as the highest calling; they believe it to be a sacred duty to protect and serve our masters and"—he bowed deeply, the hem of his kilt sweeping across his bare toes—"our Mondo Mistresses." Crossing one of his arms diagonally across his chest, he leaned back to stare into Pandora's eyes and said, "We pledge ourselves to protect you to the death, Your Ultimate Thuleness. To. The. Death." Then he lowered his voice and added, "So, if you could possibly pick a fight quite soon with some neighboring giants, my men and I would be awfully grateful." And using his pickup-stick spear as a pole, the warrior vaulted off Pandora's shoulder, ran across the floor, and, in seconds, had vanished down a crack in the floorboards.

In the End,
a Beginning

Wrapped in their separate miseries, Damp and Ffup leafed through the book of fairy tales, barely aware of what they were looking at. Every illustration of mothers and babies caused Damp's emotional barometer to plummet still further; each tableau of loving couples united in the happily-ever-after made Ffup literally incandescent with rage. Thus, when Damp finally turned the last page, Ffup reached out a talon and said, "There. Let's go *there*."

The illustration she indicated was a black-and-white woodcut depicting an island. It was no more than a tailpiece, a little decorative squiggle included as more of an afterthought than an illustration of any of the stories in the book. Under the island was the word

but since Damp couldn't read yet and Ffup had no understanding of Latin, neither of them knew that what they were
looking at was "The End," written in an obsolete tongue.

Moments later, as the dragon and child paddled ashore to
the island, it wasn't toward The End, but toward a new beginning. A new game to distract both of them from the betrayals
they'd left behind at StregaSchloss. The water lapped round
Damp's knees, wavelets soaking the hem of her down-filled
jacket, turning its pale outer fabric transparent and exposing
the curled feathers within. Beside her, Ffup's talons left
crescent-shaped gouges on the sandy seafloor. Their progress
was somewhat erratic, the dragon pausing occasionally to remove entangled seaweed from her feet or flail ineffectively at
the clouds of midges hovering around her head. The air felt
balmy and the water barely cool; on the island, the few trees
were shyly leaved in pale green, as if spring had arrived that
day. Ffup spun slowly in a circle, taking in a three-hundred-
and-sixty-degree view before concluding that wherever they
were, it wasn't StregaSchloss.

"I mean, *think*," the dragon squeaked. "We left a blizzard behind. Last time I looked out of a window, it was dropping
flakes as big as prawn crackers and it was freezing cold. Er . . .
talking of prawn crackers . . ."

Paying no attention to this, Damp plodded ahead, wishing
she'd thought to remove her Wellies *before* attempting to wade
ashore. Her feet made revoltingly slurpy sucking noises until
she finally reached the high-tide mark and sat down to remove

her Wellies and empty them out. Ffup slumped on the dry sand beside her, moaning fitfully.

"I wish we'd thought to pack some food. Don't suppose you've got anything to eat in that jacket of yours? I'm *ravenous.*"

Damp plunged her hands into her pockets and shook her head. *She* wasn't ravenous. She was sad. Damp felt as if a huge hole had sprouted in the middle of her body, a huge hole that couldn't ever be filled up again. Every time she thought about the new baby, the hole grew bigger and bigger. Staring at nothing, she imagined that by the time her parents came home from hostiple with that baby, there would only be a huge hole left to remind them that they used to have a daughter called Damp. This thought made her feel even more sad and cross, so she thumped the heels of her Wellies in the sand and frowned like a gargoyle.

Just like Damp, Ffup felt as if she too had a huge hole in the middle of her body. However, unlike Damp, Ffup knew exactly how to fill it up again. For the dragon, food was the most important reason for getting out of bed in the morning, and thus its absence on the island was a cause for major upset.

"We have to go back home immediately," she decided, heaving herself upright and glaring down to where Damp sat propped against a gnarled blade of driftwood that was poking out of the sand like a broken tooth.

"Well, come *on*," Ffup insisted. "Stir your stumps, girl. The longer we wait, the less chance there is that your beast of a brother will have left us anything decent to eat. . . ."

Unfortunately, this only served to remind Damp of her other brother: the small, newly born one. The one who had stolen her mother away and sent her to a hostiple. Damp's brows plunged.

"Not wantit, lunch," she stated. "Not want beastie brother. *Not* go home."

"What?" Ffup squawked. "What's this 'Not wantit go home' rubbish? *'Course* you want to go home."

"Not wantit, home," muttered Damp, snatching a pebble and glaring at it before hurling it at the incoming waves.

"Come on, kid. Get a grip," Ffup snapped.

"Not get grip," Damp insisted. "Want to stay here."

"Give me strength," Ffup snarled. "Of all the places you could have chosen, you *had* to pick this desolate lump of god-forsaken rock to stage your big I'm-leaving-and-I'm-never-coming-back drama. Why here? Why now? Why not wait till we're within walking distance of my lunch, and then go for it?" Seeing Damp's locked-and-shuttered expression, Ffup stamped her feet and immediately gave a deafening shriek. Toppling sideways, she fell onto the sand, howling in agony.

"Whatsamatter?" Damp was by her side in a flash. "Where's it hurty at?"

By way of an answer, Ffup wailed even louder, clutching one of her feet and rocking from side to side.

"Poor toes?" Damp guessed, trying to see if there was sufficient blood to justify the volume of the dragon's complaint. The pads beneath Ffup's talons were so wrinkled that it would have been impossible to see any evidence of a cut or tear, but the pebbles beneath her were smeared with red. At least, most of the pebbles were. Damp caught her breath. In the middle of a long line of bloody stones, one of them was glowing a dazzlingly bright neon pink.

"Pretty . . . ," Damp breathed, reaching out to pick it up.

Through her histrionics, Ffup sensed that despite her best efforts, she was no longer center stage. Snapping her mouth shut, and thereby prematurely stifling a particularly fine example of a low and quivering moan, the dragon sat up, slitted her eyes, and peered at the radiant pink stone in Damp's hands.

"Wow," she gasped, not yet comprehending what a terrible find they had stumbled upon. It would take a seawater douche to remove the traces of dragon's blood that had caused the stone to fluoresce. It would also take a few seconds thereafter for Ffup to recognize the stone as being the diamond from the center of her missing engagement ring. When Ffup and Damp triumphantly made their way back home for lunch, it would be too late to undo the dreadful harm done by their unwittingly returning the Chronostone to StregaSchloss.

X Marks the Spot

In Mrs. McLachlan's bedroom, the nanny and Latch were having a cup of tea. A lingering smell of singed carpet hung in the air, overlaid with the tarry aroma of Lapsang Souchong wafting out of the teapot that steamed gently by the fireplace. Serene and permanently unflappable, Mrs. Flora McLachlan was enjoying the ritual of morning tea, a habit that Latch suspected she wouldn't break even if the barbarians were sailing up the loch, the turrets of StregaSchloss were tumbling to the ground, and the world was due to end at lunchtime. Even then, Flora would still be sipping Lapsang at precisely eleven-thirty, come Hell or high water.

"A wee date scone, dear?"

Latch frowned. How, he wondered, could she do this? He'd just given her an edited version of what Mr. Grabbit, the lawyer,

had told him in the privacy of the Discouraging Room. Subsequently, it hadn't been the damp chill in that room that had caused Latch to shiver. If what Mr. Grabbit said was true, the entire family were in deep peril. And here was Flora, offering him a *scone*? Of course, that would come in *really* handy during the threatened invasion by Don Lucifer's hired assassins. As if reading his mind, Flora McLachlan smiled and reached forward to pat his hand.

"I wasn't suggesting you use my date scone as a weapon, *dear*. Armies march on their stomachs, I've been led to believe, and if Mr. Grabbit is correct, we adults must behave like an army to protect the three children in our care. Eat up, do."

Obediently, Latch took a bite. Warm, chewy, and deliciously sweet, the date scone immediately made him feel better, despite the fear clawing at his stomach.

"Now, then," Flora continued, topping up both their cups and adding two lumps of sugar to Latch's. "We can't leave. At least, not by road. Ffup couldn't carry us all and, lacking wings of our own, our only other means of escape would be young Titus's boat. With four adults and three children on board, I fear it would be so low in the water that it would capsize immediately." Having delivered this rather gloomy assessment of their current situation, Mrs. McLachlan briskly stirred Latch's tea and fixed him with a hard stare. "Dear," she began, "until the snow melts, we are effectively under siege. We must defend ourselves as best we can. Without knowing from where the first attack might come, or indeed when, I suggest that we prepare ourselves to hole up in the map room for a while."

Latch felt his stomach plummet, and his heart clenched with fear. "I *loathe* the map room," he whispered, taking a deep and scalding swallow of tea to fortify himself.

"There is no other room as easily defended," Mrs. McLachlan reminded him. "Stone walls, no windows, one small door; the corridor leading to it is too narrow to allow the passage of more than one person at a time. . . ."

"Dark, claustrophobic, tomblike . . ." Latch shuddered. "I'm a Highlander by birth, Flora—my kin are allergic to wee dark cavey things. I want to meet my end out in the open air—"

"We are *not* going to be meeting any ends, dear," Mrs. McLachlan interrupted. "And your lovely open air currently has a blizzard blowing in it, in case you'd forgotten. Historically, even the most claustrophobic members of your clan were forced into wee dark cavey things in the winter, were they not?" She reached out and grasped both Latch's hands, and he found himself reminded that for all her enormous courage, she was still the selfsame Flora he had asked to marry him all those months ago. . . .

"Dearest . . . ," he began, just as there came a tentative knock on the door. Their eyes met, locked, and, just as quickly, disengaged. Latch stood up and crossed the room in three strides, opening the door to reveal Miss Araminta standing outside.

"We have a problem," the young nanny said. "Damp has vanished."

Now Latch noticed that Minty was ashen-faced, and as her words sank in, he felt his heart kick hard against his breastbone.

"You've looked in . . . ?" he started to say, on the point of running through a checklist of places where a determined toddler might hide herself, but then he stopped. Minty was shaking her head.

"We've really lost her this time," she whispered, looking past Latch to where Mrs. McLachlan was, halfway out of her chair.

"Gone?" she demanded, her gaze raking Minty like a searchlight. "And I imagine Ffup as well?"

Minty nodded, biting her bottom lip. "I . . . ah . . ." She took a deep breath and continued, looking from Flora to Latch and back again. "I'm pretty sure that they're not out in the snowstorm. I checked for footprints in the snow all round the house and there are none, nor are there any signs of dragon droppings, so they haven't gone out via the doors. Which means . . ." Minty frowned and shook her head in bewilderment. "I know this must sound mad, but I think Damp has found a portal." And here she paused, partly to give Mrs. McLachlan and Latch time to absorb this statement, and partly to allow them to run screaming from the room to escape the ravings of the lunatic in their midst. To Minty's relief, they held their ground, blinking slightly, but both wearing similar expressions of faint encouragement.

"Go on, dear," Mrs. McLachlan said mildly, her knuckles white as she clasped her hands together.

"I don't know if you're aware that this house—actually, the entire StregaSchloss estate—is riddled with portals. It's got so many, it looks like a Swiss cheese. . . ."

Despite everything, Mrs. McLachlan nearly smiled: Minty's choice of a culinary metaphor was refreshingly down-to-earth, considering she was trying to describe something beyond the realm of the senses.

"I stumbled through one in my bedroom when I'd only been at StregaSchloss for a few days," Minty continued, causing Latch to frown and hold up a hand to halt the flow of what was, to him, incomprehensible gibberish.

"Forgive me if I'm being a bit dense," he said, "but what is a 'portal,' exactly? I know what the word means, in the sense that a portal is a gateway, but—"

"You're quite right, dear," Mrs. McLachlan interrupted. "They are gates of a sort. I prefer to think of them as points where worlds meet and merge, places where one can cross between."

Latch looked, if anything, even more confused. Seeing this, Minty tried to help.

"To give you an example"—she smiled—"the portals in *my* room are in the oil paintings. They look like perfectly ordinary oil paintings: old, dark, full of chaps and battles and dinners. . . ."

The Ancestors' Room had never been a suitable bedroom for the fainthearted, Latch thought, distracted from Minty's words by a wave of guilt. He remembered the day the young nanny had first arrived at StregaSchloss. He'd been instructed to put her in the Lilac Room, but he had decided to find out what she was made of, see how she responded to a challenge and thus discover if she really was suitable to be caretaker to the toddler witch Damp. Minty, to her credit, had passed Latch's test with flying colors—a test that Latch would rather have eaten slugs than take himself. Truth was, the Ancestors' Room gave him the creeps, but he wouldn't have admitted that to a living soul. It was lined with ancient portraits of long-dead Borgias, and every time Latch had been in the room for longer than five minutes, he'd been sure that the painted heads behind his back were coming to life. Here, now, was evidence that he'd been right all along, although this knowledge came freighted with deep shame for his part in putting Minty through what sounded like a terrifying ordeal.

". . . When the picture came to life and spoke, I thought I was going to pass out," she continued. "Then I climbed into it, into a hot-air balloon flown by Apollonius 'The Greek' Borgia, a man who died hundreds of years ago; *then* I was sure that I was definitely going to pass out." Minty gave a most unladylike snort of laughter and added, "And *that* was before I looked over the edge of the balloon gondola and saw how terrifyingly high up we were. . . ."

Latch cringed inwardly. This had all been his fault. If Minty had been given the Lilac Room as Signora Strega-Borgia had intended, none of this would have hap—

"I suppose I'm too curious for my own good," Minty admitted. "But having found *one* portal, I thought there might be more." She bit her lip again and took a steadying breath. "My bedroom—the Ancestors' Room—it's absolutely *riddled* with them. *All* the portraits of long-dead ancestors are portals. That made me wonder if every single picture hanging at Strega-

Schloss was a portal as well, but I was wrong. I've only found one other, and that's the reproduction of the *Mona Lisa* in Damp's old bedroom. However, no two portals are the same, nor are their passengers; portals come in different sizes, as if much smaller creatures use them as well. . . ."

Mrs. McLachlan smiled. "Yes, dear. I noticed that Tarantella has one in her teapot on the kitchen cupboard, which she uses when she thinks we're not looking."

"Tarantella? The teapot?" Latch's head swam; he was aghast that a mere spider had more knowledge of multidimensional travel than he did. "But—but why? . . . How?"

"I haven't had time to comb the entire house and gardens for any more," Minty confessed, "so I haven't a clue which one Damp used. Until we work that out, we won't be able to find her . . ."

". . . and until we find her"—Mrs. McLachlan completed this thought—"we can neither leave StregaSchloss nor retreat to one easily defended room, because that would mean leaving her behind."

"Leaving them *both* behind," Minty reminded her. "I can't tell if I'm glad that Ffup is with her or not. At times, that dragon can be more of a liability than an asset—"

Mrs. McLachlan groaned out loud. At this, Latch was beside her in an instant. "Flora? What is it? What's wrong?"

Mrs. McLachlan covered her eyes with one hand as if unable to bear what she saw. In her mind's eye she had glimpsed a child and a dragon innocently paddling ashore onto an island: the island the coordinates of which corresponded exactly with the "X Marks the Spot" on a demonic treasure map, the very same island where she'd buried the missing gem from Ffup's engagement ring, otherwise known as the Chrono-stone. In a voice that sounded as if she were clawing it out of her own viscera with fishhooks, Mrs. McLachlan said, "I don't know which portal they used, but I have a very good idea where they've gone."

What Big Eyes You Have

Titus barely looked up when Pandora came into his bedroom. He hadn't heard her—his headphones were clamped to his ears—but he had felt the cold rush of air from the corridor outside as she closed the door behind her.

"Ugh—it's like a furnace in here." Pandora fanned herself with her free hand, the other holding a brick-sized wooden box against her chest. "How can you stand it? It's unbearable." She crossed the room to the window, and then, as if struck by something, turned back. "Hello? Cloth ears? Are you in there? Is there life?"

Titus ignored her, his head bent over a notebook in which he was scribbling a single word over and over again in uncharacteristically tiny, crabbed handwriting.

"Why are you writing 'Eternity' a thousand times over?" Pandora demanded, leaning over his shoulder just as Titus snapped his book shut and removed his headphones.

"What?" he mumbled.

"I feel so . . . um . . . privileged to have you as a brother." Pandora sat down on the edge of the desk facing Titus, swinging her legs back and forth in time to her words. "There you are, lost in thought, creating your literary masterwork in your overheated bedroom, literally sweating out each word . . . for which future generations will thank you, nations will call you blessed, and . . . and why do I have the distinct feeling that you're not listening to a word I say?"

"Are you still talking?" Titus said wearily, his face milk-white despite the terrific heat in the room.

"I've found something I want you to have a look at." Pandora opened the lid of her wooden box and from inside removed a dark gray velvet bag.

Titus's face betrayed no curiosity, no interest, nothing at all. His expression was inscrutable, as fixed and inanimate as a mask. Something of this must have snagged Pandora's attention, because she peered at him sideways and said, "Are you okay? Forgive me for mentioning it, but you look a bit spaced out. As if you're not really here. . . ." She tailed off, lacking the language to express what she could only define as an absence.

"I'm fine," Titus muttered, not feeling even remotely fine, but fiercely determined not to share this with Pandora. At least, not yet. In truth, he'd been feeling decidedly weird, off and on, ever since they'd gone to visit Mum and the new baby that morning. It was nothing serious—at least, he hoped not—

but he'd felt shivery and just . . . *off*. Like a flu thing, but not: he'd felt freezing cold, as if his veins were steadily silting up with icy slush. He couldn't blame the ambient temperature either: Pan was rapidly removing layers and moaning about the heat. God. He was still *freezing*, despite having turned the radiator up to high. And one of his eyes still really hurt, for no reason he could think of. Earlier he'd looked in the mirror, tried to see if he'd picked up a bit of grit—although it felt nastier than that; more like a shard of glass, cold as ice—but his reflection had stared back at him, giving no clue whatsoever as to what ailed him.

Squinting at Pandora, he realized she was holding something out for inspection.

"Pretty cool, huh?" She raised her eyebrows and added, although the object spoke for itself even if Titus wasn't doing so, "It's a snow-globe thing. A whatchamacallit. Come *on*, Titus, you know this stuff. . . ."

"A *boule de neige*," Titus muttered, rubbing his sore eye.

"Don't sound so excited. Jeez, you're *such* hard work right now. What *is* it with you? Don't tell me it's the baby?"

"Don't be stupid," Titus snapped, stung at last into a normal reaction. "The baby's just . . . a baby. I'm glad both it—I mean *he*—and Mum are okay. Okay? I'm not jealous, if that's what you're hinting at."

Pandora stared at him, her swinging legs slowing to a halt. "Actually, Mr. Hyper-Paranoid, I wasn't hinting. I was wondering out loud. I did think the baby was really sweet, though. It looked just like a wee version of you—"

"Thanks a bunch—"

"Well, you said that about me and Damp when she was a new baby, and *boy*, was she ugly."

"And she wailed the house down," Titus added with a shudder. "Ugh. Babies are such a *pain*."

"Now you're talking." Pandora smiled. "Anyway, check this out. I found it in the game room."

"Yeah. The snow scene. And your point is . . . ?"

"*So* impatient. Okay, so look more closely. It's not just any old snow scene, is it?"

Titus forced his injured eye to focus, causing it to water prodigiously. Through a smear of tears, he tried to see what lay inside the little glass dome, his difficulty compounded by the fact that the snow inside it was swirling around like a bonsai blizzard. Then he got it.

"Wow. Cool," he breathed, wondering when the flakes would settle down on the bottom of the dome and allow him to examine the miniature scene more closely.

"What d'you think those wee black things are?" Pandora asked, pointing to a clump of little black dots swirling through the snow toward the beautifully rendered tiny StregaSchloss.

"Gnats?" Titus guessed, although how the snow globe could have suffered an invasion by Scotland's perennial summer blight was hard to imagine.

"I don't think so," Pandora whispered. "Look again. They're circling the house."

"It's totally realistic, isn't it?" Titus said, fascinated by the oddness of holding a shrunken version of his home in his hands and idly wondering how much longer it was going to take for the tiny snowstorm to stop. He had a vague memory of owning a snow scene before, but he was almost certain that it hadn't been a super-swirly one like this. In fact, he was positive that he'd developed major arm strain from continually having to jiggle and shake its sluggish snowflakes into some semblance of a blizzard. Assuming that the storm would settle faster if he wasn't holding the snow dome in his wobbly hands, Titus laid it on his desk and turned to see Pandora framed at the window.

"Not gnats," she managed to gasp, her throat suddenly so dry that she could barely get the words out. She was saved from further explanations as a long, blood-chilling howl sounded from outside, followed by another . . . and another.

As he joined his sister by the window, Titus could make out dark shapes in the garden through the swirl of snowflakes. Looking up at the windows of StregaSchloss through hungry yellow eyes was a vast pack of wolves, silent now as they paced outside the house, silent with the certainty that what they sought lay within its walls. Desperately, Pandora tried to remember if Minty or Damp had shut the door to the kitchen garden earlier that morning—really shut it, as opposed to just pulling it to. Fear clawed at her as she realized she hadn't seen Damp or Minty for ages, and then, from downstairs, she heard a confusion of feral snarls and scufflings, followed by a muffled crack.

"DAMP?" she screamed, already halfway down the corridor before she'd even had time to think, hoping that the thudding footprints behind her were Titus's and not those of a pack of underfed wolves delighted that lunch had finally been served. Skidding downstairs shrieking Damp's name, aware that she was a hairsbreadth away from total hysteria, Pandora didn't pause to consider what she was going to do if she found the great hall thronging with fanged beasts. All she could think of was how Damp wouldn't have known that the big gray dogs were dangerous—not until the first one knocked her to the ground and sank its teeth into—

There were more snarls and hideous clotted rending noises, and as Pan rounded the corner of the landing, she could see the grisly remains of one wolf below, lying in a pool of blood on the floor of the great hall. Then came another crack, and another, closer, much louder—

"DAMP!" Pandora bawled, just as Titus caught up and grabbed her.

"Try not to panic, but there's a wolf behind me," he hissed, his fingers digging into the flesh of Pandora's arm. "Don't make any sudden movements," he continued. "Don't look at it. Try and act as if it isn't there. . . . Just keep on walking downstairs. And breathe. Yeah, breathing's good. In, out, and all that stuff. Good. Great. You're doing brilliantly. Keep going. Yup. Let's try for the kitchen, shall we?"

They were stepping gingerly over the corpse of the fallen wolf when a blurred shape came at them from the darkness of the boot cupboard. With no time to think, Titus and Pandora fled shrieking down the corridor and into the kitchen, slamming the door behind them. From somewhere nearby came a series of loud cracks, but by then they had realized that they'd made a fatal error. The kitchen was freezing cold, and just as they wondered why this should be so, round the open back door came a questing muzzle, above which glinted two cold yellow eyes. The pack leader shuffled into the kitchen, followed by two of the biggest wolves Titus and Pandora had ever seen. As if this wasn't bad enough, a further two wolves, unwilling to queue for lunch by the back door, decided to shortcut the whole process by jumping straight through the window into the kitchen sink in an earsplitting explosion of broken glass.

For one frozen moment Pandora stared straight into the eyes of the pack leader as it paused to savor her scent. Things flashed past in Pandora's mind: the smell of lavender, her mother's smile, Damp's infectious laughter, the sound of waves crashing on the white stones rimming Lochna-gargoyle . . .

. . . and then, with a grunt of effort, the wolf jumped, its heavy body, for that instant, almost graceful as it arced toward Pandora.

Some Baby

The woman behind the car-rental desk watched the approach of a man carrying a crying baby. The infant's mouth was opening and shutting like a fish's. As the door to the car-rental office opened to admit them, the volume of the baby's wails increased a thousandfold, causing the woman to sigh heavily, roll her eyes, and give her chewing gum three vicious chugs. Smiling insincerely, she launched into her greeting.

"Good afternoon, sir. How may I be of assistance?"

"I want to rent a car," Isagoth said, his jaw clenched so tight it ached. "Frankly, I'd've thought that was obvious enough. Why else would anyone bother to come through your door?"

Ah, the woman thought. A joker. Oh, joy. Oh well, pal. Two can play at that game.

"Terribly sorry, sir, I'm afraid they're all out at present. . . ."

116

This blatant lie didn't even cause her to blush, so expert had she become at dealing with members of the general public from the shallow end of the gene pool. She was about to smile once more when a searing pain ripped across the middle of her chest. As she fell, gasping, across her desk, the man stepped forward and grabbed her by her hair, forcing her to look at him.

"What I want is a car. What I do not want is to be jerked around. Now, are you going to rent me one or . . . ?"

The pain increased to a pitch where she began to white out. Black spots danced before her eyes and she tried to speak, to call out, to make him stop whatever it was he was doing—

"And let me just point out that you're going to be in a whole world of pain if you tell another living soul about this." And then he let go and stood back to hush his howling baby.

The office door opened to reveal a young couple maneuvering large suitcases on wheels behind them. The woman behind the desk realized that she probably owed them her life for arriving at that moment. By the time the couple had succeeded in dragging all their luggage into the office, Scary Man with Baby was dangling a set of car keys from one hand and flashing everyone the tired smile of a harassed parent.

"Got to go"—Isagoth sighed—"get this little fellow back to his mummy. Thanks for your help. 'Preciate this. . . ." And with a final despairing bleat from the baby, he was gone.

The hotel receptionist at the Auchenlochtermuchty Arms leaned forward to stroke the baby's cheek and forced herself not to recoil at the sulfurous stench that suddenly filled her nostrils. Poor *baby*, she thought, forcing a smile onto her face and mouth-breathing as she cooed insincerely.

"Who's a dear wee baby, then? Lovely navy blue eyes. And what's your name, pet?"

Isagoth's brain seized up. What the hell should he say? Babies' names weren't his thing. Obviously.

"Er, yeah. He's ... uh ... called"—his eyes fastened on his car-key fob—"*Hertz*. His name is Hertz."

The receptionist frowned.

"Dutch," Isagoth muttered. "It's an old Dutch name, Hertz. On my mother's side." Then, aware that he was beginning to babble, he clamped his mouth shut.

"Er ... lovely," the receptionist managed. "And you'll be wanting the room for ... ?" She allowed this question to dangle while secretly taking in a huge lungful of air through her mouth. Ugh. Talk about evil diapers. *That* one takes the biscuit.

"Initially, a week." Isagoth produced a credit card and slid it across the counter to the receptionist. While she made a copy of his details, he smiled to himself, delighted by the ease with which he'd invisibly rejoined human society. The baby was the single most useful accessory he'd ever had. If anyone was asking too many questions or proving too interested in details of Isagoth's hastily forged human identity, all the demon had to do was pinch the baby hard, and immediately people couldn't get rid of him fast enough. Fact was, for all their mealy-mouthed love of all things small and squeaky, most human beings would rather have flossed with a circular sander than spend more than twenty seconds within earshot of a wailing infant.

... Twice Shy

Unaccustomed to deceiving his wife, Luciano felt his head spin with the effort of sustaining two huge lies. Not only had he not told Baci about the Mafia menace heading their way, but he also had neglected to mention the biting baby. Not yet, he decided, bringing the Volvo to a halt on the rose quartz drive outside Strega-Schloss's front door. He pulled on the hand brake while he gathered his thoughts. *Tried* to gather his thoughts. *Is it ... asleep? Please, God, let it be asleep. Don't think I can cope if it looks at me again with those* pizza di pomodoro *eyes. ... And its teeth? Dear God, no, don't think about those. Think, think ... Think a happy thought, Luciano,* he commanded himself. *Think of ... sunshine, laughter, children, babies—no, not babies. No. Come on, man, pull yourself together or Baci will wonder what on earth is the matter.*

Minutes later, in the privacy of his room, Isagoth found himself experiencing the undiluted ferocity of Baby Strega-Borgia's displeasure. Despite being a senior demon who'd spent many millennia inflicting pain, spreading terror, and corrupting innocence; despite being the kind of entity you most certainly wouldn't want to get on the wrong side of; despite his reputation as the Arch-Bogeyman, a reputation that sent a shudder through even the vilest infant demons spawned in the nurseries of Hades—despite all of these, Isagoth felt his heart miss a beat as the tiny baby took another deep lungful and let rip from both ends.

Aghast, Isagoth undid the stained Onesie and peered uncertainly at what lay inside. The baby appeared to be wearing a dirty plastic bag around its bottom, a bag that, when opened by means of two blue tapes on each side, turned out to be full of the weirdest stuff Isagoth had ever seen. Black, sticky, and relatively odor-free, what it lacked in smell it more than made up for in quantity. And more was to come.

"STOP, I command you," he roared in vain as the baby frowned and bore down.

"Surely there cannot be *more?*" the demon wondered out loud as the plastic bag proved itself to be woefully inadequate for the task.

"Where is it all coming from?" Isagoth mused, trying to grasp how it could be that such a tiny creature could turn itself into such a prodigious poo factory without completely deflating like a human whoopee cushion.

Moments later, the show was over. The baby, his diaper, his Onesie, and most of the facing parts of his totally inadequate caretaker were coated in a thick and rubbery layer of meconium—the impossible-to-remove contents of every new-born human's bowels, the black poo from hell. With a faint squeak of satisfaction, the baby fell asleep, a perfectly justifiable grin hovering around his mouth. Mission accomplished.

Babies, 1; Demons, 0.

A Hole in Time

As the wolf leapt toward Pandora, Ludo Grabbit stepped out from behind the door to the wine cellar, his antique rifle raised to his shoulder in readiness. The air suddenly filled with a metallic-smelling red mist, and something knocked Pandora sideways. She fell over and crashed against the china cupboard, rattling everything on its shelves—including Tarantella, who'd been fast asleep, curled up inside her favorite teapot. Three hairy legs appeared over its porcelain rim, followed by a body, mouthparts gathered in a peeved pout.

"Turn it *down*," the tarantula moaned. "Some of us are attempting to catch up on our beauty sleep. Some of us bitterly resent the intrusion of giant bipeds"—she peered at Pandora and shuddered—"bipeds adorned in lumps of gore. . . . Did you

know you were wearing wolf tripe? Is this intentional? A fashion statement?"

Pandora sat up, pushing the dead wolf off with some difficulty. She found that she was shaking so hard she couldn't speak, and as for standing up, her legs simply refused to bear her weight. Ludo was by her side in an instant, followed by Titus.

"We've got to get out of here," the lawyer said, hauling Pandora upright and propping her against the cupboard. "Tell me, is there any way out through the dungeons, or are they a complete dead end?"

"Out?" Titus waved a hand in the direction of the open door to the kitchen garden. "It's blowing a blizzard out there. We'll freeze to death. That is, if the wolves don't get us first."

"We're going to die, aren't we?" Pandora whispered, her voice kitten-weak and shaky. "If not with the wolves, then we'll die out there in the snowstorm. No one will find our deep-frozen bodies until—"

"What a dear little ray of sunshine you've turned out to be, girl," muttered Tarantella. "I'm so glad to be on your team. With your kind of positive attitude on board, I just know we're bound for victo—" The tarantula broke off in mid-sentence as Pandora scooped her off the cupboard and transferred her to a perch on her shoulder.

"There, pet lamb," she said inaccurately, tenderly stroking the spider's furry body with a trembling hand. "Now you can nag me in comfort. You won't even have to raise your voice beyond a shrill cackle."

Tarantella peered at Pandora with new respect. "My, my, my. Who's been sharpening their razor tongue, then? Tell me, O Snark Queen, which of the multiple options open to us are we going to select, hmm?"

Before Pandora could compose a suitably acid reply, the sound of many scuffling, skidding claws came from the kitchen garden; the door to the corridor shuddered, as if something heavy was being repeatedly flung against it; and, to Pandora's horror, another frosted muzzle poked through the broken window over the sink. With Ludo bringing up the rear, they fled through the wine cellar to the dungeons, not daring to look behind and see if they were being followed in case they slipped and fell down the mossy stairs into the depths of StregaSchloss.

"Dark," complained Pandora, groping her way hand over hand along a cold stone wall.

"Observant, huh?" remarked Tarantella to no one in particular, her many eyes fixed simultaneously on the gloom ahead, the darkness behind, and the velvety black above and below.

"Wait up," Ludo called, some distance behind the children, his voice bouncing off the walls to be immediately swallowed by the silence.

"Sssspoook-eee," hissed Tarantella, clinging to Pandora's collar and hastily spinning a length of spider silk for extra anchorage. "Just think of that immense weight of soil right above our heads . . . and while we're at it, let's hope your forebears knew what they were doing when they built this place. . . ."

"Can't you make her shut up?" Titus said through gritted teeth, already unnerved by having to grope his way along a particularly slimy section of wall. "This is bad enough without having to put up with that spider's doom-laden obs—"

"Shh," Ludo commanded. "Listen. Can you hear that?"

"What? Hear what?" Pandora spun round to face where she imagined Ludo's voice had come from. Disorientated by the oppressive darkness, she realized she'd let go of the wall that had been her only means of navigation. Fumbling blindly, pawing the darkness, she reached out a hand to try and reorientate herself with the wall, but groped only air. The first sour mouthful of terror rose to the back of her throat, forcing her to swallow hard. "Er . . . ," she managed, both arms windmilling in slow motion as she tried and failed to find the wall again. "Titus?" she whispered, struggling to make her voice sound normal, desperately striving to breathe with lungs that were failing to draw the thickening air into them. "Titus? I'm very scared, Titus. Hello? Please?" And then the fear was all over her, uncontrollable—clabbering at her throat, her mouth; crushing her chest and squeezing the breath from her lungs. As she twisted round in a slow, collapsing coil of her own limbs, her nostrils suddenly filled with the resinous scent of pine sap, and her last conscious thought was a confused sensory-impression of dappled light and voices rushing toward her.

"Where? What?" Pandora struggled to sit up, but something was keeping her pinned to the ground. Overhead, sunlight winked through a mesh of tree branches, sunshine so dazzlingly bright that she had to close her eyes against the glare.

"Pan?" Titus's voice was close to her ear. "I seem to be making a habit of telling you not to panic, but we're not in the dungeons anymore. I don't know where we are, but you've got to wake up and get moving nowwwww—"

There was a blast of intense heat, followed by a vaguely familiar thrumming, beating sound. *Where* had she heard that before? Pandora opened her eyes and rolled from her back onto her side. Beneath her lay a thick carpet of leaves and pine needles. Raising her head, she saw several things in quick succession: Titus's face, pale as milk; tree trunks stretching into the distance behind him like an infinite bar code; and finally, worryingly, a vast, scaly pillar of a leg, terminating in a paw the size of a car tire—a paw that was drumming its deadly talons on the ground in front of Pandora in a decidedly tetchy manner.

Another blast of heat, this time close enough to set fire to a large swath of forest floor and confirm just what exactly was towering over both her and her brother. A vast dragon peered down at Pandora, visibly confused by a repeat appearance of this dwarfish snack. Months ago, Pandora had borrowed Mrs. McLachlan's Alarming Clock and had found herself traveling back to a time when dragons roosted in Argyll. Back then, she'd narrowly escaped being toasted by this particular specimen of dragonhood; somehow she doubted whether her luck was going to hold for an encore.

"Mair bluidy stunted DWARVES!" the dragon roared, its tone indicating just how exceedingly delighted it wasn't.

Pandora craned her head back, squinting against the sunlight, all the better to see the owner of the roar.

"AYE. And twa WEE ones, at that. No' a SCRAP of meat on eithera rem, I'll warrant...." And with another incendiary snort, the monstrous dragon turned its back on Titus and Pandora to address its complaints to someone as yet unseen. "HOW am I supposed tae keep body and SOWL together if you keep sending me MALNOURISHED DWARVES? Twa wee skittery mouthfuls of skin and bone won't go far in *my* roost. I tell you, crone, we DRAGONS are headet for EXTINGUISHMENT if THIS is the best you can do...." Muttering to itself and emitting small snorts of flame, it rummaged behind a tree, producing a lethal assortment of kitchen implements that looked as if they'd been hewn out of granite by a homicidally inclined Neanderthal. It rattled these in a menacing fashion and continued, "I *could* shave them very thinly over ma GRUEL, but frankly they're hardly worth the effort. They're not RIPE yet, so they'll not taste of very much at all. See, what I NEED, crone, is something SUBSTATIONAL to feed my family. A nice fat baawool, or an UDDERMOO—och, we could even make do with a RAMBLEAT if we hadty. A few dozen cluckstones or a flocka GOBBLEHISSES . . . even a maiden would do at a pinch, but only a PLUMPTIOUS one, mind, not a gaunt wee GOBLINETTE like this one here...." And to Pandora's horror, the dragon turned round and plucked her off the ground, clasping her in its scaly paw for a heart-stopping moment before thrusting her toward a figure that stood some way off in the deckled shadow of the trees.

The figure came toward her, moving slowly as if it feared

that too sudden a movement might make it shatter into a thousand pieces. It raised an arm, and in a quavery voice as familiar to Pandora as her own breathing, said, "Stop drooling, dragon. What you clasp in your paws is *not* a posset or a breakfast. This human child is my kin. Or . . . at least, she *will* be. Several hundred years from now, she will be my great-great-great-great-great-great-granddaughter. Therefore I command you to put her down at once."

"Your *kin*? Why didn't you say so BEFORE?" the dragon gasped, carefully depositing Pandora in front of her great-great-great-great-great-great-grandmother, Strega-Nonna.

Pandora blinked. Although she was deeply grateful to Strega-Nonna for saving her from being turned into a blackened crisp, she was completely confused by finding her great-great-great-great-great-great-grandmother popping up in the middle of the forest. What was the old lady doing *here*? For all of Pandora's life, Strega-Nonna had lived in the freezer at StregaSchloss; only on special occasions would she appear, defrosted and dripping, ready to pull crackers or blow out cake candles before tottering back to her icy bed. Fortunately for Pandora, this was not a special occasion, and Strega-Nonna appeared to have no intention of returning to her freezer.

"*Quiet*, beast," the old lady snapped, turning away from the dragon to peer at Pandora as if she couldn't quite believe what she saw. "You? Here? Both of you?" Her voice had dropped to a whisper as she gazed beyond Pandora to where Titus stood, rubbing at his eye while trying to keep as much distance as possible between himself and the dragon. "You cannot be here," Strega-Nonna mumbled to herself. "Cannot. The children of the future have no place here in the past."

Titus stepped forward, still keeping as much air between himself and the now unashamedly dribbly dragon. He rubbed his eye and squinted at Strega-Nonna, as if unable to see her clearly.

"Nonna? You've lived round here for centuries, haven't you? I mean, if anyone knows StregaSchloss, it's you, isn't it? Reason I'm asking is that I'm beginning to think that there have always been . . . sort of . . . holes—holes in time here at StregaSchloss." Titus shook his head and rubbed his eye again. "Uh, I'm not explaining this very well—"

"Telling *me*!" muttered Tarantella, emerging from the collar of Pandora's shirt and opening her mouthparts in an exaggerated yawn. "Do go on," she said, waving a hairy leg in Titus's direction.

Titus's mouth shut with a snap. He glared at Tarantella, then hissed through clenched teeth, "Right, spider. If you're so damn smart, you take over. You explain it for us all."

Tarantella sighed. "Dear boy, metaphysics never was my strong suit. In my humble way, with my teeny-weeny, itsy-bitsy arachnid brain, what I think you're trying to describe are StregaSchloss's time portals. Yes?"

"Whatever," Titus mumbled, somehow managing with just one word to radiate complete and total lack of interest, coupled with deeply contemptuous teenage disdain.

"Thank you, thank you for being *such* a great audience here today." Tarantella arranged her mouthparts in an approximation of a leer. "As I was saying before I was deafened by your applause, time portals are like doors leading to the past or the future. What has happened here is that you and your sister have accidentally blundered through a portal. How, when, and *if* you return to your own time is another matter completely. . . ." She heaved a theatrical sigh and batted her many eyelashes at Titus. "I suppose you'll simply have to thrash around here in this limitless forest until you either accidentally stumble back out the way you came in or get eaten up by one of our friend here's less biddable friends and relations. . . ."

Titus paled and edged further away from the dragon.

"Enough." Strega-Nonna wagged her finger in rebuke at Tarantella. "You'll scare the boy half to death. *I* will lead the children back to their own time. I know the way."

It was Pandora's turn to blanch as she remembered the invasion of wolves that had made them flee to the dungeons in the first place. "We *can't* go back." She shuddered, wrapping her arms around herself for comfort. "The house is full of *wolves*—we came down here to the dungeons to escape them."

"Wolves?" The old lady smiled. "I haven't seen a wolf at StregaSchloss for hundreds of years. I hadn't thought to see them ever again. . . ."

"I like WOLFIES," the dragon said thoughtfully. "Providing they haven't suffered too lean a winter before I sling them in ma casserole."

Titus gazed up at the giant beast with revolted admiration. "You . . . you *eat* wolves?" he managed at length.

"Not raw yins," the dragon snorted. "PERSONALITY, I

like them spit-roasted. Not like your sister, who seems tae prefer them drippin' wi' gore."

Pandora closed her eyes and swallowed. The smell of wolf blood rose up from her clothes and nearly made her gag as she remembered the wolf Ludo had shot— She turned to Titus and gasped, "Mr. Grabbit! What happened to *him*? Oh God, Titus, we left him behind, on his own, with the wolves. . . . We have to go back."

A View of the Island

I ntent on rescuing Damp, neither Mrs. McLachlan nor Minty was aware that Titus and Pandora were in immediate danger as well. Oblivious to the wolves closing in on StregaSchloss, Minty ushered Mrs. McLachlan and Latch into her bedroom and closed the door behind them. Over the months she'd been employed at StregaSchloss, Minty had grown accustomed to the weirdness of using the Ancestors' Room as her bedroom. In turn, the ancestors had learned to live with Minty in their midst. After a month, their painted heads barely turned when she entered the room. Chivalrously, all eyes in the portraits would simultaneously snap shut when she disrobed at bedtime. Minty no longer awoke feeling unaccountably ravenous in the middle of

nights when the long-dead ancestors decided to throw a party and roast a boar, and her sleep was untroubled by nightmares, even when men in armor reached out of their frames to switch her bedside light on and off, simply because such electrical wonders hadn't existed in their lifetimes. Therefore she was perfectly at ease as she stood in front of the portrait of Malvolio di S'Enchantedino Borgia, Strega-Nonna's long-dead grandson; and Malvolio, in turn, responded to Minty's attentions by bestowing on her, Latch, and Mrs. McLachlan a smile that would have been dazzling had twenty-first-century cosmetic dentistry been available in the sixteen hundreds. As it was, Latch shuddered at the sight of the ancestor's dreadful brown teeth, shuddered at the impossibility of witnessing an oil painting come to life, and shuddered at the sure and certain knowledge that he was hearing a dead man speak.

Behind Malvolio's grinning head lay a window framing a birchwood beyond. In the painting, even though the window was barely the size of a hardcover novel, the painter had captured every detail of the view beyond: the pale green of the first leaves of spring, the dazzling shimmer of sunshine glinting off the loch behind the trees, and the crisp silhouette of the little island set in the distant water. It was, Mrs. McLachlan decided, too far away to see whether the island was currently inhabited by a pregnant dragon in the company of a little girl, but she had her suspicions. Taking a deep breath and knowing that Latch was going to be severely ticked off at her, Mrs. McLachlan stepped forward.

There was a sensation like spiderwebs brushing across her

face; then she found her way blocked by a heavy oak table. She looked down at a pewter plate, on which lay the remains of lunch, seventeenth-century style.

"Very nice, dear," she managed. "Roast swan, was it? You must get your cook to give me the recipe sometime. . . ."

Latch stood on the other side of the painting, his expression unreadable. What was she *thinking* of? She was supposed to be recuperating, not off gadding about with people who shouldn't, *couldn't* exist. Hitching up her skirts and climbing into paintings was just one of the many things he'd never suspected the outwardly respectable Flora McLachlan might be capable of doing. He'd hoped their life together would be less . . . unpredictable. He'd even allowed himself to fantasize that one day they might retire together to a wee cottage somewhere on the StregaSchloss estate; raise chickens and roses; plant a vegetable garden; sit of a summer's evening in their garden, shelling peas and planning . . . planning *what*? Which painting to invade next? Bleakly, Latch imagined the sheer impossibility of ever visiting an art gallery with Flora McLachlan. Ever. It simply didn't bear thinking about. He turned to share this thought with Miss Araminta, only to discover that *she'd* gone too. Into a different picture—stepping into the huge battle scene that hung over the fireplace, her blond hair like a burning candle in the middle of the smoke-blackened gloom of *The Battle for Mhoire Ochone, 1675*.

Unwilling to be outdone by the two women, Latch steeled himself to follow Flora into her painting—follow her and try to persuade her to return to the land of the living. Then came the sound of gunfire from downstairs, followed by a scream of terror. Torn between love and duty, he spun round and caught sight of movement outside, in the real world beyond the real windows—the dark shadows of wolves coursing across the snowy lawn toward StregaSchloss. From downstairs came more gunfire and, with a single backward glance—

Flora and Malvolio at the window; Miss Araminta talking intently to a mounted man in armor—

Latch ran to help.

S'tan's
Deepest Fear

From: dutydemon@deeppit
To: S'tan@bbc.co.uk/
totallytoast

Hi Boss

Sorry 2 interrupt yr prog o igenous One but things are getting realie bad here. The furrnaces have all gone out, there are rumurs of angels ice-skating on the Hades Orbital, and the volcanic slopes of Mount Heinous are 100s of feet deep under snow. At this rate we're going to have 2 use fossle fules by the weekend if we want to keep on toasting sinners as per u.

Note: do we *have* any fossle fules?

Qestions are being asked at meetings of the Hadean Execyutiv——questions like

what the H**ven is happening to Hades? Has S'tan lost it? (Begging your pardon, Your Gastly Gruesomeness, this is them, not me.) Should we elect another First Minster? Is the Boss groing soft? O Your Imperial Inflammablness, I beg U, come home. Your Empire needs U.

Grovle, grovle,

D. Demon 666

"Ready in five, Stan baby."

The Devil's head snapped upright and He spun round to face the young assistant producer, unfortunately forgetting to compose His features beforehand.

"Oh my God!" she shrieked, covering her eyes in horror. "We need to get makeup in here right now. What *have* you been up to, my darling?" Without waiting for a reply, she spoke into her headset, her voice urgent, her expression remarkably calm considering the monstrous vision in front of her: S'tan unmasked, His yellow teeth bared in a frozen snarl, His awful eyes—

"You've been painting the town red again, haven't you, you naughty boy?" Clucking, the makeup artist grasped S'tan's chin in her hand, turning His face this way and that under her critical eye before pronouncing, "You're a mess, me old duck, but no matter—that's why I'm here with me powders and paints at the ready: to repair the damage and plaster over the rest...." As she talked, she was already smearing pale green gloop across S'tan's face, spreading every inch of His outraged red skin with the color-corrective paste, hardly pausing to draw breath before inviting the Arch-Fiend to pop a pair of green contacts into His crimson eyes and simultaneously persuading Him to tuck His tail into His chef's trousers.

Was He losing it? He wondered, ushered down the dark corridors toward the *Totally Toast* studio by a chattering clutch of young BBC technicians, none of whom was paying Him the slightest bit of attention, not even when He tripped over a cable and let rip with an oath that caused one of the acoustic tiles in the ceiling to melt and curl up like a pretzel. Somehow He got through the next half hour of rehearsals, and when the camera finally broadcast His face live to the nation, it was the serene, squeaky-clean, oath-free Stan that the nation beheld. Stan, the best and funniest TV chef ever to grace the United Kingdom's television sets. *Totally Toast* had achieved such stellar ratings that already there were plans for the *Some Extra Slices of Totally Toast* cookery book, another *A Round of Totally Toast* series, and a weekly "A Slice of Totally Toast" cookery column to be syndicated across the planet in its Sunday papers. On balance, His success was bizarre, freakish even, since on *Totally Toast* most of the food was burned, dropped on the floor, or had its moldy bits scraped off on camera. And despite the BBC makeup department's best efforts, Stan always looked as if *He'd* been burned, been dropped on the floor, and had barely managed to scrape His moldy bits off before the spotlight turned on Him. In close-up, His hairy hands revealed the grime of ages stratified in black layers beneath His fingernails, and it was obvious to all but the color-blind that Stan was a cook with a seriously finger-staining, lung-furring, cancer-causing nicotine addiction. Miraculous, then, that *anyone* took Him seriously, far less endeavored to imitate His cooking style. There He would be, every Thursday lunchtime, leering out at His audience, one unsanitary fist wrapped around a knife, the other waving a toasting fork, on the end of which would be a black, charred, smoldering lump of something best described as carbon.

The nation loved Him: fan letters poured into the BBC, and admirers blocked the road outside the studios; the smell of charred meat drifted from tens of thousands of kitchen ventilating fans and outdoor barbecues every Thursday as the nation tried out Stan's latest burnt offering. The current program was subtitled "Awesomely Offal," and as Stan put the finishing touches to His Deviled Kidneys in a Gland *Jus* on a Blackened Pancake Stack, such was His professionalism that no one could have guessed that His mind was on other things entirely. The moment the program went off the air, S'tan barreled through the throng of producers, editors, cameramen, makeup artists, sound technicians, and fawning executives; fled down the darkened corridors of the BBC; and locked Himself behind the door of dressing room 2.

He pulled a mobile phone from His pocket, keyed in a number, and waited to be connected. He *was* losing it, He decided. Time was, He wouldn't have needed the aid of man-made telecommunications to contact His demon underlings. When the Chronostone had been in His possession, all He had to do was *think* of a demon and wherever that demon was, it would know the Boss wanted a quick word. Moreover, back then, S'tan knew exactly what was going through the minds of each and every one of His subjects: knew where they were without the aid of GPS and knew that their loyalty to Him was absolute. . . . Now they had to use *e-mail* to alert Him to their plight. Hades freezing over? Less than a century ago, that would have been unthinkable. Back then, Hades was hot as . . . as . . . as Hell, actually. Come to think of it, S'tan reminded Himself, back then He was pretty hot as well.

Looking down to where His feet were hidden by the swell of His stomach, He saw himself all too clearly: a fat, pathetic lump of a demon; a figure bearing more resemblance to an aging heavyweight boxer than the onetime fearsome, awesome, terrifying, petrifying S't—

"This mobile may be switched off. Please try later or send a text."

S'tan swore: a single utterance, one word translated from the original Babylonian into an expletive so foul and repellent that in front of Him, the mirror turned black with shame and the toilet in His suite flushed itself repeatedly in an attempt to wash the word away. Laboriously, muttering to Himself, S'tan keyed in a text to Isagoth, His defense minister, His greasy, lard-coated fingers leaving opaque smears all over His phone, His thumbnails clattering on the tiny keys.

where r u? have u xtermin8ed that t d us mr borgia
yet?
phone me @ 1ce.
S

There. Concise and to the point. If Isagoth didn't get back to Him within, say, ten minutes, S'tan was going in. No more faffing around, waiting for a lesser demon to do his work for Him. If the job was to be done properly, He was going to have to do it Himself.

Several months ago, S'tan had made His first pact with a human since that unmentionable snake-and-apple fiasco back in the dawn of mankind. In return for being fast-tracked onto BBC TV and given His own cookery program, S'tan had promised to destroy His human benefactor's half brother, Luciano. Trouble was, eight weeks on, the supposedly doomed Luciano was still alive and well. Consequently, S'tan's notoriety as the Big Bad Beast had taken another hammering, and if He didn't do something soon, His reputation was going to be so ruined that the only way humans would ever summon Him again would be by pouring a saucerful of milk and calling, "Heeeere, puss-puss pussy. Heeere, kitty kitty kitty."

Suppressing a howl, S'tan glared at His phone, as if by eyeball energy alone He could force it to ring. Unsurprisingly, it remained mute, but on its screen, under a lardy smear, was a little envelope icon indicating that He had a text message waiting. Isagoth? Already? Deeply impressed despite Himself at His defense minister's speedy reply, S'tan prodded a key and the text appeared.

Oh dear.

It was most emphatically not from Isagoth. Despite being the Fount of All Fear, the Prince of Darkness, the Emperor of

Endless Evil, and other assorted scary titles, S'tan felt a tiny frisson of terror. The text message was from Don Lucifer di S'Embowelli Borgia, the rat-faced, insanely vengeful uncle of Titus, Pandora, and Damp, half brother of Luciano Strega-Borgia, and, most important, the summoner of S'tan. His text message was, like him, short and brutal. It read:

signore satan.
we no longer have a deal.
your concrete overshoes are ready for collection.
capisce?

With a squeak of dismay, S'tan dropped His phone on the floor, suddenly aware that, in common with all cell phones, it was broadcasting a signal that pinpointed exactly where He was every time He switched it on. And *that* meant that, at this very moment, Don Lucifer might be sending his henchmen round to BBC dressing room 2 for a personal, one-on-one concrete overshoe fitting. . . .

After a moment's reflection S'tan picked His phone up and removed it to his private bathroom, where He tried to flush it down the toilet; somewhat unsurprisingly, it failed to disappear. This was *dreadful*. As if being without His Chronostone wasn't bad enough, He now had a Mafia contract out on Him. Could life hold any more?

Apparently it could: muffled weirdly by the water in the toilet bowl, His phone was ringing, its vibrating alert making it rattle as if it were trying to drill its way out through the porcelain. Completely unnerved, S'tan fled, bolting along corridors, pushing past security guards, skidding past the doorman and out into the snowstorm, nearly mowing down the throng of frozen *Totally Toast* fans before hailing a taxi and vanishing into its interior.

What Big Teeth You Have

In the low afternoon sunshine, the northwestern coast of Argyll resembled a Christmas card: snow capped the mountains of the Bengormless Range, dusted the Scotch pines, and graciously allowed the passage of a fleet of snowplows trailing long lines of delayed traffic in their wake. Twenty-three cars behind one of these snowplows was the Strega-Borgias' Volvo sports wagon, its interior still bearing witness to the recent birth of their youngest child. Staring into the brake lights of the car ahead, Luciano forced himself to keep calm and concentrate on driving. Despite his best intentions, his thoughts kept running off down dark avenues of possibility, all of which terminated with the same awful question: What if Latch and

Ludo could not defend StregaSchloss? The thought of Titus and his sisters alone, vulnerable, defenseless, with Mafia assassins closing in on them— *No, no, no. Think of something else, Luciano,* he commanded himself. Sneaking a glance at Baci in the rear seat, he took a deep breath. She didn't know. Miraculously, he'd managed to shield her from the truth. Baci had no idea what was really going on. As befitted a newly delivered *mama,* her thoughts were almost entirely focused on the small bundle strapped into the front passenger seat in a rear-facing baby carrier. Swaddled in a Shetland shawl of such gossamer delicacy that it could, in its entirety, be passed through the circle of a wedding ring was the changeling, eyes squinched shut, mouth wide open, and lungs in fine working order. Beside the wailing baby, Luciano gritted his teeth, clutched the steering wheel, and devoutly wished himself elsewhere.

"SHALL I JUST FEED HIM AGAIN?" Baci yelled from the rear, struggling to make herself heard over the infant's din.

"YOU JUST DID," Luciano roared, taking one hand off the wheel to stroke the baby's tearstained and quivering cheek.

"MAYBE HE'S GOT COLIC?" Baci shrieked, worn down to a nubbin by the unceasing, never-ending, grinding racket of the baby's displeasure. Being trapped in a car in a long line of slow-moving traffic was bad enough, but having also to endure the tortured screams coming from what looked like the product of a union between a purple goblin and a fat, woolly maggot was quite beyond human endurance.

Longingly, Luciano thought of the deep masculine silence of his study, a totally baby-free zone. He also briefly considered the child-exempt seclusion of his half-assembled home gymnasium before remembering exactly why it was that he needed a home gym in the first place. He had to get home. Had to gather his beloved family all together under one roof and . . .

. . . and what? What on earth was he going to do? All the sit-ups and workouts in the world weren't going to make a blind bit of difference to a bullet with his name on it. As for protecting his family—Baci, the children—his eyes prickled, his mind beset by hideous, unwelcome images of their slaughtered bodies lying in pools of blood; their dead eyes, slack mouths—

With a sickening jolt, Luciano snatched his hand back from where he had been mindlessly stroking the howling baby's face. He'd been *bitten*. The baby had *bitten* him. Uncomprehending and utterly aghast, he looked from his bleeding—*bleeding*—finger into the face of his youngest child. What he saw there was so shocking that for an instant he nearly lost control of the car. The baby stopped screaming as if it had been gagged. In the ensuing eerie silence, it opened blood-red eyes and hissed at him, its tiny mouth curled up in a sneer, its lips rolled back to expose a row of black needle-pointed teeth.

Unaware that his home was currently under siege by a ravening wolf pack, Nestor the baby dragon lay awake in his nest in the dungeons, wondering if it was worth the effort of going upstairs to the cloakroom as instructed by Minty, or whether to pretend he'd forgotten her advice and go for a quick poo somewhere dark and out of the way in the dungeons. As he gnawed thoughtfully on a stolen hiking boot, he decided, on balance, that the dungeons were the better option, toilet-wise. Riddled with blind tunnels, catacombs, crypts, fallen arches, vast caverns, and priest holes, the dungeon offered a huge variety of places where no one would ever think to go looking for one teeny-weeny little dragon dump.

Padding off down a tunnel, Nestor chewed meditatively and peered into the darkness in search of the perfect pit stop. There. Ideal. He swallowed the last morsel of boot leather and Gore-Tex, burped delicately, and reversed with some difficulty into a deep recess. Lifting his tail, he was just about to close his eyes and bear down when an unknown voice broke the silence.

"*What* the HELL—?"

And then came a flash and a loud bang as something hot and shiny whined past his head at such speed that Nestor let rip from both ends in terror.

With his night vision utterly destroyed by Nestor's dazzling burst of dragon flame, Ludo Grabbit dived out of range of what he mistakenly assumed to be a rather underpowered flamethrower. Seconds later, the lawyer revised his assumptions downward. The stench now drifting toward him out of the darkness made him realize that whatever was out there was far more afraid of him than he was of it. Sighting down the barrel of his rifle and breathing through his mouth to avoid inhaling the dreadful smell, Ludo yelled, "Come on out with your hands in the air!"

Obediently, Nestor tiptoed forward, hoping that whoever this was shouting at him, he wouldn't tell Minty about the temporary lapse in his toilet training.

Pressed with his back up against the china cupboard, Latch was trying to remember if he knew anything about wolf behavior. He suspected that paddling about in the blood of a dead wolf would not increase his popularity within the wolf pack. The wolves were spread out around him in a semicircle, tracking his every movement with their yellow eyes. At times they turned away to snap at each other, giving Latch an opportunity to see just what big teeth they had. Then a ripple seemed to go through the pack, as if their interest in Latch-as-lunch was eclipsed by the simultaneous arrival of two more edible parties: one, from the dungeons, was Mr. Grabbit, trailed by a disconsolate Nestor, and the other . . .

"FLORA! NO!" Latch howled, lunging forward in a heroic attempt to put himself between the wolves and his beloved Flora.

It could have all gone very badly wrong at this point: hackles up, the wolves were poised to attack; Ludo had his gun aimed and ready; and Latch suddenly realized that his future hung by a thread. There was a moment that lasted several lifetimes; then Flora crouched down among the wolves and, with an introductory growl, addressed them in a low, urgent voice.

"Down. Lie down while I sort out this confusion with my pack."

In the absolute hush, Latch imagined he could hear his own

heart thudding against his breastbone. What *was* this? At his feet, all around, the wolves were obeying; were lying down and ignoring him completely, all eyes on the small woman who unaccountably held them in thrall.

"F-F-Flora?" His voice was emerging as a boyish squeak. He took a deep shuddering breath and was about to try again when Ludo spoke.

"Just stand up very, very slowly and move away from them." He smiled encouragingly at Mrs. McLachlan and continued, "Don't, whatever you do, make any sudden movements. I think I can buy you both enough time to get you out of the door and down the corrid—"

"*Mister* Grabbit!" Mrs. McLachlan's voice was sharp, but nothing like as pointed as the look with which she skewered the lawyer. "Please. *Don't* presume to tell me how to behave with our allies here. D'you not think you've done quite enough damage for one day?"

At this, as if in complete understanding, the wolves pointed their muzzles toward the ceiling and howled. The volume was deafening, unbearably loud within the confines of the kitchen: waves of sound beating off the walls and floor, making any further human communication impossible. Nestor clung round-eyed with wonder to Ludo's leg, and Latch stared at Flora in complete confusion as the wolf pack mourned their fallen members.

"Quite," said Mrs. McLachlan after a suitably respectful length of time had passed. "Now, while Mr. Grabbit demonstrates his genuine remorsefulness by digging a grave for his victims, I shall require your help, dear, to prepare for the siege."

Latch's eyes goggled, but he wisely held his tongue; not so Ludo, whose legal training made him automatically challenge any command, no matter how just or unjust it might be.

"For God's sake, woman," he spluttered. "They're *wolves*. So *what* if I shot a couple of them? What did you expect me to do when they burst into the house uninvited? Ask them to stay to tea?"

Mrs. McLachlan looked up at Ludo, her hand stroking the head of a giant brindled wolf. "That, Mr. Grabbit, would have been a very good start indeed."

Bats Redux

They walked in single file through the monotonous, endless forest: Strega-Nonna, Titus, Pandora, and, some way behind, crashing through the trees, the hungry dragon.

"Are WEES no there yet?" it demanded, its voice, to Titus's ears, growing ever more strident as the hours dragged by.

Not only was Strega-Nonna's grip surprisingly strong for such an antique ancestor, Titus was stunned by her unstoppable energy as she dragged him behind her through the birchwood. Titus had lost track of time, but it felt as if they'd been walking for ages, and to his dismay he'd started stumbling and crashing into tree trunks, aware that the pain in his eye was growing worse. Not only that; it had spread to his other eye, and, if he wasn't mistaken, his sight was fading. Pandora was following him, and he was behind Strega-

Nonna, both of them relying on the old lady to find the portal or whatever it was and take them back to their own time. However, Titus noticed that little by little it was growing dark; there was less daylight filtering down through the birch leaves, and the shadows were merging together into an endless gray fog. Even then, it hadn't occurred to him what was really happening until Pandora stopped and turned round; at least, that's what he assumed she'd done—he couldn't actually *see* her properly—but her voice sounded like she was facing him, and she moaned something about wishing she'd brought sunglasses because the sun was too bright. Sun? Bright? He'd thought *night* was falling. That was when he was overcome by such a wave of fear that he walked straight into a tree, just like he was . . . blind.

At this point, the giant dragon bringing up the rear of their little portal-seeking procession nearly stood on him, and for a moment chaos ruled, during which time Titus learned a few very choice oaths he never thought to hear, especially not from the mouth of his sweet little great-great-great-great-great-great-grandmother. Then Strega-Nonna seized him by the hand and forced him to half run, half walk beside her, all the time talking nonstop and filling Titus's terrible darkness with words. Three-quarters of what she said sounded like complete nonsense, but now and then would come a phrase or an idea that would take Titus's breath away.

". . . Of course, most of this is your younger sister's doing. She was born with the Gift, as you know, but the Gift is a terrible thing to be given to one so young. It puts so much raw power into such a tiny, untried vessel. Like the ginger beer your great-great-grandfather tried to make when he was a boy. Decanted it into earthenware jars and sealed them up tight with corks and beeswax . . . two weeks later they blew apart—too much fizz in too small a space. That's what I mean about the Gift. Is that dragon still behind us? Good. Useful creatures, dragons. We'll be needing all our beasts about us, boy. Mark my words. Now. Back to your sister . . . where was I? Ah, yes. Yes. Her spells. Have you noticed that she weaves her spells out of what she knows and loves? Like a little magpie, taking shiny things to make its own. Just as *she* does, collecting shiny, sparkly things to weave her spells with. Except your little sister collects stories, not things. Heaven knows which story we're in just now—in this wood, the wolves beyond, and you, with your poor frozen eyes. . . . It's a mix of fairy tales, all stirred together. I think it's 'Red Riding Hood' combined with 'The Snow Queen,' for which we must give thanks, because last summer, if you recall, thanks to her, we had 'Thumbelina' mixed up with 'Sleeping Beauty,' and *that* was a trial. Keep up, laddie, you've much to do before you rest; miles to go and promises to keep. Did I mention that you're the spitting image of my son? It's miraculous how the centuries can pass, the sands of time sifting over the graves of those we loved, shifting and settling until our dead become part of the land in which they lie, with their cities crumbled and forgotten, their names vanished from the Earth, and then, as if preordained, a child will come, bearing the face of one whom we never thought to see . . . ever again."

Strega-Nonna stopped and turned round and placed her

quivering hand on Titus's chest. Titus felt his heart leap, as if the old woman had sent a bolt of electricity through him. Abruptly, she grabbed his hands and put them on either side of her face.

"See? Or since you cannot *see*, feel," she demanded. "And you took me for a dried and withered crone. Yet even from this desiccated twig comes some sap. Feel this water, Titus, son of Luciano. Know that you are the great-great-great-great-great-grandson of Raphael di Clemente Borgia, and you not only carry him in your blood, you also bear his features as your birthright. Feel my old woman's tears and, with them, melt the ice that binds your heart and mind. You are not blind, but frozen."

Titus would have fallen then, collapsed on the forest floor, had it not been for Strega-Nonna's clasping his shoulders and forcing him to stay upright to feel the full force of her words.

"Aaah," he groaned, hit by a wave of the most unbearable sorrow, finding himself helpless to resist as he was dragged under by a riptide of grief that, in all his sheltered thirteen years on the planet, he hadn't known existed. He was swept up in the agony suffered by countless parents who had watched their children die, the pain of lovers torn apart by death, the endless mourning of Strega-Nonna's centuries of loneliness as, time and time again, she defied Death and, in doing so, lost everything she had ever held dear. His hands wet with her tears, her face growing wet with his own, Titus stood weeping, blinded, and dumbfounded as feelings he couldn't even begin to define washed through him.

"What?" he managed, his voice unrecognizable.

"Don't be ashamed of your tears, child," Strega-Nonna whispered. "Be proud. Even the best of grown men weep. With your tears you melt the icy enchantment that binds your heart and soul."

Titus blinked at the old lady, trying to bring her into focus through the shimmering dazzle of tears that clung to his lashes. If ever he'd wished for the privacy afforded by sunglasses, now was the time. Unaccustomed to crying, his eyes felt as if they'd shriveled up like raisins. And it was *bright*. Overhead, sunshine was beating down through the tree canopy, spangling him with lozenges of light, of—

"NONNA!" he roared, so loudly that the dragon tiptoeing behind him gave a startled snort and set a tree alight with its nasal flamethrowers. "Nonna! IcanseeIcanseeIcansee!" And to everyone's surprise, especially his own, Titus wrapped his arms around Strega-Nonna and spun her round in a circle, yelling, "Thankyouthankyouthankyou!" before planting a smacking kiss on her pleated brow and gently returning her to the ground.

"What was all *that* about?" Pandora hissed as they raced through the woods after the now remarkably sprightly Strega-Nonna.

"I, um—can I explain later?" Titus gasped, his chest heaving with the effort of keeping up with the old woman's accelerated pace. "I'm not—I'm, ah . . . I don't think I understand . . . yet."

The light grew brighter as the forest thinned out; then suddenly they emerged from the trees, out onto a stony path cut into the side of a hill. To their right, the land fell away, down to where a stream wound through rocks and clumps of grass and heather. Ahead, the path was intimidatingly steep, a narrow deer track, well-defined but so awash with water that it appeared to be more of a waterfall than a footpath. Undeterred, Strega-Nonna struck off up the hillside, her feet splashing through puddles and sending small rocks bouncing downhill to where the others labored breathlessly behind. Higher and higher they climbed, until they reached a coire scooped into the hillside where, mercifully, Strega-Nonna stopped, and moments later, red-faced and breathless, Titus, Pandora, and the dragon caught up. Tarantella emerged, blinking, from the depths of Pandora's shirt and scanned her surroundings.

"Dear me," she said, eyes swiveling disconcertingly in several directions at once.

"What now?" Pandora glared at her.

"Oh . . . nothing." Tarantella sighed. "Just . . . well . . . Oh, come *on*, team. Is this *it*? This godforsaken spot is the reason we've been running flat out for what feels like several lifet—"

"We? Running?" Titus interrupted. "Spider, the only thing about you that's been running are your mouthparts."

"It's not a godforsaken spot either, spider," said a scratchy little voice. *"It's our blessed, heaven-sent home, actually."*

Pandora gasped out loud. Suddenly, several things fell into place. She knew where she was. Exactly where she was. Last time she'd been here, in Coire Crone—

"—was last summer, when you were hiding from that dreadful little terrorist. Welcome back, child."

"Pandora?" Titus's voice vibrated, pitched high as if strung too tightly. "Who *is* that? Who's speaking? What *is* this place?"

"*Relative of yours, I take it?*" the voice continued. "*Better hope he's not afraid of bats, hmm?*" And with no warning, the sky above their heads darkened as thousands of ragged black shapes took to the air.

"Darling?"

"*Cara mia?*"

"Is there something the matter?" In the backseat, Baci was gathering her wraps and gloves, her bag and the infernal goblin's—*No, no, no, Luciano, the baby's*—travel bag, and smiling at her husband's reflection in the rearview mirror.

Luciano forced a smile onto his face, forced a lightness into his voice, and forced himself not to dwell upon the huge deception he was practicing on his poor, innocent wife. "Heavens, no, Baci. You, my darling wife, you have made me the happiest, the *proudest* man in all of Scotland. *Four* fine childr—" Was that a hiss? Had that vile monstrosity dared to hiss at him? Luciano's eyes slid sideways to where *it* sat, strapped in, leering at him. No teeth visible, thankfully—

"Oh, look, Luciano, he's *smiling* at you. Ahhhhh, how adorable."

Adorable, thought Luciano woodenly, his eyes firmly fixed on the rearview mirror. *No. Not even remotely adorable, that thing. Repulsive, terrifying, bowel-clenchingly, monstrously wrong—but adorable? Never.*

"Never what?" Baci looked up, puzzled. "I didn't quite catch that. Sorry, darling. Too busy making sure that I've got all my stuff from the hospital. Honestly—I was only *in* for what, twenty-four hours, and in that time somehow I managed to acquire six bouquets of flowers, four boxes of chocolates, a ton of magazines, and enough bath foam to cover StregaSchloss in suds from top to bott— What's that sound? That weird hissing noise? What on earth is it, Luciano?"

It was doing it again. *Think, man. Don't just* sit *there,* say *something.*

"Slow puncture. Or . . . or . . . ah . . . maybe it's the, um"—
Luciano cudgeled his brains for what little he remembered of
the oily bits under the hood—"the, er, cylinder-head-rotor-
arm-carburetor-valve . . . gasket."

Baci's eyes rolled. Fortunately for Luciano, his wife's
knowledge of mechanical engineering made his look positively encyclopedic.

"Gosh. Sounds fearsomely expensive. Oh, look, here's
Minty come to welcome the new baby." And blessedly, so distracted was Baci that she failed to notice the red eyes that rapidly opened and closed again, scanning the new arrival in one
blink.

The smell of baking drifted enticingly upstairs, a tendril of
warm vanilla curling itself around the open door of Damp's
new bedroom, where, as if borne on a strong wind, it was
sucked toward the abandoned picture book lying on the rag
rug by the bed. The vanilla scent spiraled down onto the final
page of the book and vanished into the little illustration above
the word

finis

Paddling round the island's shoreline for what felt like the
millionth time, Ffup suddenly stopped and sniffed the air. She
sniffed again . . . and again, a wide grin spreading across her
mouth, her drooping wings springing upright.

"Ooooh, yesss!" she squealed. "Yes, yes, yes. Ffup, the great navigator, does it again. Without compass, map, Sherpas, or even radar, I've found the way home. What a *nose*, huh? And what's more, some kind soul is baking white-chocolate-and-vanilla brownies back at the happy homestead. . . . Oh YES, YES, YES, I'm *there*. Wait for meeee. Don't eat them all before we get there. . . ."

Wading rapidly through the shallows, the dragon scooped up Damp and, following the scent of baking, delivered them both back to StregaSchloss in time, she hoped, for lunch. Trading the island's chilly shoreline for the rag rug in Damp's bedroom, Ffup blessed the good fortune that had brought them safely home. It had been deceptively easy to travel *to* the island; the problem had been trying to retrace their steps. In fact, just before Ffup's nose had picked up the smell of vanilla, the dragon had wondered if they'd *ever* be able to go home; wondered if the millions of mussels clinging to the rocks of the island were in *any* way edible; and, finally, had wondered if falling out with her fiancé hadn't been A Very Bad Idea indeed. Stomach growling loudly, Ffup was following Damp downstairs, lost in thought, when she remembered the stone clutched in her hot little paw. Uh-oh. Bother. That would never do. She was totally useless at telling lies. Mrs. McLachlan would be bound to ask her if she'd had any luck in finding her missing engagement ring, and she would be totally incapable of saying, "Who, *me*? *What* engagement ring?" without literally bursting into flames of embarrassment.

"You go on downstairs," she said to Damp. "I need a pee."

And as if to prove her point about being a hopeless liar, a little flame of shame at this fib popped out of one of her nostrils. Ffup fled upstairs before Damp could notice and bolted into the little girl's bedroom, closing the door behind her.

Where? Where could she hide it? Chest heaving, the dragon scanned the bedroom for good places. Inside one of the Russian dolls frowning from the lineup on top of the chest of drawers? Brilliant. Ffup seized the largest doll and tried to unscrew its head from its base. To her horror, the wooden shape splintered in her paws. Oh heck. Oh bother, bother, bother. Oh *ouch*, she whimpered, picking hand-painted splinters out of her tender paw pads and poking the shattered remains of the doll down the back of the chest of drawers. Now what? Under the pillow? Too obvious, and way too "Princess and the Pea"–like to boot. In Damp's toy box? No. Might be found by accident. Ffup groaned, staring at Damp's bed for inspiration. Ahh. There. Inside her pajama-case piglet. Perfect. The very thing. Damp never ever used it for pajamas, mainly because every time the alarmingly furry pink pig was unzipped, a hidden sensor launched the whole thing into a loud chorus of—

"I'm PRETTY and PINK!!
I'm just a PIG, just watch me WALLOW—"

"Shut up, shut up—oh, for heaven's *sake*," Ffup moaned, grabbing the pajama case, stuffing the stone into it, zipping it shut, and hurling it back under Damp's bed with a squeak of relief.

Moments later she rejoined the little girl at the head of the stairs leading down to the great hall.

"Thanks for waiting. Shall we go and see if there's any lunch?"

Damp frowned up at Ffup and sighed. "Didn't flushit," she observed, adding, "Not washit hands, dirty."

"Whaaaat?" Ffup roared. "What is this? Boot camp? Boarding school? D'you think you're a matron or something?"

"Not matron," Damp said sadly, reminded of Sister Passterre, and thus of the new baby. "Not wantit, matron. Don't *care. Be* a dirty dragon. Germy paws. Dirty, dirrrty, *dirrrrr*—"

"Damp, my wee pet," said Mrs. McLachlan, appearing at the foot of the stairs, her smile showing just how delighted she was to see the little girl home safely. "And Ffup too? Marvelous. Now, *dears*, I'm sure you're going to tell us *all* about your adventures, but first let's wash our hands and paws, shall we? Heaven knows where they, or you, have been, but we wouldn't like to get nasty, dirty germs on the new baby, would we?"

Oh brother, thought Ffup, realizing why the nanny's voice had been so artificially upbeat when by rights she should have been demanding where on earth they had been. The front door stood open, revealing Signor and Signora Strega-Borgia, followed by Minty, who was holding a tiny shawled bundle in her arms.

Seeing the glad faces waiting to greet him, Luciano felt he was choking on his own lies. Everyone looked so . . . normal.

Evidently none of them suspected a thing. His gaze fell across first Damp and then Baci, and for one brief moment he saw them drenched in blood. Then the thing in Minty's arms poked a tiny fist out of its shawl, Damp's face crumpled, and, giving a loud wail, she fled back upstairs to her bedroom.

"I'll go to her, dear." Mrs. McLachlan took Baci's coat and steered her away from the stairs. "Just leave her to me. Now, Latch has lit the fire in the drawing room for you and the wee baby, and we thought you might like to feed the wee mite in privacy before supper—"

"NO!" Luciano realized he'd shouted out loud. The prospect of Baci being left alone with that . . . that *thing* was unbearable. But how on earth would he, could he—and now everyone was staring at him, puzzled by his shout of denial. *Think, Luciano. Say something. Anything.* "I mean, no. Baci is exhausted. The journey, the traffic, the snow— No, darling." He held up a hand as Baci began to protest. "Please, allow me to take charge. I want you to have a little lie-down: put your feet up, relax. The baby is fine; look, he's sleeping contentedly in Minty's arms. Why not just use this opportunity to unwind?"

Baci was about to object, about to explain that she was currently so unwound that she felt like an unraveled strand of overcooked spaghetti, when the baby took matters into its own hands.

"Bwaaah," it wailed, mouth opening wide, its green eyes fixed on Minty, its expression radiating utter misery at discovering itself to be held in the wrong arms entirely. "WAAAAaaahBWaaaah," it squeaked, entirely unimpressed by the young nanny's attempts to hush, soothe, rock, and comfort it.

Before Baci practically snatched the infant out of Minty's arms, Luciano risked a peek. Shielded by its shawl from everyone's gaze but his, the baby didn't pause in the middle of its howls of outrage. Mouth wide open, tiny fists batting the air, it turned to face Luciano and winked evilly. Seconds later, Baci bore it off to the drawing room.

The Devil Boots Up

"There, you little toad," Isagoth muttered, tugging at the bottle. "Come *on*, let *go*, it's empty."

Baby Borgia ignored this plea to relinquish his grip. Instead, he sucked harder, his tiny face turning pink with effort. Loud, squeaky sucking sounds came from the empty feeding bottle as the infant dragged down lungfuls of air, an action that boded ill for his newborn digestion.

"LET GO!" Isagoth roared, startling the baby and causing him to open his mouth in distress. The bottle's flattened nipple reinflated with a small plosive *pop*, and air rushed in to fill the vacuum. Something similar happened to the baby, except he didn't go *pop*, he went *waaah*.

Isagoth clutched his head in his hands and nearly wept. Four hours. Four miserable, deafening,

ghastly, head-mangling, nerve-grating hours during which this repulsive leech of a human child had sucked down four times its own cubic capacity in warmed-over cow juice. Four hours, and fourteen diaper changes too. After the first fecal assault, Isagoth had learned fast. He'd stuffed the squelching infant inside his jacket and left the hotel to comb the shops of Auchenlochtermuchty in search of poo-containment pants. A bemused assistant in the mini-market had steered him in the direction of disposable diapers, and Isagoth had purchased what he'd innocently assumed to be a lifetime's supply. Now, unfolding the last diaper in the packet, he stifled a howl of despair. This, he decided, was simply the pits. He'd had no idea what humans went through when they were insane enough to procreate. That they should *willingly* put themselves through childbirth and its gruesomely milk- and feces-stained aftermath was simply unbelievable. Isagoth gazed at the baby, aghast that something so small and weak could possibly make so much noise.

"Please," he begged. "Stop! Desist! ENOUGH!" He picked up the child, unwittingly setting off a slow-wave motion deep within its infant gut. Still Baby Borgia wailed, batting at the demon's face with tiny fists, drawing his little legs up to his distended tummy in the universal baby signal for being in possession of copious amounts of gas.

"Hush, shush, wheesht, SHHHHHH," muttered Isagoth, entirely oblivious to the meaning of universal baby signals and regarding the baby's drawn-up legs as proof positive that it was indeed a toad. He clutched the wailing blob under one arm as he struggled back into his jacket, patting his pockets to ensure that he had the keys for the car. "Let's hit the high street, toad-child," Isagoth said under his breath; then, opening the bedroom door and heading out into the public spaces of the Auchenlochtermuchty Arms, in a voice meant for public consumption, "More diapers, eh, my dear little Hertzy-Pops?" And fixing an approximation of an I've-been-up-all-night-with-this-baby-so-don't-even-*think*-about-talking-to-me expression on his face, he took the stairs three at a time, causing the milk-and-air mixture wallowing around in the baby's stomach to froth up like yeast. The child's redoubled wails echoed round the hotel, drawing disapproving grimaces from a quartet of crusty colonels playing a rubber of bridge in the residents' lounge.

"Will you be joining us for DINNER TONIGHT?" yelled the receptionist, struggling to make herself heard above the baby's shrieks. Unsurprisingly, Isagoth didn't respond, not having heard a word. Unsurprisingly, the receptionist didn't repeat her invitation, having no wish to spend any more time than strictly necessary within earshot of the wailing baby. She watched without interest as Isagoth stepped into the revolving doors leading out to the parking lot and then perked up a fraction as the glass door suddenly turned white.

Trapped inside a transparent wedge of revolving door, Isagoth had inadvertently squeezed the baby's abdomen as he pushed onward through a half revolution. The baby stopped in mid-shriek and, with an expression of deepest relief, erupted. Before Isagoth could duck, flee, or even point the infant's head in a different direction, he found himself unaccountably covered from collar to belt in what looked like his own weight in sour-smelling cottage cheese. In his arms, the now-diminished baby gave a final dainty little belch by way of epilogue and immediately fell fast asleep.

Babies, 2; Demons, 0.

"Have ah no seen youse on TV?"

"YES. POSSIBLY. TAKE MY BAG, WOULD YOU?"

"Why? Where're youse wantin' to go, like?"

S'tan sighed deeply. This little excursion was turning out to be an epic voyage on a par with Columbus's trip to the Americas. Scotland had turned out to be an awfully long way away from the BBC in London. So far away that the first taxi driver had refused point-blank to drive Him there, dropping Him off outside Terminal One at Heathrow Airport and suggesting that He catch a plane instead. Consequently He'd had to stand in queues and endure the rigors of business-class travel, at every stage of which He'd been forced to sign autographs and shake hands with His adoring public. And now, in Scotland, *still* with a long journey ahead, it was beginning to look like He was expected to converse with this dreadful taxi driver all the way to His destination.

"So, whit brings a dead-famous bloke like youse up here, eh?"

"I'M THINKING OF MAKING A KILLING IN ARGYLL." S'tan met the taxi driver's eyes with the kind of stare that carried a subliminal KEEP OFF warning. Insensitive clod that he was, the driver paid no attention.

"Zat right, eh? How're youse gonny dae that? I could use a

few tips, me. Wishta wis clever like youse. See, when wese get tae where youse wanty go, I'd be dead chuffed if youse'd gie me your autograph. Ah really liked your recipie fir boiled pig testicles in yon fancy wine, eh no? Pure dead brilliant, so it wis. The wifey made it fir me the ither night an' it wis jis magic, so it was—"

The driver had his back turned to S'tan and, unfortunately for him, the parking lot was temporarily deserted, so there were no witnesses to what happened next.

The demon sprang forward and slammed the lid of the trunk shut. There was a cut-off scream followed by a muffled thud; then the driver's headless body collapsed in a heap at S'tan's feet. Staggering back from the car, S'tan at first couldn't comprehend how He'd made such a ghastly mistake. He'd only intended to knock the taxi driver out, not decapitate him. Minutes later, speeding along the motorway, sitting behind the wheel and humming along with a tune on the taxi's radio, S'tan was feeling positively tip-top. He swerved to overtake a Mercedes with blacked-out windows that had been crawling along at a snail-like ninety-five miles an hour, and nearly hugged Himself with glee.

The Chronostone was *back*. Somehow it had returned to Earth— He didn't care how or why; just the mere fact of its being within range was enough. The minute He'd slammed the taxi's trunk shut, He'd known. Such a surge of power had flowed through Him that He almost felt Himself crackle with energy. He could feel it. Hell, He could practically *see* its force radiating from His fingertips like spokes on a wheel. His brain fizzed with ideas and He knew, without a shadow of a doubt, that nothing could stand in His way. Not now. Not with the stone back on Earth, radiating power like a malign reactor, filling Him with its raw energy. Without it, He'd been reduced to a pale shadow of His former Vileness. But now . . .

First, the deal with Don Lucifer. Even though he was the First Minister of the Hadean Executive, S'tan wasn't about to renege on a pact. After all, Don Lucifer had kept his side of the bargain, pulling strings and greasing palms to get Him His cookery show on TV, so S'tan was going to do His bit. He was going to wipe out the Borgia brother, closely followed by Isagoth, the incompetent assassin. Then another attempt to locate the exact whereabouts of the Chronostone, followed by a triumphant return to Hades to sort out the traitors who said He was past His sell-by date. Perhaps if He wasn't too tired by then, He might sow the seeds for a major war on Earth as well. It *had* been a while, after all. And with the ear of the nation via His cookery show, it would be risibly easy to brainwash His viewers into doing just about anything He desired. After all, He had persuaded them all to butcher cows, pigs, and sheep and devour their unmentionable parts, so how hard could it be to persuade them to butcher each other? Maybe even do it live on camera? Reality butchery? Now *there* was an idea.

Absorbed in His own brand of S'tanic darkness, plotting mankind's demise, S'tan paid no attention whatsoever to the Mercedes with blacked-out windows, which followed him like a shadow; not even when, like Him, it took the seldom-used B-road out of Auchenlochtermuchty toward the Strega-Schloss estate.

The same could not be said for the occupants of the Mercedes. All three of the men inside it were paying very close attention to S'tan's taxi as it sped along the track up ahead. However, this was for no other reason than the fact that the taxi was blocking the road. The track leading to StregaSchloss was far too narrow to permit overtaking, except at infrequent passing places where the rutted track widened just enough to permit the passage of two vehicles, either traveling in different directions or one pulling over and allowing the other to overtake. Problem was, S'tan's taxi wasn't doing the decent thing and pulling over, and consequently, the mood within the Mercedes was turning ugly. Of the car's two passengers, the one in the rear was by far the more trigger-happy. Desperate to demonstrate his impeccable marksmanship, he repeatedly flicked off the safety catch on his gun and squinted down its barrel, unconsciously licking his lips as he lined up the target.

"Eh, Santino, d'you wanta me to blow outta its tires?"

"No."

"Aw, c'mon. Maybe you letta me take the driver outta the picture, huh? Whaddya think?"

"No, Bruno."

Bruno subsided in the backseat, pouting like a thwarted toddler. Ahead, as the taxi bounced and swerved along the track, waves of muddy water and slushy snowmelt sprayed up out of potholes, and huge gritty droplets hit the windshield of the Mercedes with a loud *splat*. At this, the otherwise silent passenger in the front would utter a piercing squeak of displeasure, and Santino the driver would use the wipers to clear their view once more.

"Hey. Santino. Whaddya say we ram this joker offa the road, huh?"

"No, Bruno. You think I'm gonna risk hurting my car? You think I wanna scrape my paintwork? Benda my fenda?" The driver's voice was rising higher with each question, and to Bruno's alarm, Santino twisted round in his seat to stare straight at him—which meant that he'd completely taken his eyes off the ro—

"EEK eek IP IP!"

Santino spun back round just in time to avoid plowing the car straight into a line of ancient oaks marking the outermost boundary of the StregaSchloss estate. The Mercedes skidded through an open wrought-iron gate, ignoring the sign warning off trespassers, the car's brake lights flashing red as Santino brought the steering under control once more.

"Sorry, boss," he said, darting a sideways glance to where Don Lucifer di S'Embowelli Borgia sat rigidly in the passenger seat, displaying less animation than a sack of potatoes. In truth, Santino had privately decided that Don Lucifer looked exactly like a prosperous heavyweight boxer who'd suffered a catastrophic encounter with a rocket-propelled rodent. Right in the middle of the Don's face, where one might reasonably expect to find a nose, was a long, twitchy, bewhiskered snout, looking for all the world as if a rat had burst, at great speed, straight through Don Lucifer's face, traveling from the inside out. None of the Don's employees, from his gun-toting bodyguards to his tailor, were ever permitted to refer to his rat snout or to make any mention of the terrible medical blunder that had turned a routine surgical procedure into what was coyly termed "a maxillofacial mutilation with rodent complications."

Now, to Santino's discomfiture, the Don's nose was twitching nonstop, hinting at some deep volcanic rage bubbling just below the surface of that impeccably tailored suit. Praying that when it erupted, the rage wouldn't be directed at him, Santino drove on, keeping his eyes fixed firmly on the car ahead, so that when S'tan abruptly turned onto a wide sweep of rose quartz and slammed on His brakes, Santino followed suit, the two cars coming to a standstill, nose to tail, right outside the front door of StregaSchloss.

The Portable Portal

The changeling lay against Baci's breast and gazed up at her face, a barely audible hiss emerging from its half-open mouth. Baci slept, exhausted despite her earlier protestations to the contrary. The drawing room was warm, filled with the scent of a huge ash log that was crumbling to rose and silver embers in the grate. Surrounded by duckdown cushions and horsehair bolsters, her shoulders wrapped in a purple cashmere shawl, Baci drifted in and out of dreams, unaware that in her arms she held the stuff of nightmares.

Mrs. McLachlan smoothed Damp's hair away from her forehead and bent down to kiss her. No wonder the poor little mite was so tired; after her magical excursion with Ffup, Damp had wept non-

stop for twenty minutes, raging against the arrival of the new-born at StregaSchloss and her consequent loss of status as the baby of the family.

"Not NOT wantit hobbible BABY!" she insisted, her words muffled in the pink furry folds of her piggy pajama case, her face hot, furious, and practically glowing in the darkness of the stuffy cave she'd retreated to beneath her bed. When Mrs. McLachlan finally found her, the little girl was so prostrate with heat exhaustion that she fell asleep within minutes. Tip-toeing out of Damp's bedroom, Mrs. McLachlan discovered Signor Strega-Borgia lurking outside, waiting for her in the corridor.

"Flora," he began, "I . . . I have no idea how to . . . you're go-ing to think I'm quite mad. . . . I . . . I . . . ."

Mrs. McLachlan frowned, distracted by the distant sound of a car engine.

"It's the baby," Luciano blurted. "It's . . . Oh, how can I put this? It . . . it's . . . ."

"Signor. Surely not *it*. He's a little *boy*. Delightful. You must be so . . . proud." Sensing his distress, Mrs. McLachlan made an effort to focus on what her employer was trying to tell her. But she *had* heard an engine. Two, in fact. She could definitely hear two distinct engine notes.

"No. That's the problem, you see, Flora. It's *not* a 'he.' The baby's not . . . it's not *human*."

Mrs. McLachlan's head jerked up and she looked straight into Luciano's eyes. All other thoughts were driven straight out of her mind by this bizarre statement. Luciano was sheet-white, as if he'd gone through some ghastly transformation since Mrs. McLachlan had last really paid him any attention.

"It's a *monster*, Flora. It hides what it is from Baci, from Minty, but not . . . not from me. Oh God, I don't know what to do. Baci's all alone with it— I need—can you— Oh, Flora, help us—"

"Show me." Mrs. McLachlan ran past Luciano and was halfway down the stairs when car headlights swept across the great hall.

Titus had managed, with difficulty, not to scream his head off when several of the bats of Coire Crone fluttered down to cling to his shoulders, the leathery membranes of their wings folding up like fans, thereby indicating that they intended to hang on to him for a while. However, he decided, compared to Strega-Nonna he'd got off lightly: her body was almost completely shrouded in bats. Then, when Titus looked again, staring at the old woman as he tried to pick an easy route down the hillside, he saw that the bats were actually *carrying* Strega-Nonna, their combined wing power keeping her feet hovering above the path. Now they were heading for the river, sliding uncontrollably down a very steep and crumbly scree slope that felt, to Titus, alarmingly like skiing down an avalanche of pebbles. Several times he saw Pandora slip, her arms windmilling in an attempt to regain her balance. Several times Titus was convinced that he was about to plunge to his doom, rolling head over heels to the bottom, a course of action that would leave his broken body generously, if a tad gruesomely, distributed across the rocks of the river below. Over their heads, the giant dragon flew in a lazy circle, effortlessly demonstrating its species' superiority to man in terms of aerodynamic capabilities. Clinging to the humans, the little bats demonstrated their superiority to everyone by simply bumming a lift.

Digging her heels into the scree and raising a cloud of dust, Pandora stopped, undid her shirt, and fanned herself with her hands.

"Do you *mind?*" came an outraged squawk. "First you drip sweat all over me, then you pepper me with grit, and finally you compound the insult by whipping up a Force Ten gale. . . ." Leg by leg, Tarantella crawled out from beneath Pandora's collar and shot the bats a look of loathing. "You do realize," she continued, "that I'm now forced into direct competition with all these dreadful creatures for what little food there is?"

"Whatever," groaned Pandora, wearily assessing how much further they had to go until they reached the bottom. Titus skidded to a standstill behind her.

"Pan? Where on earth are we going? This isn't the way we came here. . . . I wish I knew what was going on. I feel like we've been walking forever. And I'm *ravenous.* Lunch must've been hours ago."

Tarantella grinned evilly. "Buster, have *you* got a surprise coming. *I* may have to slug it out with these winged mice mutants in order to eat, but you're going to have to compete with our friendly flamethrower overhead."

As if to underline Tarantella's point, the gigantic shadow of the dragon scudded across the scree, followed by an even bigger shadow, which, in the initial confusion, resembled nothing so much as a vast speech bubble. Titus's head jerked upward just as a large shape slid across, temporarily casting its shadow over him. Beside him, Pandora's mouth fell open as a massive hot-air balloon dropped silently out of the sky toward them.

"Catch hold," called a voice, and a man appeared over the rim of the balloon's gondola, holding a bundle of rope and sticks out to them. As Titus and Pandora hesitated, the bundle unwound in mid-air and revealed itself to be a rope ladder that unfurled in front of them. Below them, Strega-Nonna glided toward the balloon under bat power, waving her hands as she approached, and called up to the balloonist:

"Whatever took you so *long,* boy? We've been on this blasted hill for hours, waiting for you."

Have we? wondered Pandora, seizing hold of the ladder in a complete daze and beginning to climb, the narrow rungs painful under her feet and her hands slick with the sweat of fear.

The ladder jolted below her as first Titus, then Strega-Nonna, climbed aboard. Then, with a dizzying rush, they were aloft, the balloon rising into the sky as if their added weight had given it wings. Pandora clung on tight, inching upward one rung at a time until her head was level with the gondola's base. Pausing for a moment to catch her breath and wipe her slippery palms one at a time on her shirt, she made the mistake of looking down at the abyss between her feet. Below, the ground spun sickeningly; Titus's face frowned up at her; Strega-Nonna shouted something she couldn't hear; a wave of dizziness rushed up from her chest to her head—an oncoming darkness in which she found herself unable to summon the will to keep going, to hang on. . . .

A hand grabbed her wrist and hauled her upward, another hand fastening on the waistband of her jeans, dragging her in a most inelegant fashion up and over the wicker rim of the gondola and into the tar-scented safety within. Pandora opened her eyes; saw a jumble of ropes and sandbags; felt the heat from a charcoal burner positioned in the center of the gondola's floor; craned her neck to look up at a vast canopy of swelling silk overhead; and then, at last, turned her head to look at where the pilot stood with his back to her as he helped first Titus, then Strega-Nonna, aboard.

"I . . . I *know* you," Pandora blurted, shading her eyes against the sun and gazing at a face almost as familiar to her as her own.

"You know *of* me, perhaps," the pilot said with breathtaking self-confidence before helping her to stand up. Pandora swayed, clutching one of the ropes that tethered the balloon to its gondola, as she caught a brief glimpse of the dizzying drop to the land below.

"Let me introduce myself properly," the pilot said. "I am Apollonius Borgia, known far and wide as Apollonius 'The Greek,' at your service."

Despite his somewhat haughty delivery, his tone was playful, and his eyes sparkled as he bent at the waist to sweep one hand across the floor in a deep bow that encompassed first Pandora and then Titus. Strega-Nonna gave a disgusted *"Tchhhh"* and stepped forward.

"You're late, boy," she stated. "Enough of your folderol. Children, this is your great-great-great-grandfather, Apollonius. Or is it four *greats*? I forget. It is of no importance. However great you may have been, boy, your timekeeping has always been appalling. What d'you have to say for yourself?"

Faced with such an enraged prune of a woman, even the greatest of heroes has been known to quail. No longer quite so proud as his portrait in the Ancestors' Room had led Pandora to believe, Apollonius hung his head and mumbled something inaudible.

"Speak up, lad. I didn't hear you." Strega-Nonna was rummaging amongst the ropes and sailcloths littering the gondola floor, muttering balefully to herself, "Where *is* it, boy? Don't tell me you've forgotten to bring the confounded portal? First rule of being an ancestor: Never forget to bring your own escape route. Never. *That* was what nearly lost us the battle of Mhoire Ochone—"

At this, Apollonius clapped his hands over his eyes as if to block out an unwanted vision. "Stop, *vecchia*, I beg you. Enough. Do not remind me. That time was a black chapter in our history, and one to which I have no desire to return. You do me an injustice, besides—for here, I have the portal beside me. And"—Apollonius bent forward and hauled a large gilded picture frame upright from where it had lain unobserved at their feet—"I apologize for my tardiness, but I was delayed, unavoidably, by this . . . this vision here."

And there, framed by the carved gilt of Apollonius's portal, was Minty, her face drawn and pale, a crowd of dark shadows milling behind, her spill of golden hair the only point of light in the midwinter gloom of the Ancestors' Room. She reached out to help Pandora climb through the picture frame, and it wasn't until she finally stood beside her that Pandora realized what the dark shadows really were. For hundreds of years, all the picture frames had held portraits of long-dead Borgias, but now they were deserted, their canvases devoid of people. Their belongings, goods, chattels, homes, lands, and mountains—all of these were still rendered in oil and tempera, but of the ancestors not a single brushstroke of paint remained. Instead, somewhat constrained by the size of Minty's bedroom, every one of them nodded and smiled and shuffled their feet as first Titus, then Strega-Nonna, climbed through the portal into their own time, only to discover that the past had decided to come and visit. Not only the past, but its dogs and horses as well, a fact that did not escape the attention of the huge dragon attempting to squeeze through the frame after Apollonius.

"Desist in your dribbling, dragon," Apollonius commanded, trying to push the vast beast backward in a vain attempt to dissuade it from following. "Stay!" he barked as the gilded frame began to creak ominously around the dragon's midriff. "No! Beast—you shall not pass."

"Hang on." Pandora turned back and tugged at Apollonius's arm. "Let it come through. We could use its help with our wolf problem, and besides, our own dragon would probably enjoy the company."

The door to Minty's bedroom opened, and as if summoned, Ffup's head appeared in the gap.

"Fooood," she caroled happily; then, noticing how many humans she was addressing, her face fell. "Heavens. Where did you lot spring from? There's *never* going to be enough for us all." Then she stopped, her mouth opening wide, her wings frozen like twin exclamation points as she caught sight of the huge dragon trying to squeeze its rear through the picture frame.

"MUM?" Ffup managed, her voice betraying that here was a surprise that was about as welcome as the Black Death. "Gosh!" she squeaked, pearls of sweat popping out all down her nose, her eyes swiveling from side to side as she tried and failed to find an escape route. "How . . . how ab— How absolutely fu-fuh-*fabulous* to see you again." And unable to entirely conceal her true feelings, Ffup felt her nose and vent erupt simultaneously into flames of deep embarrassment.

Return of the Prodigal

There had been a hissed and squeaky conference on the rose quartz outside StregaSchloss between S'tan and Don Lucifer, following which an uneasy truce was reached. Don Lucifer's original threat to dispose of S'tan by encasing His feet in concrete was something of a nonstarter: for one thing, S'tan was a hundred times more convincingly evil than the Chronostone-free demon lite He'd been when Lucifer had last seen Him; and for another, He didn't have feet, He had two cloven hooves. Upon catching sight of these satanic appendages, both Santino and Bruno had fled howling, leaving Lucifer and S'tan face to face outside Strega-Schloss's front door. Before they could formulate a plan, the front door flew open and there, standing in front of them, was their intended victim, Luciano Perii Strega-Borgia, small, weak, and, unaccountably, *smiling*.

S'tan and Lucifer barely had time to register their victim's perplexing sangfroid when Luciano stepped forward and embraced his half brother, planting a smacking kiss on both his cheeks before saying, "Big *brother*! How *tremendous* to see you again after all this time! You're looking so *well*. And you've brought a friend too. Welcome, *signore*, welcome to my little Scottish home—come in, come in, both of you. Let me close the door and keep the heat in. . . . There, marvelous. Baci, darling, look who's dropped in to visit."

And knowing full well that Baci would not respond—would, in fact, be unable to respond—Luciano drew his unresisting half brother and the scowling Devil into the great hall and launched into the performance of his life, the vast surges of adrenaline coursing through his body giving him the courage to continue babbling like a maniac. "BACI? Honestly, Lucifer, *signore*, I do apologize. She's probably gone upstairs to feed the new baby. She'll be with us in a minute."

And that, he prayed, simply wasn't going to happen, since, if all had gone according to plan, Baci was currently behind a golden frame in the Ancestors' Room while the changeling was hissing and spitting in a cradle in the nursery.

"Come in, come in. Come and meet the rest of the family. Let me take your coats. Lucifer, *signore*, fantastic fur coat you have there—and Lucifer, what a big gun you have, big brother, but you know, there's no need for such things here—"

"SHUT UP. Just shut *up*, Luciano." Don Lucifer hung on

tightly to his gun, clutching it in both hands, his beetle brows drawn so far down they almost touched his nose.

His nose.

Don Lucifer's eyes widened and his hands flew up to the middle of his face, his gun falling, unnoticed, to the floor.

"MY *NOSE!*" he roared. "IT'S A NOSE!"

"Ye-e-e-es, Lucifer. It *is* a nose." Luciano smiled, winking at S'tan and tapping the side of his own head in the universal mime for don't-say-anything-but-poor-old-Lucifer's-finally-lost-the-plot-big-time before stooping down to pluck his half brother's gun off the floor and hooking it on the coatrack beside the many jackets, waterproofs, furs, and assorted coats hanging there already. "There. Perfectly safe," he lied, leading the way across the great hall before either Lucifer or S'tan noticed that one of the fur coats hanging on the rack was actually Knot the yeti, who reached out for the gun and disposed of it by simply tipping it down his throat.

"I wonder what culinary delights are in store for us today. . . ." Luciano strode down the corridor toward the kitchen, followed by his stunned and unresisting guests.

"Look at me," Lucifer whispered to S'tan. "Tell me, is this a proper nose I got, or am I hallucinating?"

"I THOUGHT WE WEREN'T ALLOWED TO TALK ABOUT YOUR NOSE," S'tan hissed. "SO WHAT? YOU'VE GOT A NORMAL NOSE AGAIN. GO FIGURE."

"But . . . what the hell's going on?" Lucifer bleated. "Like, two minutes ago I'm giving it *'Eek eek ike squee'* like some kinda demented rodent, and now—"

"Now, big brother, remember your niece and nephew? This fine young man is my elder boy, Titus, and this beauty is my elder daughter, Pandora. Children, look, what a surprise— here is your uncle Lucifer come to visit."

Curled in a tiny ball of fright inside her teapot on the china cupboard, Tarantella devoutly wished herself elsewhere. Even if her host family were behaving as if they were blind to the dangers facing them, *she* wasn't. The kitchen was so full of menace, it was almost impossible to breathe, and yet there they were, the mad Borgia bipeds, inviting the Devil and his pal round for supper. . . . With an inaudible *tchhhh*, Tarantella scuttled off through her own teapot portal, heading for a safer place where, with luck, she might be able to find reinforcements.

Titus stepped forward and gave a little stiff bow. "Good of you to drop in, Uncle Lucifer. How's my old inheritance doing? Did you manage to put it to good use? Hope you didn't blow it *all* on whiskey, wine, and wild, wild women. *Joke,*" he added hastily as Don Lucifer's face colored.

"My brother, what a kidder." Pandora sighed, stroking the heads of the two enormous dogs that flanked her, their yellow eyes firmly fastened on the Don and S'tan. "Such a tease, our Titus. Don't pay any attention, Unks—he really doesn't mean it."

Unks? Titus bit his bottom lip. Pandora always had to go that one step too far. For a moment no one could say a word. Struck by an overwhelming desire to snort with laughter, Titus managed to wrest control over his vocal cords.

"Drinks. Dad? Can I help?" Were the occasion not so fraught with peril, the temporary appearance of Titus's deep and blokeish voice rather than his normal boyishly high-pitched version would have been cause for celebration, but here and now, in front of his evil uncle and his uncle's repellent fat friend, Titus could find no cause for rejoicing whatsoever. Waiting for the unwelcome visitors to hang up their coats and follow Luciano into the kitchen, Mrs. McLachlan had counseled the children to remain calm and do their bit, but that had been before she'd clapped eyes on Don Lucifer's accomplice. Now even Titus could sense her fear, and if the unflappable Mrs. McLachlan was having a temporary case of the wobblies, then shouldn't they all be pressing the panic button?

"Titus, dear"—Mrs. McLachlan laid a hand on his arm—"would you be so kind as to go and fetch a couple of bottles of champagne from the cellar?" The hand trembled, but meeting Mrs. McLachlan's eyes, Titus caught sight of her granite-hard will. "After all, it's not every day that we have a family reunion, is it, Mr. di S'Embowelli? And if I may say, you are looking ever so much better than the last time we met. . . ."

Despite her brave words, Mrs. McLachlan had never before felt such profound fear. She forced herself to be calm and not react. *Flora Morag Fionn Mhairi ben McLachlan-Morangie-Fiddach,* she recited to herself, the cadences of her own names slowing her frantic breath and stilling her thoughts. *Flora, my dear,* she told herself, *you do not have the power to overcome this devil, but you do have something far better. You are wise, far wiser than that Hell-born thing that makes you so very afraid. In your wisdom, you know that you must observe its actions; watch as it lowers its corrupted self into a chair at the kitchen table; watch and wait, observe what it does next; marshal your strength and, when the time is right . . . act.*

As Titus headed obediently for the cellar, Pandora also forced herself to be calm. Even though Mrs. McLachlan had warned them all to expect the unexpected and to try and follow her conversational lead, this . . . this sucking up to Don Wotsit was hard to stomach. Last time they'd seen *him,* he'd had a nose like a rat, he'd been holding a gun to Mum's head, and the only way they'd managed to get rid of him was by wiring all Titus's inheritance of millions into the Don's bank account. And yet here was Mrs. McLachlan, offering him the finest champagne in the cellar and heaping compliments on his ugly head. Still, even Pandora had to admit that Mrs. McLachlan had a point: the loss of the rat nose *was* an improvement. But the other guy . . .

Pandora's eyes slid toward the man who'd helped himself to a seat at the head of the kitchen table and appeared to be falling asleep with his head balanced on his steepled fingers and his eyes shut. He was massively overweight, a fact that might have been explained by the stained chef's uniform stretched to bursting across his chest and thighs. Why exactly her criminally inclined uncle had chosen to team up with this obese cook was something of a mystery—especially since the cook and the uncle appeared to loathe each other, if the glances they had been exchanging earlier were anything to go by. . . .

Pandora shivered and looked away, her gaze falling on the glass-paneled doors of the cabinet that housed StregaSchloss's hundreds of cookery books—a collection of stained and well-used volumes lying higgledy-piggledy across the shelves, books that bore witness to thousands of meals eaten by generations of Strega-Borgias over several centuries. Pandora shivered again, her thoughts returning to the stranger at their table. There was something indefinably . . . *dark* about the fat man, she decided, trying to pin down what exactly she meant. It was as if he were a one-man dead zone, as if he came from somewhere other than Earth, somewhere in which light and sound traveled differently. . . .

All at once she realized two things: one, she hadn't heard him say a word; and two, although she could see everyone in the kitchen reflected in the glass doors of the cabinet, she couldn't see *him* anywhere. By rights he should have been visible, seated in the carver chair in between Strega-Nonna and her dad. However, according to the glass, the carver chair was empty. Pandora was just about to try and whisper this to Mrs. McLachlan when the fat man's eyes slid open and he stared straight at her. In that instant, Pandora felt a moment of fear so intense that, to her horror, she realized she was about to throw up. . . .

"DON'T WASTE YOUR BREATH." The hideous voice seemed to broadcast itself from every direction at once, as if someone had installed hundreds of speakers on every available surface in the kitchen.

"LET'S JUST CUT TO THE CHASE, SHALL WE?" it

continued as Pandora ran for the sink, constrained even under such dreadful circumstances by the kind of upbringing that forbade her to throw up over her shoes. "I KNOW YOU'VE GOT MY STONE HIDDEN HERE, AND I WANT IT BACK. AT LEAST ONE OF YOU KNOWS WHAT I'M TALKING ABOUT, SO I'M JUST GOING TO ASK YOU ALL A FEW SIMPLE QUESTIONS UNTIL ONE OF YOU TELLS ME WHAT I NEED TO KNOW."

In the stunned silence that followed this utterance, everyone in the kitchen was unable to avoid hearing Pandora being violently sick in the compost bucket.

Close to the Brink

"Shut up, shut up, shut up," Isagoth hissed, fumbling in his sodden coat pocket for the key to his rented car. After the vomiting-in-revolving-door incident, Baby Borgia had slept deeply for approximately forty-five seconds before waking up and starting to shriek all over again. Despite himself, Isagoth was deeply impressed: the newborn baby had a prodigious talent for howling like a soul in torment. In times gone by, Isagoth used to visit the barbecues of Hades, just for the pleasure of listening to the sinners howl and shriek as the duty demons roasted them on spits. But this ... this tiny purple-faced boy was a born screamer. What range, what volume, what ... What the hell was he *doing* trapped in a car with this deafening human dwarf?

Isagoth leaned forward, rested his forehead against the steering wheel, and found himself unable to stifle a sob of despair. Briefly, he toyed with the idea of running away—simply undoing his seat belt, opening the driver's door, and legging it . . . sprinting flat-out to . . . to . . . to *any*where the baby wasn't. However, he reminded himself, *that* wasn't an option. Fool that he was, he'd promised S'tan to personally oversee the destruction of Luciano Strega-Borgia. So unless he wanted to spend the remainder of eternity turned into a tub of low-calorie dairy product—turned into the very substance he appeared to be *coated* in—then he'd better Get On With It.

Drawing in a contaminated lungful of sour air, Isagoth winced at the sight of the stringy white curds dotted across his jacket. Not only was the infernal infant loud and squeaky, he also appeared to be stuffed to bursting with disgustingly rancid, wet cottage cheese—a singularly charmless substance that had erupted from the baby with no warning whatsoever. . . . Still, the sooner he got the job done, the sooner he could get rid of the baby and change out of these revolting rags. Gritting his teeth, he poked his key into the ignition, turned it, and . . . and absolutely nothing. Biting down on a howl of frustration, Isagoth tried again. Still nothing. Further attempts were equally fruitless. The car was dead. Now, when he needed it most, it wasn't working. Isagoth rolled his eyes and took a deep, shuddering breath. Had ever a demon suffered so much in the cause of spreading a little unhappiness? Could things possibly get any worse? As Isagoth stared bleakly through the windshield onto the vista of the Auchenlochtermuchty Arms parking lot, the sullen November sky gave him an answer. Rain, at first in spits and spots, then drops, then sheets, began to fall, pockmarking the snow, exposing the tarmac beneath, hammering on the car roof, pouring along gutters and down pipes and swirling past the rented car in which Isagoth and the baby sat, competing with each other to see who could howl louder and longer.

After twenty-three-and-a-half minutes, Isagoth had to admit that the baby had, once more, got the better of him.

Babies, 3; Demons, 0.

Damp had woken up to the sound of the new baby screaming in the nursery. Hugging her pajama-case piggy for protection, she had listened with increasing horror as it hissed and spat and swore, its infant vocabulary encompassing several words that Damp just *knew* were very bad words indeed. Pulling pajama-pig closer, Damp did her best not to listen. She stuck her fingers in her ears and hummed loudly, trying to drown out the baby with songs and stories. First a rousing chorus of "It's Raining, It's Pouring," which flowed into a dramatic "Hickory Dickory Dock" and then a wee spot of "Hushabye Baby" for afters. Thanks to Damp, rain poured down outside and, all round StregaSchloss, the clocks joined in to encourage the nursery-rhyme mouse; but, proving that the baby was immune to hushabyes, squeals, oaths, and hisses still echoed along the corridor from the nursery. Rolling her eyes, Damp pretended to be Cinderella's fairy godmother dealing with a particularly foul-mouthed rat, a spell that transformed Don

Lucifer's rodent nose but left the new baby unchanged, unrepentant, and determinedly swearing and cursing, until finally Damp could take no more.

"HOBBIBLE baby," she decided, pulling a hideous face and slipping out of bed to investigate.

As Damp tiptoed along the corridor, she heard an unfamiliar voice coming from the baby's room. Her eyes grew wide. *More* bad words, and this time from a growed-up. Puzzled, she halted outside the open nursery door and risked a quick peek. One glance was all it took. Don Lucifer di S'Embowelli stood with his back to Damp, but slung over his shoulder was the new baby, its face crumpled like a collapsed pumpkin lantern, its mouth a torn gash of impotent fury. As it caught sight of Damp standing in the doorway, its shrieks abruptly ceased. Just before she turned and fled, the baby grinned at her, a feral, snaggletoothed rictus of pure, unadulterated hate.

Sobbing with terror—"*Bad* baby, *bad* baby"—Damp half fell, half slid down the stairs to the great hall, where she stood, chest heaving, nose running, her arms tightly wrapped around the one constant in this awful afternoon: her pajama-case piggy. Around her, the hall was empty, the house uncannily silent. Where *was* everyone? Didn't they know there was a bad baby upstairs? Warily, she crept down the corridor to the kitchen and stopped outside the door. She would never know what sixth sense made her not turn the door handle and unwittingly deliver the Chronostone hidden in her pajama case straight across to the Dark Side. Years later, when she had grown into her own considerable powers as a magus, Damp would awake in the dead hours of night, trembling with the knowledge of disaster so narrowly averted. Whatever or whoever it was, *some*thing made Damp stop on the threshold of the kitchen and look up . . .

. . . and there, dangling in their thousands from the ceiling of the corridor, were the bats of Coire Crone, their wings unmoving, their eyes fastened on her, slowly blinking in the deep shadows of that midwinter evening.

A soft thud on her shoulder announced the arrival of her very own bat familiar, Vesper. He placed a warning wing over her mouth and whispered, "Stand away from the door, ma'am. We need to back away, niiice and easy, that's it— Whoo-hoo, take it reeeeeeal slowwww."

Damp obeyed, not because she was in the habit of taking orders from Vesper but because she had felt something infinitely *wrong* coming from the kitchen. She backed away, hoping that whatever *it* was, it wouldn't sense her presence on the other side of the door. She had no idea what was lurking in there; she just had the sneaking suspicion that whatever it was had big pointy teeth and black dripping claws, and did not have her future welfare at heart.

"Let's hit the highway and get the heck outta Dodge, ma'am," Vesper prompted, his tiny thumbs gesturing toward the front door. Clutching her piggy with white-knuckled fists, Damp was halfway across the hall when she heard a hideous scream coming from the kitchen. She froze, then spun round as the shadow of Don Lucifer and the baby began to descend the stairs toward her.

Damp needed no further encouragement. Skidding across the hall, she grabbed the heavy iron latch to the front door, lifted it, hauled with all her might, and, checking that Vesper was with her, fled from whatever evil lay behind in Strega-Schloss.

Their Deepest Fears

S'tan had learned a great deal from twenty-first-century torturers when it came to extracting information. Not for Him the brutal, blood-stained torture methods of medieval times. He didn't need to use pliers, racks, or thumbscrews to persuade His victims to sing like canaries. As He'd been fond of pointing out to His students back when He used to teach the degree course in Advanced Pain at the University of Hades, all that was required to turn victims into sobbing, blurting, willing confessors was the application of a little insight, coupled with a few handy techniques He'd garnered from jails and detention centers back on Earth. Here in the kitchen at StregaSchloss, He was about to put some of these lessons to good use, but first He had to make sure that these

stupid humans didn't rush suicidally to each other's defense. To prevent this from happening, He stopped Time.

This was a trick He could only have pulled off when the Chronostone was very near indeed; within, say, a few yards of where He stood. Stopping Time had the double benefit of freeze-framing everyone in the kitchen, wolves and all, *and* proving without a doubt that He was very close indeed to his quarry.

"Ooooh, S'tan baby, You're sssssssso *hot*," He hissed, walking round the deathly still figures arranged like statues in a tableau of *How Humans Used to Live Before S'tan Ran Things*. "Hot, hot, HOT," He gloated, bending over each figure in turn and sniffing for the unmistakable signs of who was most afraid.

The boy, he decided, stopping beside Titus, who'd just returned from the wine cellar when Time stopped. There he stood, a bottle of decidedly average champagne in each hand—the calculated insult wasn't lost on S'tan, who there and then decided to make Titus pay big-time—his stupid face moon-pale, his T-shirt soaked with what S'tan assumed had to be the sweat of true terror.

"Perrrrfect," S'tan purred, reaching out to poke two inquiring fingers into Titus's unresisting mouth. This, He'd discovered, was by far the simplest way to establish a psychic connection with a victim. He delicately prodded the arched roof of Titus's mouth until, with only a scant few fractions of an inch of bone separating His fingers from the meat of Titus's brain, He felt the boy's psyche open up like a flower. A quick trawl round his synapses and seconds later He had His answer.

. . . Something had gone wrong, he guessed, trying hard in the pitch darkness not to give way to panic. Like, one minute he'd been down in the wine cellar selecting the naffest fizz he could find . . . or had he? Was that part of the dream? Ever since the balloon and the weirdness of meeting a long-dead ancestor, Titus had felt as if he'd been sleepwalking. Now this, this darkness. It made his head hurt just thinking about it. Anyway, something had gone wrong, badly wrong, and now, without the faintest idea of how he'd got here, he found himself trapped . . . imprisoned in what felt like either a very small stone box or . . . an average-sized stone box. All right, say it. Not a box, a crypt; and yeah, not imprisoned but . . . buried. He was buried in what he suspected had to be the family crypt in Auchenlochtermuchty. And now he badly wanted to scream his head off, but he was all too aware that he had to conserve what little oxygen there was, in order to escape. But how? How had this happened to him? *Whatever were his parents thinking of, dumping him in the crypt without taking the trouble to check if he was alive or not? I mean, that was a bit much. That's like carelessness of a whole new order . . . or—the thought popped into his head—or perhaps they didn't know he was here. Perhaps they were dead too?*

NOOOOOOOOOOO.

Don't go there. I really *don't want that thought anywhere near me right now.*

Right, Titus. Get a grip. Concentrate. Engage boot-camp mode. Find whatever internal sergeant major/personal trainer you need to get you out of here. Do whatever it takes, but just do it. Knees drawn up against your stunningly weedy and underdeveloped pecs.

Tighten abdominals. Just remember, this is going to be the toughest workout you've ever done, and don't, repeat don't, even think about giving up. You only need to move the lid of the crypt enough to let air in. At first. You can survive for a good long time if you have air. Without air . . . right. There's another thought you don't want anywhere within range. Go. C'mon, Titus. Go, Go, GO. Put your back into it. PUUUUUUUUUSSSSSSSSHHHHHHHHH.

*And push he most certainly did. Veins bulged in his head and capillaries burst behind his eyes, and he could feel his clenched teeth creak . . . but he pushed his feet up and away, and after several increasingly desperate attempts, he was rewarded. A tiny slit appeared in the absolute blackness above. He felt the blessing of a chill draft, felt its touch on the sweat on his face, felt his skin cooling under its welcome caress. He lay gasping for air, still trapped but triumphant. Head pounding with what promised to be the mother of all monster headaches and legs like overcooked spaghetti, but hey . . . he was alive. Just as he was about to indulge in another moment of deserved self-congratulation—*Way to go, Titus; what cool; what strength; what—

The dim crack of light was blotted out, and all of a sudden he understood that what he'd felt before wasn't true fear, it had just been a rehearsal for when the real fear began. The crack reappeared, its silhouette reassuringly geometric, crisp, straight, and . . . oh God, there it was again, and this time he knew with total certainty what was about to happen. Knew before the first soft brush against his terrified, tortured face. Knew as, over and over and over again, the darkness came and went, as spider after spider dropped silently into the crypt beside him: thousands of them, wave upon

*wave, relentlessly dropping to their doom as he thrashed and
screamed, crushing them beneath him . . .*

*. . . until there was no room left for thrashing, and soon no air to
scream in . . .*

no—

"Neeeext." S'tan retrieved His fingers and fastidiously wiped
them on His filthy chef's trousers, His nostrils flaring as He as-
sessed whose fear he could best exploit. The father's, or the
daughter's? He considered this, strutting round the kitchen
table until He was level with where Luciano stood behind
Strega-Nonna's chair, frozen in the act of helping his aged relative to fold herself into a sitting position.

The father. Definitely. The man *reeked* of fear, despite his
earlier performance as relaxed host and delighted brother to
Don Ratface. Once more, S'tan's fingers scrabbled and poked,
forcing their way in, gate-crashing Luciano's mouth. Again,
the answer was almost immediate. Neither father nor son had
any idea of what or where the Chronostone was. Peeved by
this lack of results—after all, He was the finest of torturers
and unaccustomed to anything other than one hundred percent success—He allowed His gaze to wander around the
room. The old hag? Hardly. She looked as if one puff of wind
would blow her apart. That only left the girl and the nanny.

A few deep sniffs told Him nothing. They both smelled of
soap, not fear. Feeling vaguely uneasy, S'tan realized that there
was something about the nanny that confused Him. He
couldn't put a finger on what exactly that something was, but

as a general rule of thumb, He'd learned that things He didn't understand or found confusing were always bad news. As He was coming to this conclusion, He was already prizing Pandora's lips apart with His fingers, pressing down on her tongue and demanding entry to her thoughts. S'tan's eyes widened in shock. What? He was actually meeting with *resistance*? Hard to credit, but this . . . this impudent squirt of a girl had the temerity to stand up to Him? Impressive? Well, yeah, but also most definitely *not* to be tolerated. S'tan brought His Chronostone-enhanced will crashing down on Pandora, battering her psychic barricades and clabbering at the locks, bolts, and drawbridges of her mind.

Somewhere deep down inside herself, Pandora fought back. Refusing to admit that this terrifying face-off with her uncle's fat friend was the worst thing that had ever happened to her, she forced herself to dredge up a vivid memory out of her bank of Bad But Survivable Things I'd Rather Not Repeat. It came erupting up out of her subconscious like a bubble of marsh gas, but she clung to it as if it were a life raft.

When she was five years old, school had come as a most unwelcome shock. Plucked out of the cocoon of StregaSchloss and flung into the alien landscape of Auchenlochtermuchty Primary, she had been assured that school would be fun. After the muted monochrome of home, to be surrounded by so many dazzling colors was astonishing. Noise too: the roar of her fellow pupils; the clanging of bells telling them when to eat, when to play, and, eventually, when to go home; this too was so different from the relative hush of StregaSchloss that she found it thrilling. Collected by Luciano after her first day at school, Pandora had babbled happily all the way home, telling him about the thrilling clamor and the astonishing colors, and had fallen asleep later that night, happy in the discovery that school had been fun.

Where it had all gone catastrophically pear-shaped was that Pandora had mistakenly assumed that after one day spent in school, that was it. No more of that. Been there, done that. When Luciano delivered his red-faced, pink-eyed, and protesting daughter back to school the following day, she'd been inconsolable with grief at the prospect that the school thing was going to last for the next twelve years of her life. Luciano, practically in tears himself, was persuaded to go home, but couldn't stop himself from turning round to catch a last glimpse of his little girl's face pressed up against the window of the classroom, her eyes fixed accusingly on him, her mouth open in a downturned crescent of denial.

It remained fixed in Pandora's memory as the worst day of her life. Not because of Dad's betrayal, nor the semi-intentional thuggery of some of the nastier kids in her class: these were Bad Things, but far, far worse than these was finding out that some adults—one in particular—seemed to take great pleasure in making children utterly miserable. This grim discovery occurred in the dining hall. Standing in a straggly lunch queue, she wondered out loud what was causing the dreadful smell she'd noticed the minute she'd walked into the dining hall.

"'S like poo," she confided to the little boy in the line behind her. "Smells like dragon poo," she added, confident that she'd managed to nail down the source of the unwelcome pong.

"What did you say?" a voice demanded.

Pandora spun round, her smile fading as she realized that the adult towering over her was not amused; was in fact furious, if her pinched expression was anything to go by. Miss Clint, onetime traffic warden and now school dining hall supervisor, was a woman for whom the word bristly might have been invented. Pandora quailed, shrinking away from the advancing menace like a balloon before a hatpin.

"I, um, it smells like dragon poo, I said." Pandora spoke so softly, it was doubtful whether Miss Clint heard, but that didn't seem to matter. Before the little girl could say one more word, she found herself sitting at a table on her own in a corner of the dining room, peering in disbelief at the monstrously overloaded plate in front of her.

"But. Um. I hate cheese," she explained, glaring at the gluey plateful of macaroni and cheese, which was emitting the odd wisp of sweaty-sock stench, like a slumbering volcano. Horrible, stinky cheese. She'd rather eat bees.

"And you're not leaving the dining room till you've eaten every morsel," Miss Clint advised through lips that hardly moved.

"But I'll . . . but . . . I'LL BE SICK," Pandora blurted out, hoping that this shameful truth would melt the woman's heart and grant her an escape from death-by-ingestion-of-dairy. This was not to be.

Miss Clint folded in the middle, bending down to hiss in Pandora's face: "Stop fussing. I'm prepared to wait for as long as it takes for you to do as you're told and Clear Your Plate." But it was the expression on the woman's face, not the insanity of her words, that convinced Pandora that here was an adult who actually relished causing pain.

That had been a defining moment in Pandora's life. For the first time ever, she realized that she was on her own. At pickup time Mummy and Daddy wouldn't know what had happened to her and would have to go back home without her. She'd never be allowed to go home again and would have to spend the rest of her life staring at a moldering plate of macaroni. Her fellow pupils were trying to pretend that they hadn't witnessed the whole hideous exchange, and were looking away in case bad luck was contagious. When Miss Clint forced the first ghastly, disgusting, dragon-pooey, bad-socky forkful past her lips, Pandora had been utterly terrified.

But she still didn't swallow. She locked eyes with Miss Clint, noting, even as she began to gag, that the dining hall supervisor was changing in front of her eyes: fattening out, sprouting even more bristles on her chin—or was she a he? His face was growing uglier, his eyes were turning red. Red? She barely had time to register this horror before the tines of the fork pressing against her tongue began to soften and swell, becoming once again the fingers of her uncle's fat friend, and now the fear was almost overwhelming, coming in huge surging waves, battering at her, one after the other after the—

Now, dear, a voice said softly in her mind, *you've done marvelously. We're so proud of you. Do you think you could manage to do just one more wee thing?*

Don't ask me to swallow, Pandora begged, her eyes swiveling from side to side, trying to see where Mrs. McLachlan had sprung from, appearing as she had done in the middle of this nightmare like a very welcome gate-crasher.

No, no. Not swallow, *pet. I wouldn't ask you to do that. No. Just bite down instead. Very hard. And don't worry—Strega-Nonna and I are right behind you. So. After three, bite. One ... two ... THREE.*

Pandora did the needful. She bit down hard, but whatever was in her mouth certainly didn't feel remotely like school macaroni. There was an awful, hideous shriek—a desperate, lost howl of agony—and through it, Pandora could hear Mrs. McLachlan saying, "Well *done*, child. Now RUN!" And before Pandora could blink, she found herself stumbling to her feet, pushed and pulled out of the kitchen, along the corridor, through the great hall and out ... into the freezing chill of a darkening winter evening.

The Fallen Felled

Titus slowly regained consciousness. At first he felt completely disorientated; then, little by little, he began to piece the whole nightmare together. He wasn't, thankfully, in a stone box. Instead, he found himself lying on the freezing-cold stone flags of the kitchen floor, surrounded by broken green glass, with his head lolling in a pool of what he at first assumed to be his own blood. That was before he took a deep and calming breath and discovered that he was marinating in spilled champagne rather than his own bodily fluids. Feeling somewhat fragile, he sat up, trying to separate the awful dream from what was rapidly looking like the even *more* awful reality. Where was everybody? He looked around, blinking in disbelief. Why *was* the food mixer upside down in

the log basket? Who had smashed all the chairs round the kitchen table? And the fridge? Its door had been torn from its hinges and lay to one side as if flung there by someone strong and insanely angry.

The kitchen was . . . it was *trashed,* actually. Broken glass littered every surface, and the china cupboard looked as if the same insanely angry fridge-door ripper had swept his hands along each shelf, toppling plates and dropping bowls and platters with no regard for their value or antiquity. Even Tarantella's favorite teapot had not escaped the whirlwind of destruction. There it was on the floor, with its spout snapped off and lying beside it like an accusing finger. Unaccountably— since he didn't even like spiders, *especially* after what he'd just been through—the sight of Tarantella's broken teapot sanctuary made Titus feel desperately sorry for the tarantula. Bending down to rescue her spout and tuck it in his shirt for safekeeping, he was reminded of what else he had hidden in there. Checking that he was alone, he pulled the front of his shirt away from his chest. Yup. Safe and sound, even after the horrors of the crypt, there they all were, thawing rapidly now and soaking his shirt in the process. Titus gazed down at the tiny clones of himself and Pandora, survivors of a disastrous experiment he'd carried out nearly a year since. More recently, the clones had been tenants in Strega-Nonna's chest freezer until he'd removed them approximately half an hour ago.

What exactly he hoped to do with the fifty or so shrunken, geriatric versions of himself and his sister was as yet unclear.

However, he reminded himself, StregaSchloss was under threat, and the family needed all the help they could get, even if it came in the form of these tiny geriatrics. Tucking the broken teapot spout into the waistband of his boxer shorts like a stumpy ceramic dagger, Titus looked around, wondering if there was anything he could use to protect himself. He briefly considered helping himself to the black-handled meat cleaver, but he couldn't bring himself to pick it up. Just the thought of its being used to open up a new mouth in someone's living flesh was enough to give him a brief taste of the spins. Ugh. No *way*. However, the poultry shears were another matter entirely—sharp, strong, and useful for a variety of tasks, not all of which *had* to involve blood. . . . Titus jammed these into the back pocket of his jeans, an action that he was quite sure would have been number one in a list of Things the Manufacturer Recommends You Don't Attempt with Your New Shears. But hey. The whole ghastly scenario he was currently dealing with was right up there at number one in the Full-On Nightmare charts. Someone had to do *something*, he reckoned. Even if that something involved hurting someone before he hurts you. Even if you had to use the shears to—

The room spun around him and he staggered slightly, putting out his hands to regain his balance. His fingers slapped down on one of Mrs. McLachlan's cake tins, its lid emitting a metallic *byoing* as it was struck. Now, *there* was exactly what he needed, Titus realized. Sustenance. What the situation required was a major calorie intake to ward off the dizzy spins and cheer him up slightly. Prizing off the lid, he found the tin to be full of—oh, what joy—cappuccino muffins. He remembered Minty making these little beauties, using some of Luciano's precious hoard of dark-roast coffee to flavor them. And *what* a flavor. Titus's eyes rolled. *Phwoaaarrrr.* These were *strong. What* a kick. Wow. Right. Look out—here I come. Titus flung open the door to the kitchen garden and took deep lungfuls of the rain-drenched air. At that very moment he felt more awake than he had done for years. Invincible, or what? His senses were sharpened too. D'you know, he could almost swear he'd just heard the cappuccino muffins say, *Just one more, Titus.* It would, he reminded himself, require no more from him than a few mouthfuls. God. There it was again. . . . *Pick me up—go on, you know it makes sense. . . .* What else could he do? Titus opened the cake tin once more and obeyed. God, it tasted so *good.* Actually, that one tasted even better than the one before. He needed another for the purposes of comparison. . . .

A fat raindrop plopped onto the perfect iced top of the last one in the tin, denting its icing beyond repair. Titus felt a pang of sympathy for the poor, solitary, damaged little muffin. Nobly, he did the right thing and put it out of its misery; then, with deep reluctance, he replaced the lid on the cake tin before heading out into the rain.

S'tan's first aim when Pandora bit Him was to turn her into a little smoldering pile of carbon. However, somewhat worryingly, He'd discovered He couldn't maintain the freeze on Time *and* summon the firepower to punish the girl *plus* cope with the unbelievable agony that had erupted in His fingers when Pandora spat them back out. He'd roared with pain, crashing backward against the china cupboard and venting His rage on its contents. When the red mist finally cleared from His sight, the girl had vanished, He appeared to have destroyed the kitchen, and He found blood running down His arm. Blood? *Yes.* She'd bloodied Him, the wretch. He could barely focus through His tears, in the throes of the kind of pain that He far preferred to dish out than to receive. Halfway across the great hall, as He ran to find a bathroom where He could lick His wounds in private without anyone seeing that He—*He*—was crying like a big wuss, He realized that He'd only had to deal with this sort of pain once before, on the dreadful day when He was sent into exile. . . .

"Whaddya mean, you're downgrading me to breakfast chef? I'm every bit as good a cook as you, pal, and you know it."

The Chef had smiled kindly, parrying S'tan's words with a balloon whisk, radiating embarrassment tempered with determination.

"S'tan, S'tan, my dear colleague . . ." He wrapped a consoling arm around S'tan's shoulders and continued, all the while steering S'tan in the direction of Heaven's back door, which led directly out to the Dumpsters and Heaven's Exit. "Heyyy, we don't need to fall out over this, huh? It's simple. There can only be one Chef, and I'm It. You're good—you may even become great, given time—but your dodgy methods, your even dodgier ingredients, the way your tea towels stink and your pans don't shine . . . tchhh. You know

that only one of us is perfect. And . . ." He paused, then added, "That's Me."

They'd reached the back door, and the Chef was handing Him His papers. S'tan still couldn't believe this was happening.

"You're firing me?" He gasped.

"Oh, S'tan. Don't be so melodramatic. Think of it as a gentle roasting." The Chef twinkled. "They've got a vacancy in Hades, by the way."

The rival establishment. Grim, smoky Hades. Known far and wide as "The Pits."

Barbecues as far as the eye could see. Sizzling fat. Slabs of lard stacked a mile deep. Rack upon rack of burned meat. Could this really be happening to Him? S'tan stifled a sob. He was ruined. This was The End. Now He'd never get to run Heaven. Oh God, He was about to say—but He stopped Himself in time. Catching a glimpse of the Chef's shiny, happy face, S'tan felt a burning stab of flame in His belly, and it sure as heck didn't feel like indigestion. Right, then. If that's the way the Chef wanted to play it . . . Without another word, He spun on his hoof and stalked out of Heaven's kitchen, refusing to take the staff staircase down to the alley, but heading for the elevators instead. Right, He fumed, I'll show you, Chef. I'll prove who's the top dog round here. I'll . . .

In His rage, He was so consumed by thoughts of revenge that He failed to notice the little OUT OF ORDER sign hanging on the open door of the Heavenly lift. Sadly, the kitchens were located on Heaven's top floor, so as S'tan fell and fell and fell, He had plenty of time to reflect on how much further He still had to go before He hit the bottom. Over countless millennia, the pain from His injuries

slowly faded, but the real pain caused by His fall from grace had
ached for all Eternity, ached and burned like a never-ending flame,
never quenched, never . . .

"Never mind, dear," Mrs. McLachlan said, holding out a clean white hand towel, on which was laid a tube of antiseptic cream, three hypoallergenic bandages, and, if He wasn't imagining it, two Tylenol tablets. S'tan gazed at this offering in astonishment, stunned by the woman's kindness while simultaneously marveling at her stupidity. Didn't she *know* who she was dealing with? Offering the Devil some painkillers? It was such an insane gesture that, for a moment, He was quite nonplussed, and He stood there with His mouth open, blinking at her.

That was exactly the opportunity she'd been hoping for. As she felt His will falter, Mrs. McLachlan removed a fat white cone-shaped bag from the folds of her hand towel and, quick as a flash, she jammed the narrow end of the cone deep into S'tan's gaping mouth, almost down His throat, as with all her might she squeezed the bag dry. S'tan's eyes bulged as he realized that He'd just been force-fed. He was on the point of retaliating when whatever had been in the bag hit Him.

"What the HEh-h-h-h-h—?" he squawked, bending double over the sink and spraying it with a pink jellylike mist. By the time he managed to raise his head, Mrs. McLachlan had disappeared, but by then S'tan was too weak to do much more than hang on to the rim of the sink and groan fitfully. Tell me that isn't my insides on the *out*side, he beseeched his reflection in the mirror over the sink. His reflection stared back, an expression of utter horror appearing on it as he realized that for the first time since he'd arrived at StregaSchloss, he actually *had* a reflection. He looked down again into the sink, wondering what on earth had been in that bag. Tentatively, he reached out a finger and sampled the pink jelly, reasoning that it couldn't do him any more harm than it had done already. He brought his pink-smeared finger up to his mouth and unrolled his tongue to meet it. Hmmm. Not bad. Actually, pretty good. Yum. It—whatever it was—tasted both sweet and sour. Actually, whatever it was tasted pretty damn good. He could see its flavor working very well with cold roast ham, or with game . . . venison or wild boar. . . . Whaaaat? What the Hades did he think he was doing, thinking of food at a time like this?

S'tan slapped himself on the forehead. Gripping the edge of the sink for support, he looked up. Yes. That was him there, ugly as sin itself, but still reflected in the mirror, just like any old normal immortal. This was all so *wrong*. He was S'tan, Viscount of Vileness, Emperor of Evil, Prince of . . . Prince of . . . He caught his breath. He couldn't even remember what he'd been Prince of, for Heaven's sake. What *was* that stuff in the bag? Whatever it was, it was pretty powerful medicine. And that *woman* had administered it to him; *she'd* done it. She'd done it and *he'd* lost it. He just *knew* he'd lost his edge forever. He was doomed. He'd be the laughingstock of Hades. S'tan, onetime First Minister . . . When they stopped laughing in his face, they'd probably give him the job of manually clearing the sewage vats . . . or raking out the ashes from the Pit . . . or . . .

Or perhaps he could just stay here? Earth wasn't so different from Hades. Both places had a great deal in common: corrupt governments, terrible food, awful traffic . . . except here on Earth he could still command some respect, even if only for his skills with a gas-fired grill. . . . However, he was lacking only one thing before he achieved culinary dominion. He licked his lips and smiled. What he needed was a recipe for whatever the heck had been in that bag. Forget the Chronostone; with that recipe on board, he'd be unstoppable.

When Bad Stuff Happens to Good People

Sheltering from the rain beneath the chestnut tree, the remains of the Strega-Borgia family took stock of the situation. Over their heads, dangling from the bare branches, the bats of Coire Crone looked almost as miserable as the humans they'd sworn to protect. Tendrils of mist rolled up from Lochnagargoyle, and huge droplets of rainwater plopped down from the tree onto the figures below. In her father's arms, Damp grizzled continuously, and a coughing fit racked Strega-Nonna's frail body. Tucked inside Titus's shirt, the defrosted clones tutted to themselves, bemoaning the weather, the outside temperature, their current lodgings, and the increasingly unlikely prospect of ever being allowed to return to their lovely deep freeze.

"*My* lovely deep freeze," Strega-Nonna gasped, in between bouts of coughing that sounded as if she'd exchanged her lungs for two treacle-filled accordions. Unable to avoid listening to these ghastly squeaks and bubbles, Pandora shuddered. Poor Nonna. Poor *us,* too. This was *dreadful.* If they didn't do something soon, they were all going to die of exposure. Night had fallen, and in the headlong rush to escape from the house, none of them had thought to bring coats or jackets to keep out the winter chill. Pandora rolled her eyes. Now they just seemed to be standing there, waiting to be either rescued or picked off, one by one. As far as Pandora knew, Ludo was still guarding Baci in the Ancestors' Room, but of Latch, Minty, and Mrs. McLachlan there was no sign. They *had* to be in the house still, she reasoned; otherwise . . . otherwise. Pandora groaned. She was too cold to think straight; Damp was making things a million times worse by whining like that; and, to put the lid on it, Dad had the thousand-mile stare of a sleep-walker, gazing into the mist as if he alone could see something materializing out of the rain.

After what seemed like a lifetime of listening to Damp and waiting for whatever they were waiting for, Luciano broke the silence.

"Take care of Damp while I go and find out what's happening back at the house. I'm not entirely convinced that your mother is safe, even with Ludo, and Flora's taking a very long time. . . ." His voice tailed off. Stricken with uncertainty, he removed his sweater and tenderly wrapped it round Strega-Nonna's shoulders, blew them all a kiss, and vanished into the mist, leaving his family to be guarded by StregaSchloss's low-tech security system, which on that particular evening consisted of only two mythical beasts, neither of them remotely interested in guard duty.

Pandora groaned again. She really didn't want to listen to what, had the beasts been married, would be rapidly escalating into a loud, no-holds-barred prelude to divorce.

"You *creep*. You faithless, slimy, two-timing rat. You adulterous toad. You—"

"Aw noo, jist a minute, hen. Yer mammy's no far away, an' she'll no wanty hear youse ca'ing me aw they names, eh no?"

"I don't give a fat fig *who* hears me calling you a lying, sneaking, slippery, stinking, two-timing, faithless—"

"Youse said that before, yon time. Look, hen, could youse listen fir a wee minute, eh? And stoap it wi' the burnin' bogies—yous're settin' aw they trees on fire. Jis calm doon. . . ."

But Ffup couldn't calm down. One hour spent with her mother had been enough to set her blood pressure soaring. One hideous hour in which Mother Dragon had pointed out all daughter Ffup's shortcomings in loving detail, including said daughter's foolishness for falling out with her Sleeper.

"Just HOO many PREPOSTERALS of marriage d'you think you're going to GET, m'girl?" the older dragon demanded, poking her daughter in the chest with a nobbly talon. "That SLIPPER'S a fine young fellow of a man. You should count your BLISSINGS he's willing to take YOU on. After all, you're no OILY painting, plus you're getting on a bit and . . ." Ffup's mother fought dirty, and she paused before delivering the final assault: "You've put on WEIGHED since I last SEED you—even your SLIPPER agreed with me. . . ."

At this, Ffup's jaw dropped. What? Her mother and the Sleeper were having cozy little chats behind her back about how *fat* she was? This was the same Sleeper who was about to have his engagement ring returned with menaces due to his being romantically entangled with someone who *wasn't* his faithful fiancée, Ffup the Fat. This final betrayal by her very own mother was more than flesh and blood could stand. Flames of rage nearly consuming her, Ffup shrieked in time-honored teenage fashion, "You just don't UNDERSTAND him, Mum," before storming off in floods of tears, intent on demonstrating just how well *she* understood her fiancé by shouting at him.

"And you can take your stupid engagement ring back, you fatheaded, renegade mutant WORM."

Uh-oh, thought Pandora. This time Ffup's gone too far. This time the Sleeper's going to turn round and slip-slide back into Lochnagargoyle, and *that* will be the last we ever see of him. But to Pandora's surprise, the Sleeper refused to rise to the bait.

"Wherr is your ring, onyways, hen?" he inquired mildly. "Ah hope youse haveny loast it again."

"Lost the ring?" Ffup gave a theatrical snort to confirm just how ridiculous she considered this slur on her character. "I haven't *lost* the ring. I simply choose not to wear it anymore. Seeing as how it was given to me under false pretenses."

"Aye, hen. Youse might have a point therr. Ah never should've gi'en youse it." The Sleeper undulated with embarrassment, his vast fleshy coils slapping repeatedly onto the rain-soaked grass of the meadow and splashing him and his fiancée with chilly water, which did little to improve Ffup's temper.

"You *admit* it?" she shrieked, her head surrounded by a halo of steam from where the Sleeper's splashes met her fiery exhalations.

"That's whit ah'm tryin' tae tell youse, wumman. I wis gi'en yon ring by a wee horsy thing, a burnt liberayrian, and telt tae take guid care o' it."

Beside Ffup, Pandora gasped. A *wee horsy thing*. A *burnt librarian*. She knew *exactly* who the Sleeper was talking about. This could only be the centaur Alpha, onetime custodian of the Etheric Library and Keeper of the Chronostone. Pandora also remembered, on being introduced to the centaur, that she'd been horribly embarrassed by his complete lack of clothes and puzzled by his library's complete lack of books. Her gasp of recognition went unnoticed by Ffup, who was too blinded by jealousy to either understand or care.

"*Whaaaaaat?* You expect me to believe that slinky wee sea serpent thing I found you wrapped round is a *librarian*? Oh yeah, right. And I'm an accountant."

"Aw, c'mon, hen." The Sleeper raised his voice, goaded at last. "Get a grip, eh? Yon slinky wee sea serpent wis a *sea horse*. And youse may weel be an accountant, but youse're certainly no zoologist. *Look*. Wid youse open your eyes? The sea horse is right behint me. And *he's* brocht aw *his* freends, and they want their stone back, the noo . . ."

"They're not the only ones," said a voice. "*I* want that stone back as well." And stepping out of the mist came the demon Isagoth. Regrettably, he was still coated in baby sick despite his walk in the pouring rain all the way from Auchenlochter-muchty, but nobody noticed this lamentable lack of personal hygiene because the demon was clasping the real Baby Strega-Borgia under his arm. Titus inhaled sharply, dropping Damp's hand before launching himself in what would have been a heroic but ultimately fatal attempt to rescue his baby brother. However, Titus had reckoned without the strength of his rick-ety relative; hadn't factored Strega-Nonna into the equation at all, assuming that such a feeble old woman was more of a lia-bility than an asset.

As they all had. All except Pandora, who'd had firsthand ex-perience of what a tough old bird Strega-Nonna really was. Pandora, who alone knew the depth of the old woman's courage and who was just beginning to suspect that Nonna's love for her family was without limit.

"Nonna, no . . . ," she began, but she was light-years too late. In what now felt like slow motion, Strega-Nonna turned to Damp, unwrapped Luciano's sweater from around her own shoulders, placed it like a cloak around the child, and then bent to unzip Damp's pajama-case pig and withdraw the stone hid-den within. As if she had all the time in the world, she turned and patted first Titus's, then Pandora's cheeks in the manner of Italian grandmothers the world over; next, she stopped and waited to make absolutely sure that Isagoth could see what a treasure she held in her hand before picking up her skirt in her other hand and sprinting for the loch.

Then all was noise and confusion. Much later, when Titus and Pandora tried to piece together the ghastly chain of events that transpired, link after dark link, on that winter evening, it was Strega-Nonna's bravery that shone like a lighthouse, illuminating all their deeds like a beacon of hope in the darkness. At first Titus had had no idea what she was doing, bolting off in the mist like that. But Pandora knew—knew without doubt that Strega-Nonna was using herself as bait. Isagoth too had instantly understood what was happening. After all, he reasoned, it had all happened before, during the previous summer, when that suicidal pest of a nanny had flung herself into the loch, clutching what he was beginning to think of as *his* stone. That time, back then, he'd been too slow to stop her, but this time . . . this time he had the kid. This time *he* was in charge. Even if he did have to run like a fool to catch up. Coughing horribly, the old lady headed across the meadow, only quickening her pace when she heard the footsteps behind her.

"Hey, hag. Haven't you forgotten something?" Isagoth taunted, pointing to the baby, who bounced and jiggled in his arms. By now they'd crossed the meadow and, to his surprise, the old bag was way ahead—almost at the end of the jetty, for Pete's sake. If he didn't stop her, history was going to repeat itself, and there was no way he was going to allow *that* to happen. He stopped, dropped the baby on the grass, and extended his arms in a V shape in front of himself. There was a crackle, as if lightning had struck, and a thin black line shot out from Isagoth's fingertips, faster than the eye could follow, striking Strega-Nonna right in the middle of her throat. The old lady coughed once and slowly toppled to her knees, her hands still clutching the stone. Smoke began to coil around her, wisps of gray wreathing round her neck like a choker made of mist. Pandora screamed and then ran full tilt into the demon, shrieking Strega-Nonna's name over and over and over again; behind her, Titus scooped up his screaming baby brother into his arms and continued to run toward his dying great-great-great-great-great-great-grandmother. Flames licked around the old lady's head like a crown of fire, and her sightless eyes turned inward to some place Titus and Pandora dared not follow.

Don Lucifer di S'Embowelli held the changeling at arm's length as he paced back and forth in front of the silent pictures in the Ancestors' Room. Hoping they might be mistaken for figures made of paint rather than flesh, Baci and Ludo Grabbit hid in the deep painted shadows in the portrait of Malvolio. With no idea what was happening beyond the Ancestors' Room, they had been waiting on the other side of the portrait until someone came to let them know if the coast was clear. When Don Lucifer had appeared round the door, Baci's heart sank. StregaSchloss must still be under siege. . . . And then she saw the infant grasped in Lucifer's arms. Ludo had been ready, leaping forward to catch her, to pin her arms to her sides and stop her from rushing to the defense of the Hell-born changeling.

Now Baci was still, in the manner of a rabbit caught in a snare, poised between the world behind the portal and the world to which she yearned to return, no matter what it cost. Don Lucifer glared at the paintings, but there was no response from any of them, not even when he roared Baci's name so loudly he made the baby cry.

"I know you're in there, you stupid woman," he bawled, his ugly face contorted with rage. "If you don't show yourself, I'm gonna start on the brat, *capisce?*"

Hidden behind a tree on the other side of the frame that had once housed the likeness of Malvolio di S'Enchantedino Borgia, Baci struggled her hardest against Ludo's grip, aware of how puny her best efforts were. Tears rolled down her face as she saw her tiny baby flopping like a rag doll in the grip of his evil uncle Lucifer.

"Let me go to him, pleeeeease," she begged Ludo, her fists raining against the lawyer's chest, her voice rising to a ragged shriek. "MY BABY! YOU HAVE TO. LET. ME. GO!" And then, to her horror, she saw why Ludo wouldn't let her sacrifice herself.

Annoyed at being squeezed in the grip of the roaring man and aware that Baci, source of all good things, was somewhere nearby, the changeling decided to seize control of the situation. Before Don Lucifer could issue another threat, it reared forward in his arms and sank its teeth into the gangster's newly restored nose, biting down so hard that it was some moments before the Don could dislodge its grip, hurl the monster to the floor, and get as far away from the biting baby as possible. Blind with pain and rage, Don Lucifer crashed along the corridor, flinging open doors at random in search of something to stanch the flow of blood as well as something to numb the pain. Ten minutes later, pressing a towel to his face, he reentered the Ancestors' Room clutching a bottle of whiskey. Again the room was silent, save for the changeling hissing on the floor in front of Malvolio's portrait. Don Lucifer smiled nastily. He'd had enough messing around with biting brats and wailing women. He'd do the wife and the baby together. . . . At this thought, his smile widened and he dropped the towel. Slowly, lingeringly, he removed the cork from the bottle and let it fall to the floor. It bounced once, then rolled toward the glowing embers in the fireplace. Perfect. Don Lucifer had just worked out how to hammer the two final nails into his brother's coffin. Paying particular attention to the area of floorboards around Malvolio's portrait, Don Lucifer splashed whiskey all around, laying a trail of alcohol that led all the way back to the warm tiles surrounding the fireplace. He did this with one hand while, with his other hand, he rummaged in his pocket for his cigarette lighter.

Running across the rose quartz drive, knowing deep down that something was very wrong indeed, Luciano smelled the smoke but couldn't at first see its source. Then he heard the sound of breaking glass, and looked up just as the windows of the Ancestors' Room were illuminated by an awful flash of bloody light. As he ran, he saw two figures silhouetted in the window, backlit by leaping flames. Luciano's throat was so constricted with dread that he couldn't even say Baci's name; could do nothing other than run flat out for the front door, knowing that no matter how fast he took the stairs, nor with what degree of suicidal courage he broke into the burning room, he would forever and ever and ever be too late to save his beloved Baci.

Burn, Baby, Burn

A wave as tall as a mountain rose up out of the loch. It was like nothing Titus had ever seen before, unless he discounted the sort of tidal waves generally found in disaster movies. Except, he decided, you don't get the smell of the sea from waves in disaster movies; nor do they sound like the babble of a million voices, one on top of the other, all of them clamoring to be heard. Titus knelt beside his dead great-great-great-great-great-great-grandmother, shocked into a state of emotional numbness, hardly aware of the baby in his arms or the imminence of his own death as it rushed toward him, borne by the vast wall of water towering over the shores of the loch. He looked up from Strega-Nonna to where Pandora was struggling on the pebbly

shore with Strega-Nonna's murderer; looked to the meadow, where Ffup was rising into the air with Damp clasped in her forepaws; and finally looked back to the house, where he saw flames leaping from the windows of the Ancestors' Room.

Then something as tall and heavy as an apartment building hit him, driving him under, deep, deep down into the darkest night, and he found himself wondering, as consciousness fled, if there might be white-chocolate-and-vanilla brownies in the afterlife or if being dead was really as final as he'd been led to believe.

S'tan sat at the table reading recipe books, oblivious to the chaos surrounding him and unruffled by the wicked wind howling through the broken window by the sink. Occasionally he would lick his finger and turn a page, his entire attention focused on his search for whatever had been in Mrs. McLachlan's icing bag. Thus, when the nanny appeared in the kitchen, he didn't at first regard her as a threat, but as a welcome source of information.

"That . . . that stuff you rammed down my throat," he began, closing the recipe book and pushing it to one side before taking another from the pile of unread volumes and opening its stained cover. "It was . . . well, heck, it was *wicked*, whatever it was." He didn't look up, didn't make eye contact with the nanny; instead, his fingers continued to flip pages as he scanned the lists of ingredients, hoping against hope that Mrs. McLachlan would let him in on her secret recipe. To his delight, Mrs. McLachlan did not disappoint.

"It was just a wee rowan jelly, dear. Made from rowan berries. Of course, being a cook yourself, you'll know that a jelly made from the ripe berries is the most concentrated form of the fruit you could hope to obtain. . . ." Here Mrs. McLachlan paused and took a breath; when she spoke again, her voice had developed a marked edge. "What you *weren't* to know was that here in Scotland, we used to grow rowan trees in our graveyards to ward off evil. And very effective they were too. So a jelly made from *those* berries . . . well, I'm sure you can imagine how potent its effect would be."

Which was when he looked up and saw that Mrs. McLachlan wasn't alone. Behind her stood Minty, Latch, and the wolf pack, all of whom stared at him with flat, expressionless eyes.

"Your time's up," said Mrs. McLachlan, and as if to underline this, Minty took an egg timer out from behind her back and placed it firmly on the cupboard, where they could all watch its progress.

Clearing his throat, Latch removed a small Play-Doh figure from his pocket and met S'tan's puzzled gaze before saying, "I took the liberty of mixing some of the blood from your injured finger into this dough. I'm sure you'll appreciate the significance of what I'm talking about." And stepping to one side, the butler opened the door of the oven and held the figure uncomfortably close to the flames.

Fat beads of sweat broke out on S'tan's brow, and he held up his hands in mock surrender. "Guys, ladies, I mean . . . Sheesh. Is this aggro strictly necessary?"

Silence greeted him, and his eyes flicked from the egg timer to the oven and back. Blisters began to break out across his face, swelling up and bursting, as the silence stretched out, unbroken. Then, as if a switch had been thrown, S'tan's mood abruptly changed.

"D'you cretins really think that you can best me? ME? The Prince of Dork, the Prints of Dark . . . yeah, whatever . . ." He paused, his brow furrowed as if he were an actor who'd forgotten his lines, his whole body racked with the embarrassment of waiting for the prompt that never came. Shaking his head and sending drops of sweat spraying in all directions, S'tan stood up, and his chair went crashing to the floor behind him. His face twisted with contempt, and he closed the recipe book as if it held a story with a deeply unsatisfying conclusion. With his eyes firmly fixed on the falling level of sand in the upper chamber of the egg timer, S'tan ground out his final lines, spitting each word across the kitchen, the effort of speaking costing him dear. Latch tried to ignore the black smoke trickling out from S'tan's nostrils, just as he forced himself to ignore the pain he felt in his own hand—the hand that held the little figure over the flames. Somehow S'tan managed to force a laugh from his throat, even as his lower legs burst into flame.

"You—*you* must be out of your tiny minds if you think this is *it*. I'll boil you *alive* and suck the flesh from your *bones*. I'll make you wish you'd never been *born*. I'll give you nightmares for all eternity. And as for *you*—" At this, he lurched toward Flora, and that was enough. With a roar of rage and pain commingled, Latch flung the manikin into the oven and slammed the door shut.

There was a ghastly scream, a crackle and a hiss, and in front of their horrified eyes S'tan melted, blackened, bubbled, and turned to smoke. The smell was indescribably bad, the air so thick with cremated devil flesh that it seemed to Latch and Minty as if they would never be rid of him. S'tan coated their skin, clung to their hair, trickled down the backs of their throats, clogged their lungs; even his glowing, flaming after-image seemed to have seared itself on their retinas—but Mrs. McLachlan flung open the door to the kitchen garden and they fled blindly outside, never before so glad to be cold, wet, and alive on a winter's night in Argyll.

Even though she now understood the changeling was not her own—was some twisted stand-in for her missing baby son—still Baci was unable to ignore the little creature's shrieks and wails. The changeling shrank away from the flames that licked across the floor of the Ancestors' Room, its face a gargoyle's mask of horror, its true nature revealed by fear. Half mad with grief, Baci broke free from Ludo's grip and lunged through the gilt frame, passing through the portal between the worlds as if it were merely an ordinary doorway. She scooped up the howling changeling and ran for the window with it in her arms. Two paces behind, barely able to see through the smoke, Ludo plunged across the burning room, intent on saving Baci from herself. As the lawyer reached out to her, the velvet curtains caught fire, their moth-eaten, sunbleached fabric no match for the greedy flames. For one heart-stopping moment, Baci and the changeling were silhouetted against an unbroken wall of fire; then the curtains fell from the pelmet, spilling to the floor in a waterfall of sparks and flecks of burning velvet . . .

. . . at which point the windows imploded and Ffup crashed into the burning room, wings wide, neck outstretched, a grin stretching from ear to ear, delighted at having made the most dramatic entrance of her entire life.

"Pretty cool, huh?" she demanded, stamping on the burning curtains with her heat-resistant dragon feet, forgetting in her triumph that she was the only creature in the room in possession of heat-resistant *any*thing. Smoke filled the room; the floor was dotted with little bonfires; and glowing flakes and embers threatened bookcases and chairs, beds and wardrobes alike. Despite this, Ffup paused in front of Minty's cheval mirror and turned to one side admiringly; then, remembering the purpose behind crashing into the Ancestors' Room, she collected herself.

"Right, guys. Time to rock and roll." And grabbing Ludo, Baci, and the changeling, she ran full tilt at the window and her powerful wings bore them all out into the night.

Waiting one floor below, with his mouth submerged in the waters of the moat and the remainder of his scaly body coiled on the rose quartz drive, the vast Sleeper took Ffup's reappearance as his cue for action. He trundled forward, quartz crunching beneath his belly as he uncoiled and extended his colossal body, inching slowly up the wall beneath the Ancestors' Room. When his head was finally level with the shattered windows, he paused, took a deep breath, and then, looking more like a firefighter's hose than a mythical Scottish beast, squirted thousands of quarts of moat water straight into the burning room.

Something's Got to Give

The unmistakable smell of burned flesh hung in the darkness of the great hall as Luciano took the stairs five at a time in what he knew must be a doomed attempt to rescue his wife. Memories of her flickered across his mind: Baci crowned in cream rosebuds as his bride; Baci asleep, her body curled around the babies like a mother lion's; Baci dancing across a meadow full of cotton grass; Baci swimming in the lily pond . . .

"BACIIIIIIII," he howled, catching sight of the telltale line of wicked orange flame glowing round the doorframe of the Ancestors' Room. He could feel the heat from the other end of the corridor; knew even as he ran toward its source that the best he could hope for now was to join his dead wife, and thus leave their children completely orphaned. . . .

"BACIIIIIII," he roared, aware of a shadow passing between him and his goal. Then the shadow spoke.

"You might as well save your breath, *stupido*. Place she's gone, they don't have any ears left."

The brutality of this statement, its crude assessment of the situation, hit Luciano in the center of his chest like a sledgehammer. Lucifer di S'Embowelli Borgia stepped out of the shadows, walking toward him with a sneer on his ugly face as he'd always done when they were children, appearing at the best moment to inflict the maximum damage possible on his little brother. Hardly any surprise that he was here now, gloating while Luciano wept.

"You pathetic little worm," he observed, strolling toward Luciano, taking the time to savor his triumph. "Don't tell me you think your tears are gonna put out the flames. Is that how you're gonna save her, hero? Is that it? You're gonna snivel all over her?" He was alongside Luciano now, his changeling-bitten nose a cosmetic nightmare of blood and bruising, his yellow eyes alight with malice. "Hey. You may as well face it, Luci-boy. You ain't gonna be able to live with yourself after this. Think, my heroic brother. You did *nothing* while your lady-wife burned to death. Or did you? Oh, excuse *me*. I do apologize. You *did* do something. You . . . you *cried*. She screamed her head off and you . . . you sniveled and wept like the useless, cowardly—"

"Not another word," Luciano spat, lunging for his tormentor with one arm outstretched in front of him. "Get. Out. Of. My. Way."

"Make me." Lucifer yawned, looking down at his fingernails as if that concluded the matter.

Luciano grabbed Lucifer's shirtfront, forcing them close enough to feel each other's breath.

"Oooh, I'm wetting my pants, I'm so scared. Ooooh, little brother, you're so frightening." Lucifer made no attempt to escape his brother's grip, but stared into Luciano's eyes, his bottom jaw working from side to side until, with no warning, he reared back and spat full into Luciano's face, simultaneously shoving him so hard that he fell backward and crashed to the floor.

Lucifer's mocking laughter bounced off the suits of armor downstairs and seemed to echo endlessly in Luciano's ears as he picked himself up off the floor. Grimacing with disgust, he wiped the spit from his face, observing his own actions as if he'd somehow managed to split himself in two: into Luciano, the ice-cold witness, and Luciano, the man with the red mist rapidly occluding his sight.

Lucifer was striding past the open door to the game room when Luciano caught up with him. A monumental, unstoppable force batted Lucifer through the doorway and into the room, flung him across the carpet, and narrowly missed pitching him headfirst through the glass front of the game cabinet. Lucifer caught a brief glimpse of the hundreds of muddled-up games stacked behind the glass, games he half recognized from childhood—

He'd always cheated. Always. Thing was, it was never as much fun when your opponent was too dumb to realize you were robbing him blind. Luciano was such a knucklehead he never even guessed why he lost every game he played with his big brother. The stupid sap would just stare at the cards, or the board, or his dwindling stock of poker chips, peering at them with his big brown eyes like some sorta dumb animal, so doglike in fact that Lucifer frequently found release in kicking his kid brother until Luciano howled exactly like a dog. . . .

Lucifer was spun round and his face slammed against the wall, his nose making painful contact with the brass dome of the antique light switch. Shove. The lights came on over the billiard table. Another shove from Luciano, more agonizing contact between Lucifer's tender bitten nose and the unforgiving metal of the light switch, and off went the lights again. Shove, on. Shove, off. In the background, over his own grunts of pain and Luciano's labored breathing, Lucifer could hear a shuffling sound, as if the jumbled game pieces in the cabinet were stirring in their sleep. Then came a shove vicious enough to make him scream, a high-pitched shriek he'd never before heard coming from his own throat. . . .

He recognized it, though. He'd made Luciano squeak and squeal like a stuck pig often enough. 'Specially when the pinhead was just a baby and couldn't rat on him. Those were the best times, him and his kid brother playing the game where he'd loom over the crib in time to catch the look of utter horror as Luciano realized that here was the nightmare, back again. The rush of power he used to feel when he saw the fear in Luciano's eyes was indescribable, almost better than the feelings he had afterward. Poppa didn't notice the

bruises that sprouted all over Baby Luciano like black flowers;
Poppa was too busy trying to keep control of his Mafia empire—
besides, real men like Poppa took very little interest in their children
until they were old enough to hold a gun. . . . Not like wussy Luci,
who probably spent all his time with his squalling brats because he'd
never grown up hims—

Shove.

"AUGHHH."

"How d'you like being on the receiving end, huh?" Luciano's breath felt hot on Lucifer's face; the two brothers tangled in a mass of thrashing, wrangling limbs, a two-headed beast whose struggling shadow fell across the floor. "I *said.* How. D'you. Like. It?" Luciano demanded. "I hope you're beginning to be afraid, Lucifer. You bloody well ought to be."

"Don't be ridiculous. Me? Afraid of you?"

Shove.

"Ah, Lucifer. I'm not going to stop, see? I'm not going to quit on you now. Not now that you've killed her. Not now that there's nothing left for me."

Shove.

It hurt. It hurt Lucifer far more than anything had ever hurt him before, but he was damned if he'd ever admit it. Not to Luciano. Not ever. Never say quits. . . .

"Say it, you big baby, c'mon, say it. Let me hear you beg."

"Please, stop. Please, Lucifer, I'll do anything you want, I'll give
you anything, just stop it. You're killing me. Lucifer. PLEASE.
STOP."

He couldn't make out if the sniveling fool was crying, because Luciano was dripping wet from repeated duckings in the bath. One minute the stupid baby had been whipping up a storm of soapsuds; the next he found himself grabbed by the scruff of his scrawny neck and forced underwater. And don't think Lucifer hadn't been tempted to keep old Luciano under till the frenzy of thrashing limbs and bubbles had stopped, but that would have meant an end to the game, and it was no fun at all when games ended.

He hoped that Luciano felt the same way. Hoped that his dumb brother wasn't thinking of playing this one to the death.

"Hey. Luci. Murdering me ain't gonna bring her baa-AAUGH."

"Shut it."

"If they send you to prison, you'll never get to see your kids grow up."

"I said, *shut it.*"

"Awwww, Luciano, weedy little jerks like you get eaten *alive* in prison. Come on. You'll get over her. Plenty more where she came fr-AUGHHHH."

Clotted gargling sounds came from Lucifer's throat as Luciano dragged him choking and struggling across the room. His spine made contact with the edge of the billiard table, and Lucifer found himself bending backward under the relentless pressure of his brother's hands. Luciano's face loomed above him, but what he saw was not a brother he recognized. Even if by some miracle Lucifer had managed to force any words past his throat, Luciano was beyond reason, beyond hearing. The stupid jerk's eyes were squeezed shut, tears sliding out from under the lids; he was sobbing like the baby he'd always been, his mouth drawn up like a gargoyle's. Trying to move his head, Lucifer saw movement out of the corner of his eye. At first he couldn't work out what it was he'd seen; it looked like hundreds of toy soldiers had been laid out across the green baize of the billiard table like some sort of weird war game.

Then he realized that it wasn't a war game—wasn't a game at all. They weren't toy soldiers, they were *real*. Real soldiers, who had discovered their life's true purpose in this final battle. Real living, breathing warriors, who despite their height were no less lethal than their full-size human counterparts. Lucifer had approximately three and a half seconds to consider the vicious points on each and every one of the shrunken warriors' tiny spears before he was impaled upon them, their wicked tips penetrating skin, muscle, blood vessels, and several of his major organs simultaneously. As his blood leached out across the baize and his sight faded to black, Lucifer saw with utter clarity that, for him, the game was over.

Bless the Bed
That I Lie On

ndoubtedly it was the clones tucked inside his shirt that saved Titus and the baby from drowning when the vast wave hit them. Had it been up to him, Titus knew he couldn't have survived. After all, he'd only learned to swim earlier that year, and under Pandora's tutelage he could now barely manage a length of the moat, let alone stay afloat in this terrifying open water with a baby tucked in the crook of one arm.

Titus had no idea what had happened. Was he even alive? And if so, where on earth was he? He wasn't in Lochnagar-goyle anymore, that much was certain. And if it really was water he was currently flailing in, it was like no water he'd ever encountered. Sure, it was wet, and its salt rimed his mouth, but

it didn't *sound* like water. From all around came a faint murmur, like the sound made by thousands of hushed voices: the
noise of a vast crowd of people all talking very quietly, as if
they were in church or ... or in a library. Occasionally he
would distinguish an individual sound, even make out the
odd phrase or foreign word, but for most of the time, all
he could hear was a tangle of voices that his ears were unable
to decipher. Ahead, he caught occasional glimpses of land
he didn't recognize at all; at least, he *thought* he could see
land, but in the darkness, the most he could see was a distant
silhouette. What he *couldn't* see was Pandora, and this was
terrifying—he was positive she must have been swept away
by the same wave that had plucked both him and the baby
from the shore. Plucked him, the baby, and ... He tried his
hardest not to follow that particular thought to its tragic conclusion, but it proved unavoidable. The wave had swallowed
them all, including Strega-Nonna, crushing her limp body
under the pounding tonnage of more water than he'd seen
in his lifetime. Where Nonna might be now was anyone's
guess, but mercifully she wouldn't be needing her body any
longer. . . .

"TIIIITUUUUUUS!"

Had he heard that? His name, so faint and far away, its syl-
lables part of the wind and the waves. He trod water for a moment, his arms aching with the effort of holding the baby's
face clear of the waves slapping his face, as he strained to hear
his name once more. He was tiring, and he knew that he had
to find land soon, so he paddled on, the geriatric clones tug-

ging him forward, their weak voices occasionally gasping out the odd insult to keep him going.

"Youth of today . . . born idle."

"Call *that* swimming? I've seen faster bricks. . . ."

"Come on, you great lummox. Put some effort into it. D'you think we *enjoy* towing you ashore? You weigh a ton, you do."

"Eeeh, when I was your age, I used to swim across the loch every day with my bicycle on my back and my fishing rod between my teeth. . . ."

And then his feet smacked off a rock, closely followed by his knees, and then he heard someone yell "TIIIIITUUUUU- UUSSS!" and he knew that he hadn't dreamt his sister's voice, for there she was, fairly dancing across the waves toward him, relief writ large across her face, her skinny arms wrapping around him in a most un-Pandora-like hug.

"Thank heavens you both made it. Come on. I was terrified I'd be stuck here on my own with . . . with that horrible bloke." Seeing Titus's frown, she tried to explain, her words tumbling out one after the other in her haste. "D'you remember that weird guy, the creepy photographer who showed up last summer, the day Mrs. McLachlan vanished? Come on, Titus, *think.* The same guy who began to appear in all my photos? Yup. I thought you'd remember. Right, him. So I *knew* I'd seen him again, but I couldn't put my finger on when or where until now. It was this morning, when we went to the hospital to see Mum and the new baby and I was gazing out of the window and he was *there*, balanced on crutches, staring inside, staring at us. . . . The same guy. The same one who ki—who kill—"

She couldn't go on, and Titus couldn't finish the sentence for her. It was unthinkable that Strega-Nonna was gone forever. Neither Titus nor Pandora could even begin to imagine StregaSchloss without the old lady. Even though they rarely saw her in her thawed state—the telltale puddle of her meltwater only appeared by the range a few times a year—she was so much a part of their existence that her absence was about to rip a huge hole in the fabric of life at StregaSchloss. The baby stared up into Titus's face, watching as he blinked several times and looked out to sea, to where a last thin blade of yellow cut the sky in two.

"It's dark, Pan. Any idea where we are?"

"None whatsoever. All I know is that it's an island and that we're stuck here—at least until it gets light. There are a couple of trees and signs of an old campfire. That man—the one I was telling you about—he's over there, trying to get a fire going. The island's so small, I don't think we can avoid him, and besides . . . I'm *freezing*."

She was right, Titus realized. There was hardly any shelter on the island, and the temperature was plummeting. Plus, he imagined that babies weren't equipped to deal with extremes of temperature, so if he didn't do something and do it soon, the baby would end up joining Strega-Nonna, and *that*, he vowed, simply wasn't going to happen.

Isagoth had managed to get a fire going, but it was only a feeble little flicker that dimmed alarmingly as he balanced more layers of wet twigs over its glowing heart.

"Ignite, dammit," he commanded, kneeling down and trying to encourage flames by blowing on the embers. Smoke billowed around his head and he retreated, choking, wheezing, and enraged at the island's failure to provide dry kindling. "The wood's all *wet*," he spat.

"Funny, that," Titus muttered. "I noticed that about the water too."

Isagoth's head whipped round, and he glared into the darkness beyond his fire. "Oh, it's you two," he said, turning back to his fire-building. "Joy. You brought that infernal cheese factory along too. . . ."

At the sound of Isagoth's voice, the baby began to sob. At the sound of the baby, Pandora gave a deep and heartfelt groan and gritted her teeth. Something about the sound of weeping babies made her feel as if her eardrums were being massaged with shards of broken glass while small lions were chewing on what remained of her brain. And just when she imagined that things couldn't get any worse, the sea gave up its dead, washing Strega-Nonna's body ashore like driftwood. Pandora had turned away from the baby to face out to sea, and thus she was the first to witness the return of her ancestor. A cry must have escaped from her then, because Isagoth slitted his eyes and stared at her, before following her gaze to a bedraggled bundle of rags and tatters. In one fluid motion, the demon was on his feet and running toward the high-tide mark, bounding across the pebbly shore before Titus and Pandora realized his intention. "Ssso, let's hope you had the sense to hang on to my stone," the demon hissed, hauling Strega-Nonna's body about as if it were of no account whatsoever.

"*Stop* that!" howled Pandora, revolted by Isagoth's vulture-like behavior. "Leave her *alone*, you monster. She's *dead*. Doesn't that give her the right to rest in peace?"

Isagoth ignored her, turning the lifeless body over with his foot and swooping down to prize something from Strega-Nonna's grasp. Bile rose in Titus's throat. Even in death, the old lady's grip was so powerful that Isagoth was forced to break her fingers one by one in order to extract his prize. Frozen with horror, Titus and Pandora clung together, sobbing along with the baby they held between them.

At length the demon stood upright, his legs straddling Strega-Nonna's remains, his face illuminated with pure, undiluted hatred. It was as if he was growing in maleficence right there in front of them, sprouting like some wicked seed, his mouth opening into a crack that allowed smoke to spill forth from his interior.

"Miiine," he breathed in a voice straight from Hell. "My ssstone. At laassst MY time is come. BEHOLD, THE NEW ORDER OF THE WORLDS. WELCOME TO HELL."

Round the island's high-tide mark, pillars of flame ignited with a roar, leaping up to rim the land with red fire. Overhead, the night peeled back like the lid of a sardine tin to reveal a sky so raw it appeared to bleed. Titus and Pandora saw the land melt and turn to magma at their feet, saw gouts of flame shooting through from beneath the Earth's fragile crust. Instinctively they made for the sea, dodging erupting columns of flame, screaming in terror as they ran straight through the burning fringes of the island and floundered across its muddy shallows. But where they had expected to find water, there was only sand.

"Where's the sea *gone*?" Pandora gasped, spinning round to try and find her bearings. "Where *are* we?"

Bruised clouds scudded past overhead as, all around them, the land heaved itself aloft, taking the form of dunes, vast cliffs, and massifs, which just as swiftly blew away to re-form in sculpted curves elsewhere. Shapes appeared at their feet, rotted hulks of what might have been vehicles, and in the distance Titus was sure he saw the tumbled remains of buildings, roads, and bridges, their rusted metalwork spanning valleys of dust. The children stumbled and tripped, still running, still in flight from the horrors they had left behind, their breathing ragged as they scaled dunes and sent avalanches of sand cascading down in their wake. They gained a little height and stood panting and breathless on a ridge, but all they could see for miles around was more of the same. Ahead lay endless empty acres, wave upon wave of nothingness stretching off toward the horizon.

It was exhausting territory, Titus decided, shifting the weight of the baby to his other arm and taking a deep breath before dragging himself across a particularly soft stretch of sand. His feet slowed of their own accord; he was sinking up to his knees in sand, his mind turning in a weary gyre of one-step-more-just-one-step-more-just—

He stopped to catch his breath again. Sand ground between his teeth, and he grimaced. In his arms, the baby stirred, his dark eyes opening on the strange new world he found himself in.

"Pan . . . ," Titus found himself whispering. "D'you . . . d'you think we're de— we've di—?" He stopped, cleared his throat, and began again. "No. Well. Thought not. *Obviously* not, huh? Not dead, I mean."

Pandora stared at him, shaking her head slowly from side to side. "How d'you know?"

"The baby just peed down my arm. Somehow I'm *sure* that doesn't happen when you're dead." He looked down at the solemn baby boy in his arms and managed a wan smile. "You have your uses, squirt, even if it's only to remind us that we're still alive. Just."

"But where *are* we?" Pandora's voice was teetering on the verge of hysteria. "And where's the sea? And we left Strega-Nonna with that awful man. We didn't think about *her*. We just ran away. . . ."

Titus wasn't listening. He was staring at something over their heads, his eyes narrowed in concentration. With a trembling hand, he pointed to a small shape flying toward them, its rapid approach quickly bringing it within range and allowing them both to recognize Damp, her eyes sparkling, her arms outstretched in greeting, and her mouth open in a wide grin of delight.

"LOOK AT MEEEEEEEEE," she bawled, evidently delighted to find her siblings, even if it was in such a dismal location. "Lookit, Tyts. Look, Panda, see me!" And unable to resist showing off, Damp described a wobbly loop-the-loop before crash-landing in a giggling heap at Pandora's feet.

Dragging himself out from under the toddler, a small and

mightily peeved bat unfolded his wings, spat out a mouthful of grit, and turned to address Damp.

"Well, ma'am. I have to tellya that your flight today contravened each and every Fedril Aviation Athorty regulation ever written and some that haven't even bin thought up yet. . . ."

"Veeeesper," Damp groaned, picking herself up and greeting her stunned siblings with a grin. "Shoosh." She wobbled over to Titus and grabbed on to his arms, bringing the baby nearer to her. The baby blinked at Damp, his dark blue eyes gazing deep into her brown ones. Damp smiled. "Look, baby. I brunged your friend." And from inside the collar of her fleece she hauled out a small, wriggling salamander and unceremoniously dumped him on the baby's chest. The salamander blinked, as did the baby.

"What the he——?" Titus couldn't frame the question, couldn't get over his shock at finding his little sister appearing right in the middle of what was rapidly turning into a complete nightmare. "Where did . . . ? But why? How?"

The salamander slapped his forehead and reared up on his hind legs. "Pleath," it lisped. "Lithen. Thith ith Hell, or Hade-eeth, if you prefer. It uthed to be the domain of Death, but not anymore. The Chronothtone hath fallen under the control of the Dark Thide, and now all ith Chaoth. Patht and Future are mixthed up with Heaven and Hell——"

"Hang on, hang *on,*" Pandora begged, one hand clutching her head as she tried to make sense of what the salamander was saying. "How d'you know this is Hell? How come you're such an authority on all of this stuff? Why are you all *here*?"

"*Ahem*. If I might speak?" Vesper had clawed his way onto Damp's shoulder and was flapping his wings in agitation. "We're running outta time, folks. Save the Spanish Inquisition for later, lady. We need to get outta here. We need to pick up the dead broad and—"

"The dead *broad*?" Titus's voice had risen into a squeak of outrage. "I hope you're not meaning my great-great-great-gre—"

"Yeah, whatever, kid. She sure was greater than you'll *ever* know, but calling her a dead broad is a helluva lot faster than giving her the full title. We gotta fly. We gotta get airborne before the sea comes rushing back and—"

"Thut up, thut up, for heaventh thake." The salamander was almost beside himself with panic. "I can thmell him. The demon. He'th coming back. You're all wathting time. Are you tho blind that you can't thee?"

"No. They can't see. Or should I say 'thee'?"

Pandora nearly screamed out loud. That *voice*. It was *him*. The murderer. Skin crawling with fear, she turned round and there, towering over them, silhouetted on a ridge, was the demon Isagoth with one foot planted on the prone form of Pandora's beloved ancestor.

"You filthy *monster*," Pandora howled. "You evil, murdering, disgusting mutant FREAK." And as her words turned into inchoate, choking sobs, she ran at him, clawing her way up the dune, her eyes, nose, and mouth full of sand, blind rage alone propelling her onward, her mind full of hatred for everything Isagoth stood for.

And he laughed. The demon stood astride his victim and mocked Pandora, relishing her pain, reveling in her grief, and, above all, delighting in having turned her into some creature powered by blind hatred, just like him. Seeing this, Titus thought his heart would burst with sorrow. The pointlessness of Pandora's struggle, the mocking peals of laughter, the pathetic sight of Strega-Nonna's body lying defenseless beneath the foot of her killer: all of these conspired to crush Titus and render him impotent with despair at his inability to change the situation.

The salamander inched along the baby's body until his lagoon-blue eyes were level with the infant's own. The little creature dipped its head once, twice, and then scuttled out of sight down the neck of the baby's sleepers. The baby turned his head and looked straight at Damp, a single glance passing between them like a spark of raw energy. Damp's eyes grew wide.

"Here. Catch!" Isagoth yelled, jamming his foot beneath Strega-Nonna's ribs and, with one kick, sending her body rolling and flopping downhill like a bundle of discarded trash. Seeing this, Titus paled and Pandora turned away in horror, but Damp walked forward to meet the tumbling body as it came to a standstill.

"Jackan Jill," she said dismissively, an unreadable expression crossing her face. She looked up at the demon on top of the dune and, as if she'd come to a decision, took a deep breath and called out, "Not like it, that one. Damp do it now. Damp's turn. Damp says *Maffew, Mark, Lucan, John. . . .*"

Isagoth had been turning away when Damp's words took magical effect. His eyes flamed ruby red as he realized what the child was doing. That *spell*. That ancient spell. The White Paternoster? How the hell had she known to use it? He spun round, but it was already too late. A wind sprang up from nowhere and swirled playfully around his feet, giving the temporary illusion that he was floating above the dune, just as now, down below in the dark valley, four distinct columns of light floated around the little group of souls. Even as he shrieked in defiance, Isagoth heard Damp's voice complete the invocation, the little girl shifting fluently into the ancient Babylonian version, as taught to her by Mrs. McLachlan.

"... *then* Damp says, *Shamash ahead; behind me, Sin; Nergal to my right and Nimb by my left—*"

At this, Isagoth bent forward and vomited blood onto the sand. It was *intolerable*. That *child*, that malignant human *dwarf*, was getting the better of him. Somehow she had managed to cast the one spell that gave her and her companions absolute, one hundred percent protection against anything he could throw at them. ... Isagoth caught his breath. Hang on a *minute*. The Chronostone predated any Babylonian babble, did it not? It was around long before the Cabbalistic version Damp was now intoning.

The great names drifted up to where Isagoth shook and spasmed, spitting blood across his sandy perch: "... *Michael to my right, Gabriel to my left, Uriel in front of me, and Raphael behind* ..."

"Oh, yessss," he hissed. He held the ace. The Chronostone would break the spell, and then he'd have her, the meddling little troll. With an effort that cost him dearly, he stretched his arm back and threw the stone with all his might in a lethal trajectory straight toward Damp's head.

Time-to-Go Time

Later he would remember the awful sense of waking from a very bad dream only to find himself in the middle of an even worse nightmare, but when Luciano staggered back from his half brother's body, his first thought was to stop himself from being violently sick in reaction to what he'd done. In this, he was not successful. Between heaves, he attempted to piece together what had happened. *So, Luciano,* he told himself, *try this one on for size—your wife is dead and somehow you've killed your half brother, Lucifer.* Both of these statements were so preposterous that, for a few seconds, Luciano's mind simply refused to accept such patently false information. *System error. Incorrect data entered. Please check and try again.* Then the nausea passed and he opened his eyes on a world so transformed that he briefly entertained the idea that he'd gone insane.

Lucifer was dead, that much was certain. His body sprawled across the billiard table, his sightless eyes fixed on the ceiling, his blood pooling beneath him, turning the green baize brown and running in rivulets to drip through the mesh pockets under the table's rim and spatter the floor below. Luciano was aghast. He had done this? Somehow, in a fit of madness—for what other explanation could there be?—he had killed his half brother. Stabbed him several times, judging by the pools of gore. *But how?* Luciano wanted to scream. *With what?* Had he been so possessed with rage, so blinded by hate, that somehow he'd done this, this dreadful deed, without even being *aware* of doing it?

At this he began to shake, his castanet teeth chittering uncontrollably, his jellified legs barely able to support his weight as he was filled with the terrible knowledge of what manner of creature his blind rage had turned him into. He was a murderer. A killer. He had taken a human life. Lucifer lay dead by his hand. What kind of beast had he, Luciano Perii Strega-Borgia, become?

"Noooo," he wept, his trembling hands reaching out to touch his dead sibling. "Oh, let this not be so, please, no, not this, noooo." And then, precisely when he needed it most, he recalled something he'd read in a book. It had been in one of the dusty old leather-bound books on Roman philosophy that he habitually read during those lonely nights when he rose in the darkness and tiptoed down to his study to find comfort in the words of long-dead wise men. The words did not fail him now; they reached out across the centuries to give the weeping Luciano precisely the comfort that he craved:

"Nothing happens to any man which he is not formed by nature to bear."

A sob caught in Luciano's throat, and a great stillness swept over him. It was almost as if, at that precise moment, everything in his life, all that had gone before, was balanced equally against all that was yet to come, and he, Luciano, had become a human fulcrum, and was poised at the tipping point in the exact center of his life.

The stone flies through the air, its weight more than enough to shatter the delicate shell of Damp's skull and to so damage her growing brain that she would never take another step, or breathe another breath unaided.

and

In the damp twilight of the kitchen garden, Minty, Latch, and Mrs. McLachlan catch their breath, drawing sweet, deep lungfuls of the moist air and ridding themselves of the lingering taint of corruption from S'tan's final fiery departure. A line of geese stretches across the sky, their distinctive call sounding like the very essence of winter. Flora McLachlan looks up and sees where the birds describe a long cursive *l* in the sky. The nanny's hands creep up to clasp first her throat and then her mouth, as if to stopper up the words that spill forth.

"Amelia," she breathes, her eyes on the skein of geese. "Amelia, do you leave us?"

Overhead, the birds wheel and call, their line coiled upon itself into a circle, an *o* in the sky, just as, in turn, they will slowly spin and loop, their wings beating until they have spelled out a further *v* and an *e*, at which point the distance swallows them and a deep silence blankets the Earth.

and

They wait, the long-dead Borgias, wait on the shores of Lochnagargoyle, allowing no clank of metal from their armor, no creak of leather from their saddles nor the rough *whurr* of a horse's exhaled breath to break the silence. Their faces are solemn but also attentive, alert, as if they are waiting in glad anticipation of something not yet here. Nowhere is this air of joyous expectation more evident than on the features of Raphael di Clemente Borgia, beloved son of Amelia, known to her family in her later years as Strega-Nonna.

No matter what dangers may still be lurking inside Strega-Schloss, the deep chill of a winter's night is no place for a woman who has recently given birth; thus Ludo Grabbit decides to take Baci indoors, come what may. They enter Strega-Schloss by the front door, Ludo leading the way, Ffup and the Sleeper bringing up the rear, Baci bearing the watchful changeling in her arms. For a moment there is no sound, save for the mournful honking call of a flock of geese flying landward from the loch. Then the changeling whimpers, for perhaps it has caught a faint whiff of charred demon, or perhaps it simply knows that in a house where love abides, its time is nearly over. Regardless of the reason, it whimpers and Baci responds automatically, pressing it closer to her breast, closer still so that it might hear her shy lullaby, for she is too embarrassed to sing out in front of this man, this Ludo whom she hardly knows. So she sings quietly, sings the first song that comes to mind, sings:

"Matthew, Mark, Luke, and John—"

. . . a song she's often heard Mrs. McLachlan humming to Damp . . .

"Bless the bed that I lie on—"

. . . her voice so soft that, turning along the corridor at the top of the stairs, Luciano at first thinks he is dreaming . . .

"Four corners to my bed, four angels round my head."

"Oh my God. My love. BACII*iiiii*—"

One of the effects of having earlier consumed far more than his fair share of cappuccino muffins is that, despite the rigors of his swim and subsequent conquest of several sand dunes, Titus is still full of seemingly boundless, caffeine-induced energy. As the deadly stone comes flying toward Damp, Titus is automatically reaching out to intercept it. As if on rails, the Chronostone sails into his outstretched hands, docking there with an audible slap.

It is Isagoth's demented shriek of fury that tells Titus what a prize he has caught, but then he hears a distant boom that suggests the Strega-Borgias' troubles are far from over.

Vesper lurches into overdrive. "Secure the dead broad," he

bawls, and to his relief, Damp responds exactly as he has taught her.

"Check," she says, wrapping a skein of spider silk around herself and anchoring this to Strega-Nonna's lifeless body.

At this, Pandora's mouth falls open. "Where did you learn how to do *that*?"

"Tan'tella showed me," Damp says, extruding more silk and wrapping it around herself, Titus, the baby, and, finally, Pandora, before returning to Strega-Nonna and repeating the entire procedure. Titus looks as if he might be about to vomit.

"I don't want to even *begin* to find out where that *stuff* is coming from." He shudders, trying and failing to extricate himself from its adhesive clasp.

"Jeez. You *guys*," Vesper groans. "Just cool it, huh? Save your energies."

"Here comth the wavth again," the salamander says, somewhat redundantly, because as Isagoth's Chronostone-enhanced power falls away, the old order comes crashing back, and the Light gains ascendancy over the Dark. The babbling seas return once more to replace Isagoth's Chronostone-enhanced vision of Hell, washing it away, brushing it aside as if it were no more than a bad dream.

This time the tide that comes foaming toward them is led by a vast, innumerable herd of white horses. Orynx is overjoyed, recognizing these beautiful creatures for what they really are: colleagues and descendants of the last Etheric Librarian, the one who Orynx witnessed refusing to give up the whereabouts of the Chronostone, even when his demon torturers set him alight. Orynx knows the Librarian only as "the one who got away," but Pandora knew him as the onetime custodian of the Chronostone, having once accompanied Mrs. McLachlan to the Etheric Library before its destruction by demons. Pandora knows more—knows the Librarian's name, which she now says out loud.

"Alpha?" she says, her voice hoarse with fear as the first wave of horses surges all around them, sweeping their feet out from under them as Pandora repeats the Librarian's name, screams it, all to no avail as they are pounded beneath white hooves and dragged under by a towering white tidal race. "ALPHAAAAAA?"

"Alpha is the beginning," Strega-Nonna explains, her voice kindly in Pandora's ears. "It is the first letter of the Greek alphabet, the place where everything has its birth."

A pause; then: "Child? I have the sense that you are drifting away, your thoughts elsewhere."

"Sorry," Pandora mumbles. "It's just . . . well . . . I don't want to sound rude or anything, but . . . I'm drowning here."

"Nonsense," Strega-Nonna snaps. "You cannot drown here, although some have tried. This is the sea of knowledge, a place that knows no beginning nor end."

"Nonna, I . . . er . . ." Pandora is uncertain about the rules of etiquette governing the discussion of death with one's newly deceased great-great-great-great-great-great-grandmother. On reflection, she decides that Vesper's label of "the dead broad," while woefully lacking in tact, has a great deal to recommend it in terms of brevity. All is blackness as against her a small body struggles, its weight such that it can only be Damp. Then she hears the unmistakable creak of oars in rowlocks, and hands are upon her, pulling, hauling her into a dinghy, briefly reminding her of Apollonius, of his hands dragging her into his hot-air balloon; but looking up, she sees that her current savior is no friendly ancestor. This figure, this hooded, shrouded thing hunched over the side of its rotted dinghy, is the epitome of what most humans spend their lives avoiding.

"NO!" she howls. "Get away. Get away from me—NOOO. AUGHHHHH. HELP!"

"Child. Would you calm down?" Strega-Nonna's icy hand is on hers, her face peering intently into her own. Behind her, Pandora can see Titus sitting ashen-faced in the boat's prow, and now the hooded thing is hauling Damp out of the water.

"But it's dead. And sorry, Nonna, but I was so sure you were de— de—"

"Quite," Strega-Nonna mutters. "He is, and I am too. Dead. Tact was never your strong suit, child."

Pandora tries to drag her gaze away from the fatal black mark in the middle of Strega-Nonna's throat.

"But the demon, Nonna. Where is—?"

"He'll be along presently," Strega-Nonna sighs. "I'm afraid we won't get rid of him that easily. However, thanks to your little sister, he can't touch us."

"Damp?" Pandora frowns. "What did she do?"

Strega-Nonna smiles. "So many questions. Always such an inquisitive child. Why don't you ask her? Maybe she'll teach you. But you'll have to wait. There isn't time now. We're here."

And the boat bumped ashore, back on the island once again.

Waiting for them by the fire was a thin man dressed in an impeccably tailored gray suit. He nodded to them in greeting, watching while they made their way toward him. As she approached, Pandora felt her blood turn to ice. It was as if she'd always known that one day, no matter what she did, she would come to stand in front of this person, bleating her excuses, avoiding his eyes, and utterly desperate to postpone the inevitable conclusion—

"My poor Pandora, you look like a rabbit caught in the headlights, and you, Titus, dear boy, calm yourself. Your presences here are accidental. Or should I say 'incidental'? *In* time, you will return to your lives, and *with* time, you will forget that you were ever my guests." The man bowed, his gray eyes heavy with foreknowledge, his expression full of compassion. Then he pulled himself up to his full height and turned to Strega-Nonna, but now his face was wreathed in smiles.

"My dearest lady," he said, his voice like liquid velvet, "I am delighted to welcome you into my realm at last."

Strega-Nonna hung her head in embarrassment, aware of how strenuously she'd sought to avoid this moment; how, in fact, she'd spent centuries evading this man, finding ever-more-elaborate ways to ensure she didn't end up as his guest.

"Now, now," he chided. "Don't be bashful. I know you've been avoiding me, and I've tried my hardest not to take it personally, but, Amelia, truly the only person you've been avoiding is yourself."

Strega-Nonna's shoulders began to shake as the man continued, his voice softer now, almost aching with sympathy. "All those hundreds of lonely years, Amelia. All those nights alone, dreaming of those you loved . . . and lost."

Strega-Nonna wept openly, and neither the presence of the baby boy in her arms nor that of Titus, Pandora, and Damp hugging her tight appeared to give her comfort.

"But you are out of your own time, Amelia. You have been lost in time for so long now, you cannot remember what it is not to be homesick. I can bring you release. I alone can bring you home. Come, my dear, lay down your burden, take my hand, and let me lead you home."

"STOP RIGHT THERE." A ghastly voice bellied out of the darkness, a voice that set Titus's teeth on edge and advanced the dial on his internal terror meter several notches into the red. "GIVE ME MY STONE," it continued, assaulting their eardrums, the words distorted by the raw power behind their projection.

"Quickly"—the man in the suit spread his hands wide— "the sooner you come to me and pass over that pesky stone for safekeeping, the sooner we can dispatch that demon back to where he belongs."

"Ba-bye," Damp whispered, her face upturned to Strega-Nonna as if trying to imprint the old lady's face forever in her memory.

"YOU STUPID OLD *WITCH*," the voice roared. "YOU THINK YOU CAN DEFY ME?"

"Nonna"—Pandora realized she was crying—"I love you. We all love you, we always will, but . . . you *must* go. Now."

"YES," the voice mocked. *"YOU GO, AND I'LL EAT THE KIDS. SO GET A MOVE ON. STIR YOUR STUMPS, BE-CAUSE I'M GETTING A TAD PECKISH HERE. FEE, FI, FO, FUM . . ."*

"Don't be silly." Damp heaved a sigh, mortally affronted at this misusage of one of her favorite fairy tales. "We're not playing 'Jackan Binstork.' We're doing *Maffew, Mark, Lucan, John.*"

Isagoth froze, his face a picture of horror. There it was again. That awful spell. Deep inside, he knew he wouldn't be able to survive hearing it a second time. He was already running into the water as Damp reached the third stanza. "AUGHHH. STOP. NO. SHUT THE *TROLL* UP. Make it STO-OP. My poor *ears.* Aaaaaughh—" The hateful voice abruptly cut off as Isagoth dived beneath the surface in an attempt to put himself beyond the range of Damp's unbeliev-ably potent spell.

"Nonna"—Titus's voice was thick with unshed tears—"give me the baby and go. Don't worry. We'll be fine. We'll never forget you. We love you. *Go.*"

Strega-Nonna stood, hesitating for one second, drinking in the features of her youngest descendant before passing him over to Titus. He, in turn, removed the Chronostone from his pocket and handed it over to the gray-eyed man.

"Blasted nuisance, this," the man muttered to himself, tuck-ing it into his pocket and returning his attention to Strega-Nonna. "Come on, then, m'dear. Let's be having you."

As if unconsciously following instructions for a rite of

passage, Titus solemnly removed the poultry shears from his back pocket and cut the thread of spider silk binding Strega-Nonna to her living kin. From overhead came the lonesome calls of geese flying inland, their flock arranged in a broken circle like a lion's head.

Strega-Nonna smiled, stepped forward into the elegant embrace of Death . . .

. . . and was gone.

The Past Is Another Country

A smell of wet ashes and old bonfires clung to the air as Mrs. McLachlan peered round the door into the wreckage of the Ancestors' Room. Paintings hung askew, some so blackened by smoke that it was impossible to tell what their subjects had ever been. Wings drooping, Ffup crept through the doorway behind the nanny, visibly aghast at the damage done.

"What a *mess*," the dragon breathed, slowly turning full circle, her golden eyes wide. Icy rain blew through huge holes in the masonry where Ffup had smashed through walls and windows in her haste to reach Baci and Ludo. Decaying lily pads from the moat were smeared across the walls after they'd been vacuumed up and hosed back out by the Sleeper in his role as chief fire-fighter.

Mrs. McLachlan didn't appear to notice; she picked her way across swampy wet carpets and squeezed past toppled furniture until she reached the fireplace. It was as if a vast bonfire had blazed there, the floorboards burned away entirely to expose the beams beneath, the wooden skeleton of Strega-Schloss. The walls to either side of the fireplace were sticky with tar, the silk fleur-de-lis wallpaper burned away to reveal twisted veins of electrical wiring that poked out from the cracked plaster. Flora McLachlan moaned, reaching out to place one hand against the wall for support.

"It's okay. Don't panic. I'm rrright here." Ffup crashed toward the nanny, her paws splashing across the sodden carpets. "Talk about overkill, huh?" she prattled nervously, guiltily aware that she and the Sleeper had caused far more damage by their fire-extinguishing efforts than the actual fire itself. "I'm sure I could dry out some of these wet rugs myself, if that would help. . . . You know, sort of gently toast them, with both nostrils . . ." Her voice tailed off as she saw that Mrs. McLachlan's face was awash with tears. "Awww, no," she whispered. "Don't cry. It'll be all right. We can make it better. Don't worry. It's okay." And running out of words of comfort, the dragon awkwardly folded the weeping nanny into the vast embrace of her wings.

It was this strange tableau that greeted Latch as he came along the corridor toward the Ancestors' Room. Its door lay open, and he could see Ffup and Flora framed therein, the blackened walls only enhancing the funereal air of deep sadness that hung over StregaSchloss that evening. Latch had just come upstairs after making a pot of tea in the wreckage of the kitchen and taking a tray through to the library, where his employers sat mute and ghostlike, their hands clasped, their eyes rimmed with red. Ludo Grabbit and Miss Araminta had also fallen silent, their tentative words of comfort falling on deaf ears as Signor and Signora Strega-Borgia came to terms with the knowledge that their deepest fears had been realized.

All the children gone, Latch thought. All gone, save for that changeling monstrosity lying in a baby carrier in a corner of the library, its continued presence an affront to the grieving Strega-Borgias. He'd come upstairs to find Flora, to beg her to use whatever magical powers she had to bring the children back. For Latch had been forced to realize that Flora was a witch, and though he wished it were not so, he knew in his secret heart that she would *always* be one; would always belong to some secret club to which he could never gain entry. In his naiveté, he'd half hoped that by becoming his betrothed, she'd miraculously undergo a complete personality change—like a leopard losing its spots, or a selkie choosing a permanent human form. . . . But Latch now knew that this would never happen. A part of Flora would always be beyond him, of this he was certain; he'd seen her eyes when she believed herself to be unobserved, fixed upon some distant place to which he, with his brief human life span, would be unable to travel. He'd hoped . . .

Och, but there was no place for him or his foolish hopes now. Flora was the one person who stood any chance of finding those poor children; not only of finding them, but of returning them to their devastated parents. He called out then, called her name and saw her break free of the dragon's embrace and turn to face him. . . . And then his heart clenched with pity, because at that moment he saw in her face no sign of sorcery, occult self-possession, or witchery; saw only a middle-aged woman whose heart appeared to be breaking as she stumbled toward him, blinded by grief and displaying a kind of vulnerability of which he had not expected her to be capable.

Embarrassed beyond words, Ffup turned her back on the couple; then she whistled loudly as she waddled around the room, righting fallen furniture and, somewhat pointlessly, straightening ruined paintings against walls so blackened by fire they were in obvious need of replastering.

"I'm . . . uh . . . aiming for a kind of minimalistic, post-modern effect here," she babbled, filling up the silence with stream-of-consciousness off-the-top-of-her-head nonsense. "You know, I'm actually rather *fond* of black as a color, really. It's sort of restful, don't you think? And I've been thinking about the furniture . . . well . . . it *was* wayyy past its sell-by date, wasn't it? All those antiques. So *gloomy*. All that heavy brocade—just a dust magnet. I think what this room really needs is a complete makeover. If it was up to me, I'd chuck everything out and start again." She came to a halt in front of the fireplace and frowned. "I've never seen that picture before," she muttered, peering at the huge canvas hanging over the mantelpiece, "and I *know* I'd remember seeing it, because it's all about food. . . ." The dragon leaned forward, her long nose nearly touching the canvas; then she recoiled rapidly, her eyes widening in shock as she reached out a trembling paw to check whether her initial impression had been correct. "Spoookeee . . . ," she whispered, backing away from the picture and practically falling over Mrs. McLachlan in her haste.

"What's spooky, dear?"

Ffup peered at Flora and tactfully decided not to mention the fact that the nanny's eyeballs looked like they'd been marinating in tomato soup. "This painting. It's . . . the paint's still wet, like it's just been painted. . . . Look, see for yourself—"

But Flora McLachlan was there already, with Latch right behind her, both of them grabbing whatever came to hand, dragging items of furniture over to the fireplace, piling a chair on top of a desk and a footstool on top of that.

"Bring me back something to eat," Ffup wailed, realizing that she was about to be left behind, since she was far too big to squeeze through the gilt frame into the painting beyond.

The painting was a classic still life, its centerpiece a deceased fowl laid out on a pewter plate surrounded by fruits and fish and vegetables, everything chosen with an eye to composition rather than flavor. Thus, wild strawberries cozied up to a gaping sea trout, and grapes sat cheek by jowl with red onions.

Goblets filled with wine sat untouched, as if the diners, whoever they were, had been called from the table to some other, more urgent appointment, or perhaps to welcome a late-arriving guest.

For, Flora realized, her breath catching in her throat, it was a homecoming feast, and she was certain who the guest of honor would be. Turning back to check that Latch was with her, she saw the butler's ashen face, betraying his deep unease at passing through a gilt frame into the land of the paranormal. And yet, she marveled, he hadn't hesitated to come with her, even though he could have had no idea what dangers may have lain ahead. Love had brought him to her side, to this place that existed hundreds of years before he'd been born.

Latch looked at her, wondering to himself who she really was; wondering just how many lives she'd lived before she'd arrived on StregaSchloss's doorstep, slipping into his life as if she'd always been there. He'd never asked, never pried into her past, because he was afraid of what he might find; and she, in turn, had rarely spoken of her previous life; had hoped to leave the past behind when she became nanny to the Strega-Borgia children. It had been the discovery that Damp was a magus that had blown Flora's cover. To protect the little girl, she'd been forced to act in ways that demonstrated clearly that she was a great deal more than just a children's nanny: was, in fact, a sorceress in her own right. That much Latch had understood. What he had yet to discover was that Flora McLachlan was cursed with immortality. It was her fate to watch those she loved wither and die, while she was forced to live on and on forever. She was ageless and unchanging, wandering the Earth alone, yet not alone; human, yet lacking the certainty of her own death that is at the core of what it is to be human.

Thus Flora McLachlan, more than anyone, felt the loss of Strega-Nonna, her friend and companion for over six hundred years. Flora instantly recognized the food on the table, the logs burning in the brazier, the distant view of the hills through the arched window: all these were as familiar to her as her own self. She had dined in this room, long, long ago, with a younger Amelia newly delivered of a son, Raphael di Clemente, asleep at her breast, and with Amelia's young husband, yet to die in battle, his face flushed from the wine they had drunk to toast the safe arrival of their firstborn. . . .

Looking around the deserted room, Flora saw she had no place here now. The ancestors would be bringing Amelia home, all of them turning out to welcome her at last into their company. No, she did not belong here, she realized, looking up at Latch, whose eyes shone for her alone.

"I love you, lassie," he whispered, the unaccustomed words kindling a fire in the middle of his chest as he continued, "and I'll always love you, even if this is all we ever have. The short time I've known you has been better than the whole of my life was before you came. . . . I . . . you . . ."

She placed a hand over his mouth then, because his words had moved her so much it took all her self-control not to break down and weep like a baby. Later, when the children were safely home, *then* she could draw comfort from his embrace and, for a while at least, put the aching loneliness of her immortality to one side and become his wife. But for the moment, for now, they had much work to do.

Grimmer Than Grimm

Ffup crept disconsolately downstairs, avoiding the almost palpable atmosphere of grief that hung outside the library. Without words of comfort to offer her master and mistress, the dragon trailed down to the dungeons to find Nestor. She heard the murmur of voices in the dark below, and she smiled to hear the Sleeper reading a bedtime story to his little boy. When Ffup rounded the final corner and came upon the candlelit huddle curled in the straw, she saw that the Sleeper had adapted the bedtime fable from "Little Red Riding Hood" into something more along the lines of *The Company of Wolves*. Gone was the endangered child in her red cape, gone too the kindly grandmother and the heroic woodcutter. Ffup held her breath and froze, not wishing to

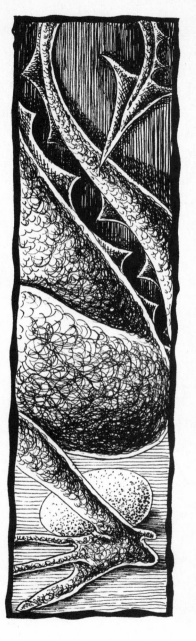

break the spell cast by the Sleeper's words, a spell that not only held Nestor in thrall but had also cast an enchantment over the many members of the wolf pack sprawling across the little dragon's nest.

"Little Red Ride in the Hood shrieked tae a stop ootside Granny's bender and rolled doon her windae. Loud thumpin' music poured oot, disturbin' a' the wee burds an' deer and aw they forest beasties fir miles aroond.

" 'Haw, Granny,' the wean yelled. 'Check this oot. This here's ma brand-new sawn-aff shotgun wi' its serial numbers filed aff. Let's go an' kill soma they wolves, eh?' "

Ffup winced. What sort of bedtime story was *this*, pray, for a little tot? Nestor would have nightmares for *weeks* if it continued. Ffup was unable to forget the time she had read him "Goldenhair and the Three Dragons," when the poor mite had been unable to be parted from his porridge bowl for *months*. No, no, no, she decided, enough of this violence. No guns, no dead wolves, no hood, no thumpy music, no . . . "AOWWWWWW!" she shrieked, bending over double, eyes crossed in agony.

Immediately, the wolves sprang to their feet, hackles up and teeth bared at the unexpected intrusion of this shrieking dragoness. The Sleeper gave a roar of alarm.

"Ehhhh? Och, *wumman*. Dinnae sneak up on us like that. You nearly made me keech ma breeks."

In between gasps, Ffup pointed out that the Sleeper didn't *wear* breeks, and if he was so inconsiderate as to *keech* in the middle of her nice clean dungeon, then he'd have to clear it up—but by then she was hardly able to speak for pain, so her domestic tirade lost something of its passion, and in fact was practically indistinguishable from her wails and sobs of agony.

"OW. Not *this* again. Oh heck. NOOOOOO. I thought second time round was s'posed to be EASY. A cakewalk, Mrs. McLachlan said. The lying toad. Ahhhhowwww."

The Sleeper dropped Nestor's storybook and was by Ffup's side in an instant. "Fit'sa matter, hen?"

"GOD! How many TIMES?" Ffup squeaked. "I'm not a bloody chicken, I'm aaaaaAAARGH, a DRAaaaaarghon." Effortfully, she hauled herself into a squatting position and, realizing that they were not alone, glared at the wolves. "Do you lot *have* to stare at me like that? If I don't die in dragon-birth, then I'll undoubtedly die of embarrassment with all of you staring at me. Shoo—go awayyy—give me some PEEEEEEace. OWwwwww. HELLLLLLLLP."

The Sleeper looked poleaxed, eyes round, mouth agape, the remains of his dinner still flecking his vast teeth with decaying greenery. Nestor had wisely turned his back on his mother's hysterics and was attempting to press a wolf into service as a pillow while persuading two more to drape themselves on top of him like hairy duvets. Then, as if he suddenly understood what was required of him, the Sleeper came out of his trance and rose to the occasion magnificently.

"Whit can ah dae to help? D'youse want a wee drinka water? Or d'youse want me tae rub yer back . . . ?"

Ffup lurched forward and clung to the Sleeper with her forepaws, her talons digging painfully into the gaps between his scales.

"No!" she squeaked. "Just . . . be . . . ready . . . tocatchthebaby."
Then all further conversation was curtailed as she concentrated on the task at hand. "Nnnngh, rrURGHH."

Catch the baby? The Sleeper was somewhat surprised by this. Was she going to fling the bairn at him? He hoped not.

"Ow, ow, ow, AUGHHHH nnngh."

Problem wis, he wis totally useless at catching things. Ham-fisted tae the max. Hand-tae-ee'n coordination never being his thing. An' he wis never picked for the football team, eh no? Whit . . . whit if he *drapped* it?

"PUFF, puff, PUFF, puffpuffpuff FFUP, ffup."

Wid it smash? Wid she ever forgive him? Widn't wee Nestor be traumatized for life at the sight of yon newborn bairn trickling across the flair? The Sleeper risked a peek at his firstborn, but the little dragon's eyes were squinched shut, his body snug under its twin-wolf duvet, one little paw clutching the ears of his hairy pillow.

"OHHHHHhhhhhhhhhhhhhhhhh," Ffup gasped, and there, with a squelch and a pop, miraculously, on the straw beneath her vent lay a beautiful speckled blush-pink egg.

The Sleeper was enchanted. "Ma wee BAIRN," he whispered, looking from the egg to its mother in amazement. "Och, pet, you're jist a wee star, so youse are. Ah'm that proud, ah could burst."

Ffup toppled sideways, her legs giving way as she collapsed onto the straw with an exhausted groan. She lay still for a moment, then stretched blissfully, able to roll onto her deflated belly for the first time in ages, luxuriating in the knowledge that she wouldn't have to do *that* again . . . at least, not for a while.

"Kin ah get youse anything, ma wee pet?" The Sleeper towered over her, his expression that of someone who has only just, by a completely happy accident, managed to successfully disarm an atom bomb. Expressions of relief, awe, gratitude, guilt, and stunned disbelief flickered across his face like shadows, and his paws were clasped together as if he were praying that Ffup would set him a task, send him on an errand, ask him to do anything that might not involve too much in the way of mopping up after dragonbirth. Ffup grinned from ear to ear. Rolling the egg toward herself, she gave a tremulous, girly sigh and sank back into the straw.

"Ohhhh," she breathed, her voice so faint that the Sleeper feared for one ghastly moment that she might expire in front of him like a snuffed candle. "That would be just sooo terribly kind of you," she whispered, deciding that a little nibble might be in order. "Let's see. . . . Well, I'd love a cup—no, a *pot*—of Lapsang Souchong tea, then . . . um . . . a round of toast—that's *six* slices—in fact, better make it *two* rounds, then, with butter and honey. That'll do for starters, but *then* I'd be ready for some bacon sandwiches—BLTs would be perfect, *if* those feckless humans have remembered to buy any L and T, not to mention the B. . . . Some cake too. A muffin or twelve: banana, vanilla, and white chocolate are my all-time favorites. . . . Er, perhaps more tea to wash that lot down, and then I think I'd be almost strong enough to move on to the champagne and smoked salmon, don't you?"

The Sleeper's mouth fell open in stunned disbelief. For a beast who'd appeared to be on Death's doorstep a scant ten seconds previously, Ffup had made an astounding recovery. And her *appetite*? This was perhaps not the best of times to remind his fiancée of her vow to squeeze into her size double-D, wedding gown, a goal that required her to eat like a sparrow instead of a tyrannosaurus. . . . Wisely, the Sleeper clamped his lips shut, dropped a kiss on Ffup's head, blew another to the new egg, and undulated off upstairs to see what he could rustle up.

Also preoccupied with the subject of food, the Strega-Borgia children huddled round the little island campfire like refugees, cold, hungry, frightened, and trying to keep the darkness at bay by telling stories. Damp clung to Pandora, and the new baby peered out from inside Titus's sweatshirt, his navy eyes wide as his big brother rolled a driftwood log into the flames and jumped back when a shower of sparks was launched into the night sky.

"When we get back," Titus said, for what had to be about the six-millionth time, "I'm going to put in a request for Mrs. McLachlan to bake a batch of her raspberry muffins—" He paused, suddenly struck by a happy thought. "Pan, *Pan!*" His voice leapt an octave with excitement. "Allrrrrright! Remember the Multiplimuffin? If there were any crumbs from it in my pockets, would they be magical like it too?"

Pandora puzzled over this, uncertain what the answer would be. The Multiplimuffin, as its name implied, was an automatically multiplying, self-regenerating cake; thus, each bite taken from it was magically replaced, so that it was impossible to consume it in its entirety. Unknown to Pandora, Titus had once decided to find out what would happen if he swallowed the whole cake in one big gulp. This was most emphatically *not* an experiment he ever cared to repeat, but it had taught him an unforgettable lesson about the dangers of greed. Now Pandora watched him as he dug through his pockets, frantically turning each one inside out in an attempt to unearth even a single, solitary crumb of magical muffin. As he sifted through his pockets, he remembered the broken teapot spout he'd tucked into his waistband some hours before. Pretty amazing that it hadn't smashed, he thought, extracting it from his jeans and wondering what on earth had possessed him to put it there in the first place. After all, he reasoned, it was a totally worthless bit of china, and he was on the point of flinging it into the sea when it spoke.

"Don't even *think* about doing that, dear boy," it had said.

Well . . . perhaps not *it*, exactly, he realized, stifling a scream of terror as a clutch of furry legs blossomed from one end of the spout, closely followed by the equally hairy abdomen of the Strega-Borgias' very own teapot-teleporting tarantula, Tarantella, spider extraordinaire. Emerging unscathed from the remains of her teapot portal, she peered around with the jaded air of a frequent flier forced to make an unscheduled landing at an airport in the back of beyond.

"*This* place," she groaned. "Lordy. Not *again*. Whatever possessed you to pitch up here?" She scampered along Titus's arm and scuttled onto his shoulder, vaulting onto his earlobe and hence onto the crown of his head, giving him the temporary appearance of a person wearing an animated topknot.

"Shame you're all such *giants*," she said, her many eyes measuring the children as if calculating exactly how many limbs they would have to shed before they conformed to her criteria. "If you were a tad smaller, we could all have squeezed into my teapot spout and traveled to somewhere less . . . watery."

Mention of Tarantella's teapot reminded Pandora of home: of the kitchen at StregaSchloss and the comfort of family rituals like dinner. Pandora's stomach growled, a long serenade to wish fulfillment, an audible tribute to her dad's authentic Italian cooking—his wine-rich pasta sauces, his saffron risottos, and his divinely garlicky rosemary-studded *arista alla fiorentina*. Then, to counterbalance this dad-based reminiscence, came a blissful memory of her mum's perfect picnics— Baci was, by tacit agreement, a dreadful cook, but she was a marvelous assembler of feasts to pack in a wicker basket. . . . Pandora could practically *see* the picnic basket now, so hungry was she. It had leather straps securing its lid, and there was always a distinctive protesting creak of wicker as she lifted the lid, the smell of picnics past rising up like ghosts from within. It was such an evocative memory that Pandora could have sworn she could hear the creaking of wicker coming from nearby, but that . . .

That wasn't possible . . .

. . . *was it?*

She looked up then, because Damp was wriggling and

struggling to escape from her arms, calling out excitedly, and Titus was actually running flat out across the pebbly shore, his arms upstretched to grab the long rope that dangled, impossibly . . .

. . . gloriously from the rim of the huge wicker gondola of a hot-air balloon that dropped out of the sky, down toward them, its silk panels illuminated in the darkness as Latch squeezed the bellows and fanned air across the charcoal burner that kept the balloon aloft.

Deep Chill

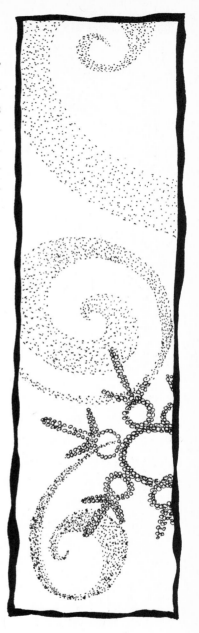

"**M**ust be my lucky day," the duty demon muttered, stomping across the dirty snow between the admissions block and the portakabin to which he and his fellow demons adjourned for their morning vitriol break. Dawn was breaking in Hades, the temperature was seventy degrees below zero, and a blizzard had just blown in from the east.

"Shut the DOOR!" shrieked the off-duty demons, all of them huddled round a brazier that, judging by the stench, was burning a heady mix of old French-fry fat, rendered trolls, and briquettes of the dried by-product of the Hadean sewage works. Despite the rank odors swirling round the portakabin, the demons had already unpacked their breakfast pails and were devouring the contents with every evidence of enjoyment.

The duty demon reached for the kettle suspended over the brazier and poured himself a steaming goblet of hot vitriol, tipping this caustic brew down his throat before attempting to speak.

"Hey, compadres, guess who's back in town?"

The off-duty demons unanimously ignored this, their entire attention focused on what really mattered: namely, the consumption of enough calories to stay alive at seventy degrees below zero.

The duty demon wasn't put off. Draining his vitriol goblet, he continued, "Whoo-eee, we sure do live in interesting times. I tell you, brothers and sisters, when the Executive find out who I have a-waiting in my little shed, the fur's really going to hit the fan. . . ."

No takers. The off-duty demons stolidly munched on, paying their colleague as much attention as if he were a strip of wallpaper.

"Fine. Suit yo'selves. When y'all can't get a ringside seat at the Public Cringe and Mortification Trial, don't come running to me. Y'all heard it here first. Or, as the case may be, y'all stopped up yo' ears and plain *refused* to hear it here first." And flinging open the door onto a shrieking swirl of snowflakes, the demon returned to his duties.

In the joy of their reunion with all four missing children, neither Latch nor Mrs. McLachlan had thought to stand guard over the balloon. Crawling out of the sea and across the pebbly shore, the demon Isagoth couldn't at first believe his good fortune. Never one to miss an opportunity, even if it was *Heaven*-sent, the demon seized this chance to escape. Before anyone realized what was going on, he had cast off the ropes tying the balloon to a tree and was aloft, soaring out over the water without so much as a backward glance or even a parting gloat. The first to notice what had happened, Titus dug deep into his cache of forbidden oaths for extreme circumstances, but even as they left his mouth, he knew he was wasting his breath. Isagoth wasn't going to come back, and without the hot-air balloon they were all marooned.

Mrs. McLachlan swaddled the new baby in her cardigan and Latch piled wood upon the fire, but it was obvious they couldn't stay outside in the cold for much longer. Titus wasn't sure, but he was beginning to suspect that immersion in the sea followed by hours inside his soaking-wet sweatshirt had been very bad for the health of the geriatric clones. He didn't want to look—he'd seen quite enough death for one day—but the complete absence of movement inside his shirt tended to indicate that the clones had perished. Soon, if they didn't find shelter, this would also become *their* fate. Pandora had fallen silent, as had Damp. Orynx and Vesper were nowhere to be seen, and even Tarantella was remarkably quiet.

Mrs. McLachlan broke the silence with a loud and heartfelt *tsssssk*.

"Oh, very *well*, then, dear," she said, shaking her head as if she were reluctantly giving permission for some as-yet-indefinable act.

Damp's face lit up.

"My wee pet," Mrs. McLachlan said. "Much as it goes against the grain to ask you to do this, I have no alternative. We need to return home by whatever means possible. Now, I know you've been itching to cast a big spell for ages, so this is your chance."

By now, Damp was practically glowing with anticipation. Inwardly ticking off spells she'd already done—*Sleeping Boaty, did that; Thumbleener, did that too; Cindreller; Snoke Ween, not wantit that one*—she looked up for inspiration just as a single snowflake drifted down from the darkness above like a white feather.

Damp stretched out her arms, took a deep breath, and spun her best and brightest enchantment ever.

There were three new admissions in Hades that morning: a human colander, a fat guy, and a big mean-looking bloke who radiated ill will. Predictably, all three were loudly demanding special treatment, as befitted their exalted status. Groaning, the duty demon stabbed at a key on his computer and invited the new admissions to step forward one at a time. It was always the same, he thought, gloomily avoiding eye contact with the three men, who were jockeying for first place in the queue and pleading ignorance of Hadean protocol. Always the same old same old. Every time. Claiming that if they'd only *known* Hell was going to be this bad, they'd've mended their ways.

Yeah, right.

The duty demon rolled his eyes in disgust and began to log

them into his computer. "Name?" he yawned into the face of the human colander.

"Don Lucifer di S'Embowelli Borgia, but there's been some kinda mistake—"

"Nope. No mistake, bud. You did the crime, now you have to do the time."

"But, but . . . I'm a very important guy. I'm a made man. I got connections all over could put you inna hospital if they heard about this. You gotta show me some respect—"

"Y'all finished yet?" The duty demon raked Don Lucifer with a withering glance. "See," he continued, his brown and stumpy teeth bared in a hideous smirk, "I've heard it all before, me. None of it cuts any ice here in the Big Freezy. Y'all got an unbreakable appointment with the barbecue pit, and me, I've got more important things to do. NEEEEEEEXT."

"Oh puhlease, don't pretend you don't recognize me." The fat man sighed. "Let's just cut to the chase, shall we?"

The duty demon made no attempt to hide his contempt. "Which name are y'all using now? S'tan? The Boss? Or"—he sniggered—"or perhaps you'd prefer to be known as our long-lost First Minestrone, the Earl of Yellow-Belly and Prince of Dorkness?"

"Yeah, yeah." The fat man shook his head sadly. "So . . . things didn't exactly work out for me, huh? But I tell you what, I've got a sensational recipe for rowan jelly. . . ."

"Manual Sewage Removal Operative for you, pal." The duty demon smiled nastily. "NEEEEEXT?"

"I THINK YOU KNOW WHO I AM." Isagoth's voice

sounded as if it was being broadcast straight out of the Abyss; it was a sound to inspire the deepest of deep fear in all who heard it, a sound that caused Don Lucifer's ears to bleed and S'tan's bowels to turn to water.

The duty demon didn't dare hesitate. Pressing the red panic button beneath his desk, he flung himself onto the floor at Isagoth's cloven feet, prostrated himself in front of Hades' one-time Defense Minister and now Prince-Apparent of Deepest Darkness. "Maaarsturrr," the demon breathed. "Y'all welcome home, hear?"

The Deepest Fear

Afraid to allow themselves to fall asleep, Baci and Luciano spent the whole of that terrible night awake, staring into the fire, as if the answers they sought lay with the silent tongues of flame flickering in the hearth. In its basket near the fireplace, the changeling slept soundly, its breath as mechanical as the ticking clock marking the hours on the mantelpiece. First Minty and then Ludo fell asleep in the fire's warm glow, too tired to keep vigil with the grieving Strega-Borgias. As the first gray light appeared in the sky, Baci and Luciano stood, stretched, and quietly left the room, tiptoeing downstairs to shroud themselves in coats and scarves before slipping outside into the cold dawn.

As they crossed the frosted meadow, Baci's hand sought

Luciano's, and hot tears began to spill down her face. Still, they did not speak, neither of them wishing to frame the terrible words to confirm all that they had lost. Their breath hung in white clouds in front of their mouths as they picked their way down the bramble-lined path to the jetty. Everywhere lay beauty: diamonds of frost studding the carpet of autumn leaves; frozen tears of rainwater beading the bare twigs of the oaks; and all around, the air so cold and sweet that each inhalation brought a reminder that they were still very much alive.

Luciano gritted his teeth, wishing he were surrounded by a landscape that mirrored his feelings—a bleak, godforsaken desert devoid of life and hope, not this exquisite vista that in happier times they had regarded as their very own Christmas card. Thoughts of Christmas caused Luciano to nearly pass out with loss—the unutterable horror of all those empty, childless days and years stretching out ahead made him wish he were dead alongside Titus, Pandora, Damp, and Little No-Name. He turned then, turned to face his wife, wondering if to fall prey to despair was really such a terrible thing, wondering if they might find a way to escape the awful heartache together. They could simply walk out onto the frozen loch, step by step, hand in hand, hoping that way to be reunited with their beloved children.

Titus, Pandora, Damp, and Little No-Name.

Baci's hand in his tightened as the first tentative flakes of snow began to fall from the sky.

Titus, Pandora, Damp, and Little No-Name—

Luciano's feet stepped in time to the litany of their names.

Now he and Baci were out on the jetty, their boots making hollow echoes across the ice imprisoning the loch shore in its frozen grasp.

Titus, Pandora, Damp, and Little No-Name—

And now they stood poised at the end of the jetty with nowhere to go but back to the unbearable pain of the days ahead or . . .

A flock of birds flew toward the shore, the beat of their laboring wings audible across the silent loch.

Seven white swans, Luciano thought, still alert to all the beauty of the world he was considering leaving.

Seven swans. Like the story, Baci thought, her eyes stinging with tears as she recalled winter evenings spent reading to all three children just as she knew in her heart she would never read the same stories ever again.

Seven swans fluttering down to land on the unfrozen water in the middle of the loch, their feet paddling frantically beneath them, voices raised in wonder at the miracle of their flight.

"Anyone got any ideas what swans eat? I'm *ravenous*."

"Oh, Latch, my dearest, if only you could have seen the look on your *face* . . ."

"That was soooo seriously cool. I've *always* wanted wings. However, my legs are totally freezing—d'you think I'd look stupid wearing tights?"

"These ridiculous birds could undoubtedly use more legs. . . . How you lot ever manage with only two is quite beyond my understanding—"

"You know, Flora, I could get used to this flying business.

And feathers? Never in my wildest dreams did I ever imagine I'd enjoy having a wee feathery undercarriage. . . ."

"Wheeee*eeee*, lookit me. Mumma, look. LOOK!"

"Waaaaaaaaaaaaaaaah . . ."

Titus, Pandora, Damp, and Little No-Name.

Luciano was running now, his voice echoing across the ice as he called his children home, reeling them ashore on the thread of their names.

As snow falls like feathers from the sky, the giant birds are surrounding him in a cloud of swirling white, their wide wings beating, beating, beating like a glad heart.

Name That Baby

Luciano stood in front of his mirror, knotting a sky-blue silk tie and trying to ignore the fact that, behind him, Baci was teetering on the brink of a full-blown wardrobe crisis.

"I'm still so *fat*," she howled, heaving at the zipper on her velvet skirt and turning pink with the effort. "Hate my bum. HUGE. Back end of a tractor trailer. God. *Why* aren't I back to normal? Ugh. LOOK, Luciano, who's that wibbly blob in the mirror? Please, tell me that's not meeeeee—"

And just before she dissolved into tears for the fourth time in as many minutes, Luciano wrapped her in his arms.

"*Cara mia,*" he breathed into her hair, "hush. It was only one week ago that you carried our Little No-Name under your own

skin—you're still a brand-new *mama*, not a supermodel, for heaven's—"

There was a warning shriek from the bedroom, and both Luciano and Baci froze.

Looking somewhat haunted, Luciano whispered, "You just *fed* him. Surely he's not due another feed for hours?"

"Are you sure that's our baby?" Baci hissed, frantically fastening buttons and dragging a brush through her hair. The warning shriek became an extended peal of outrage, and Luciano's shoulders slumped.

"No. It's the other baby," he groaned, aware that if the star of the day, Little No-Name-about-to-be-named, was still sleeping, then it meant that someone, probably him, would have to deal with the changeling instead.

"Darling"—Baci paused in mid-brush—"we really have to name them *both* today. We can't go on calling them Little No-Name and the Other Baby."

Luciano rolled his eyes at his reflection, then headed for the bedroom. Baby Borgia lay sleeping soundly in the ancestral cradle; wailing his head off in his basket was the changeling. Gritting his teeth, Luciano bent down and plucked the sobbing goblin out from its tangled shawl. Immediately, the wailing stopped, replaced by an ominous silence. From bitter experience, Luciano calculated that he had approximately two minutes to feed the changeling with an acceptable Baci substitute before it sank its needle teeth into the portion of Luciano's anatomy nearest to its gaping mouth. Holding it at arm's length, Luciano set off for the kitchen as fast as he dared.

Skidding round the balustrade at the bottom of the stairs

leading into the great hall, Luciano nearly crashed into Pandora, who had risen up out of the shadows like a wraith.

"Waaargh. *Dad*. Jeez, you nearly flattened me."

Despite the changeling hissing in his arms like a burning fuse, Luciano paused and stared. What on *earth* was she wearing? he wondered, gazing at his eldest daughter in dismay. Moths appeared to be hatching out of Pandora's—dress? coat? bathrobe? What *was* that thing?—as he watched. And black? Deepest funereal black, on today of all days. *And* eyeliner, dammit. He'd told her about makeup ages ago. Not just told her: *forbidden* her to wear it.

"*Pandora*. For *Pete's*—" Before he could complete this sentence, thus ensuring that she spent the rest of this special day in a mood every bit as black as her clothing, he was interrupted by the changeling, who demonstrated what happened when its fuse ran out. Clamping its teeth round his index finger, it leered up at him.

"AAAOWWWW—you little *monster*." He'd been about to say something far, far worse, but his daughter's presence made Luciano curb his tongue even as the changeling's teeth ground against his knuckle.

"Stop it, you disgusting little *creep*," Pandora gasped, reaching out and squeezing the changeling's nostrils shut. Unable to breathe, it let go of Luciano's finger and screamed with thwarted rage.

Luciano placed it on the floor in front of him and took several steps backward, as if afraid that the infant might explode. Pandora remained within range, shaking her head in disbelief.

"Tell me that thing isn't being named along with our baby?"

Luciano sighed. "Your mother—she has a soft heart. You know she'd feel really bad if we left it . . . that . . . the creature out."

"Dad. That's *insane*. It's not like it's a member of the family. It's a goblin, for heaven's sake. It's like something out of a book. What're you going to call it, anyway? Rumpelstiltskin?"

At this, there was a demonic shriek from the changeling as it literally turned purple with rage. It began to batter its heels and fists on the floor with such hell-bent ferocity that the very walls of StregaSchloss seemed to tremble around it. To Luciano's dismay, a huge crack appeared, zigzagging its way across the stone floor of the great hall. It gaped wider and wider until the changeling tipped over the edge, scrabbled frantically in an attempt to pull itself back out, and then, with a ghastly howl . . . was gone.

Luciano blinked. Had he really just seen that? Even as he watched, the crack began to shrink, emitting a faraway clashing, grinding sound—the noise made by tectonic plates moving far below the surface of the Earth. Just before the floor became whole again, two items of infant apparel were vomited back out of the crack, both somewhat charred: one diaper, hardly used, followed by one crumpled pair of sleepers, both utterly reeking of sulfur.

"Huh?" Luciano took a deep breath. So I married a student witch, he reminded himself. I should have expected no less. He peered at his daughter, dimly aware that he'd been about to say something deeply tedious and wrinkly-orientated about her eye shadow or her moth-eaten—what *was* that thing she was wearing?—costume. Then he pulled himself together. A scant week ago, he'd been on the verge of throwing himself into the loch because he'd lost his children. Now here they were, safe, sound, hale, hearty—and what was he doing? Nagging them about something as trivial as eye makeup?

Too right.

"Pan*dora*. Wash that muck off your face before the guests arrive—"

Ludo's Land Rover rattled across the rose quartz drive and then blithely plowed straight on to smack into an ornamental stone urn, much to the detriment of the Land Rover's front bumper.

"Bloody *hell*," Ludo moaned, climbing out to inspect the damage. For the fortieth time that morning, he patted the inside pocket of his jacket to check that the tiny green velvet box was indeed still there. It was. However, that was only half the story. He still had to remove it from his pocket and offer it to her. Would she laugh in his face? Would she gently turn him down? Would she take offense? Tell him exactly where to stick the exquisite sapphire-and-diamond ring that had been in his family since . . . since . . .

"Mr. Grabbit, your poor *car*."

Oh Lord. It would have to be her, wouldn't it? Before he could separate the bloody urn from the even bloodier bump—

"Can I help?" And there she was beside him, her impossibly lavender-blue eyes shining, as he, for the first time in his entire life, found himself absolutely at a loss for words.

"Champagne, sir?"

"Please, Latch. I'd love some. We've all got plenty to celebrate today, hmm?"

"Absolutely, sir."

Ludo waited until Latch had filled his glass before saying, "Any idea where we might find our host? Can't see him anywhere."

"I'd try the game room, sir. I believe I saw him heading in that direction a while ago."

"Splendid. And Latch?"

"Sir?"

"I'd say this family should count itself darned fortunate to have you looking after all its members. Last week. Kept your head when all around were losing theirs. Good stuff."

"Thank you, sir. Will that be all, sir?"

"Hopefully, yes. For the time being, at least."

"Very good, sir."

Luciano's voice came from beyond the open door to the game room. As Ludo approached, he could hear it, rising and falling, at times subdued, at times almost breaking with suppressed emotion.

"You know, I never meant— We never— I only wish . . . But you, you tried to kill my wife— But even so, I didn't mean to— Oh, what have I done? How can I *ever* forgive myself?"

"Forgive my interrupting, Luciano. Can I come in?" And without waiting for a reply, Ludo stepped into the game room.

Luciano looked up, his hands slowly falling away from his

face, revealing features made haggard by the cold winter light pouring through the window behind him. When he spoke, his voice was uncertain.

"Ludo. Yes. Of course. I was . . . I was just—"

"Talking to yourself. I heard. Listen to me, Luciano. No, don't turn away. Listen. My dear chap, you must stop blaming yourself for your brother's death." Ludo strode across the room to where Luciano sat hunched in the window seat, looking utterly forlorn and knotting and unknotting his silk tie while staring desperately at anything other than Ludo.

"Blame myself?" He gave a mirthless laugh. "Well, of course I do. After all, no one else killed him. I *was* there. It was just him and me in the room at the time. I . . . I can't . . . D'you know, Ludo, I can't for the life of me remember how I actually did it? Killed him. You know? One minute we're thumping about, knocking lumps out of each other; next minute he's exsanguinating all over the table and I'm looking at my hands in horror. . . ." He shuddered at the memory, unconsciously winding his tie round and round his hands as if to bind them and thus render them unable to do more harm. "Who else can I blame, if not myself?"

Ludo laid a hand over Luciano's trembling ones. "I buried your brother, Luciano. Well, not exactly *buried*. Latch and I gave him a traditional Mafia send-off with the help of your dragon. Apparently it's not the first time that butler of yours has disposed of criminal lowlifes in your loch, but that's another story. Suffice it to say, we fitted your brother with a very fine pair of concrete overshoes and sank him in the middle of Lochnagargoyle—"

"Yes. Thank you. I appreciate everything you've done, but—"

"I haven't finished yet. When Latch and I lifted your brother's body off the billiard table, the cause of his death became immediately apparent."

Luciano's breath caught in his throat as Ludo carried on.

"I'm assuming you were unaware that you were playing host to a battalion of animated model soldiers?" Taking Luciano's stunned silence for a yes, Ludo continued, "Just as I'm also assuming that you hadn't realized that the same model soldiers had vowed to defend you and your family to the death, no matter what that entailed?"

Luciano's face resembled that of a condemned man who, by some unforeseen miracle, had just been accorded a stay of execution.

"Nor, on the fatal day in question, as the two of you lurched blindly toward the billiard table, were you to know that the entire battalion were in position with their spears held upright, ready to skewer your brother like a particularly unpleasant bug on a pin. . . ." Ludo stopped and waited for Luciano to catch up.

"You're telling me I didn't do it?" Luciano whispered.

Ludo nodded. "You didn't kill your brother. However, I have to say, thank heavens someone did. Or *several* someones. One last thing, before we go downstairs and join your family: Latch and I gave the soldiers from the battalion a decent burial, with full military honors. . . ." Ludo paused, then smiled. "So next summer, if the blooms in your wife's rose garden are particularly fine, it will undoubtedly be thanks to the Fifth Battalion of the Dragon's-Tooth Engineers."

"Ishn't Nieve a girl'sh name?"

"God, Titus. Say it, don't spray it. Stop stuffing food down your neck for just one millisecond while you speak, would you?"

"You heard me."

"Does it really matter what name they give him? He'll always be the Squirt as far as I'm concerned."

"God, Pan, that's *gross*. Not while I'm eating, if you please. Talking of which, d'you think anyone'll mind me sampling the buffet before the guests arrive? Saves me having to queue later on, huh? Wow. This stuff is *sensational*. Yum. What d'you think it is? This dip thing? I could eat that entire bowl myself. Come to think of it, I nearly have. Mmmmhmmm."

"Dad's *bagna cauda*?" Pandora waited until Titus had his mouth crammed full before saying, "Uh . . . anchovies, mainly. Why d'you ask?"

"Pass me the towel, dear, would you?"

Damp obediently dragged a fluffy white towel off the radiator and delivered it to Mrs. McLachlan. She was waiting patiently to see how scratchy cardigans would go down with the new baby, waiting to see if Nieve's lungs were half as good as she suspected. Mrs. McLachlan scooped Nieve out of the bath and was about to swaddle him in the towel when Damp saw something surprising.

"What's the matter, pet?" Mrs. McLachlan peered at Damp, then turned back to the baby. "Och, he's just a wee boy, pet. They all have those. Not like wee girls at all."

Damp's eyes grew wide, but she decided not to correct Mrs. McLachlan's assumption that she'd never seen Nieve undiapered. *That* wasn't even remotely interesting. Heaving a deep sigh, she wondered if she was the only one to notice that the baby hadn't entirely lost his magical covering of swansdown after the Sevens Wan enchantment wore off. As if snowflakes had settled like a mantle round his shoulders, baby Nieve was lightly dusted with downy feathers, giving him the appearance of a small angel recently fallen to Earth.

His navy blue eyes met hers, and Damp placed a finger across her lips as if to let her baby brother know that, for the time being at least, his secret was safe with her.

"Oh, come *on*. You don't believe in all that stuff, do you?" Receiving no answer to this, Titus rolled his eyes and slumped facedown on the rug. "Come off it, Pan. Act like a rational being for once. They're dice. Lumps of inert plastic. Much as I hate to be the one to break it to you, dice are immune to a woman's charms. You can lavish kisses upon their many dear little plastic faces until Hell freezes over and angels land in Argyll, but all to no avail. Read my lips. Kissing the dice isn't going to make any difference to how they fall."

Pandora ignored this completely, rolling the dice back and forth between her hands while concentrating very hard on exactly how much she desperately needed to win. If she'd remembered correctly, there were twenty-eight thousand, nine hundred and forty-six good reasons for why she had to throw a double six right now.

One last kiss for luck, then.

"Did you hear that?" Tock paused, halfway through a mouthful of water lily sandwich.

"What? The shrieking of a thwarted man-child?" Tarantella's mouthparts curved upward with delight. "About time, too. Let's hope his sister does the decent thing and eats him up immediately."

The roar of outrage came from one of the windows on the first floor, although whether it was made by Titus or Pandora was impossible to tell; under duress, Titus's voice was still indistinguishable from that of his sister. A listener standing on the rose quartz drive outside StregaSchloss might also have made out the murmur of many voices whose owners had raised crystal flutes of *prosecco* to welcome Baby Nieve, the newest Strega-Borgia, into their company.

Far, far harder to hear was the muted chink of pewter goblets, one against the other, as, in a firelit room, the ancestors drank a toast in celebration of their oldest and most elusive member, home at long last.

But only the keenest ears of all could hear the feathery hush of snow falling, flake upon flake, all around, for some sounds are most easily and clearly heard in the realm of our imaginations: we hear them in the waiting, listening hush between the dream and the awakening; in the indrawn breath of a new day; in the quiet beating of our own private hearts.

Afterword:
The White Paternoster

amp's spell to protect her family is, no doubt, yawningly familiar to a modern reader who might unwittingly dismiss it as a mere nursery rhyme, a vaguely interesting but forgettable relic that they had thought to put behind them, alongside the indignities of toilet training and other dimly remembered horrors of early childhood. However, it might interest a reader to know that the actual rhyme is centuries old.

When Damp invoked Matthew, Mark, Luke, and John, she too would have been blissfully unaware that she was tapping into an ancient and powerful magical tradition, older than even Strega-Nonna herself. Damp's rhyme was used across medieval Europe as a common prayer—the named pairs of angels invited to take up their positions round a child's bed were expected to act as a form of verbal armor-cladding to ward off evil. These kinds of common prayers were known as Lorica, derived from the Latin word *lorica*, which means "armored breastplate." This rhyme in particular was also known as the White Paternoster—*white* symbolizing its usage by ordinary people for good purposes, as opposed to a Black Paternoster, which was undoubtedly used by ordinary demons for evil purposes and most certainly hissed over the heads of the demon babies in the nurseries of Hades.

In the unlikely event that you've managed to live your whole life until now without ever clapping eyes on Damp's spell, here it is for your protection too.

> Matthew, Mark, Luke, and John,
> Bless the bed that I lie on.
> Four angels to my bed,
> Two to bottom, two to head.
> Two to hear me when I pray.
> Two to bear my soul away.

Gliossary

BLAG: To acquire something with the aid of much wheedling, begging, and making false promises. The blagger has no intention of repaying the favor. The blaggee has no idea of this, due to the blagger's skill at blagging. Not to be confused with borrowing, but, it has to be said, not a million miles distant from stealing.

BUNG: This is something akin to a bribe that is bunged your way in return for services rendered or to ensure your tactful silence. Unsurprisingly, a BUNG is another name for a cork or stopper, or something that shuts something else up. See also COCK-A-HOOP.

CLUEDON'T: This is a board game that bears a faint resemblance to the hugely successful Cluedo (U.K.) and Clue (U.S.). Unlike these two commercially produced games, CLUEDON'T was made for the Strega-Borgia family by a grateful houseguest with, it has to be said, a particularly gruesome sense of humor. The game of CLUEDON'T differs from the original in many ways, but in the interests of not having a Gliossary that ends up being thicker than the text it is attempting to Gliossarize, we need only concern ourselves here with the differences between the brutally elegant murder weapons of Clue (the rope, wrench, candlestick, etc.) and the upstart CLUEDON'T's assortment of raggle-taggle death-dealing artifacts.

So, inside the CLUEDON'T box, you might find:

The Dodgy Hair Dryer: One imagines the houseguest was

poking fun at StregaSchloss's antique and dangerous electrical wiring by creating here a murder weapon that electrocutes its victim.

The Flask of Botulinum Toxin: Again, this is the playful houseguest referring to the strong possibility of being poisoned by dining on badly canned food while a guest at Strega-Schloss.

The Concrete Overshoes: With these murder weapons, a player of CLUEDON'T is reminded of the Strega-Borgias' connection to the Italian Mafia. Victims are weighted down with concrete blocks and dropped into canals, oceans, and lakes, where they sink to the bottom, never to appear again.

The Box Jellyfish: Imagine a transparent blob of maritime menace infamously capable of killing its victims with just one sting. In CLUEDON'T, players can float the Box Jellyfish invisibly in water in the bathtub, kitchen sink, or even, memorably, inside the water that is always present in domestic toilets.

The Headphones of Doom: When placed over a victim's ears, these appear to be normal audio accessories until the victim's music of choice reaches a crescendo. No doubt the same houseguest who designed the entire CLUEDON'T game must have grown weary of the loud *tss tsss tss* coming from Titus's head, and imagined headphones with spring-loaded spikes hidden deep inside each cup. *Tss tsss tss-AUGHHHHHH!*

The Fatal Fishbone: I have encountered this thing's closest relative, the Nearly Fatal Fishbone. Over here in Scotland, we sometimes consume a smoked fish known as a kipper for breakfast. This is a dish for the very brave or the somewhat suicidal due to the diner having to be very careful not to inhale one of the millions of tiny, hairy fishbones that hide inside the kipper's exquisite flesh. Breakfast *not* being a time of day when I am either awake or in possession of fully functioning eyesight, I have unwittingly eaten forkfuls of Nearly Fatal Fishbones and only just narrowly escaped death. My fellow diners at these near-death breakfasts have been traumatized for life at the sight of me gagging, choking, turning blue, clawing at my throat, crashing backward off my seat, and thrashing on the floor to the accompaniment of noises more commonly associated with those of an espresso machine. *Bon appétit!* More kippers, anyone?

COCK-A-HOOP: Picture the scene. Back in the Middle Ages, the highlight of a weekend's entertainment could be found by partying in a drafty castle. Deer and swans were roasted on an open fire, the contents of huge wooden beer barrels were broached, and vast quantities of food and liquor were consumed. In order to keep the beer flowing swiftly, someone would remove the stopper from the beer barrel and allow the beer to flood forth. This stopper was known as a cock. No, I don't know why either. Please don't interrupt. The cock would be placed on top of one of the large metal hoops encircling the beer barrel as a signal to everyone that it was time to get down to some serious beer drinking. Hence, COCK-A-HOOP. *That* was the historical part. The meaning of the phrase is "full of joy, jubilant and rejoicing," which, I guess, is what you probably would have been feeling back in medieval times if you liked beer. If, however, like me, you preferred sparkling mineral water, you would have rolled your eyes and wished you'd been born five hundred years later.

FAFFING: From the verb "to faff," which means, roughly, "to flutter around in a useless fashion instead of getting on with a task." There also exists the derogatory form of "faff" used as a noun, as in, "That's a right *faff*," which translates as "That is a thankless task with many wearisome details that will consume my entire life only to spit my shriveled remains back out once said hideous task is completed." The alternative Scottish word with an identical meaning is "footer." This is not to be confused with a "First-Footer," which is the name given to the first person to set foot on one's doorstep after midnight on the 31st of December.

MONOPOLY: The U.S. version versus the U.K. version. You say tuh-may-toe, we say tuh-mah-toe. Yes, it's this old thing again. Two nations divided by a common language, et cetera. Titus and Pandora's battered old Monopoly board probably looks more or less the same as yours, except the names of the streets are different. So I have to ask you to picture, if you will, the layout of a British Monopoly board. After passing Go, clutching your two hundred pounds sterling, you whiz past a round of neighborhoods arranged in an ascending spiral of desirability and expensiveness. In the U.K., just before you've performed an entire circuit of the board, you enter the dizzyingly PUKKA and exclusive neighborhoods of Mayfair and Park Lane, in which a stray metal hat, car, or oddly hollow dog would stick out like a box of Krispy Kremes at a Weight WIBBLERS Anonymous Convention. I am reliably informed that the equivalent neighborhoods on your U.S. Monopoly board go by the names Park Place and Boardwalk, in which you are pleased to dock your metal ship, press your iron, or even kick your boot.

NAFFEST FIZZ: The cheapest, nastiest, most headache-inducing and liver-rotting effervescent white wine ever to be poured into a bottle and passed off as champagne. Perfect for giving to houseguests you never wish to see again and also ideal for removing those unsightly stains from sinks and toilets.

PONG: An unpleasant smell. Not as ghastly as a stink, but along the lines of a whiffy or even a niff. One could almost say that a PONG is a NAFF NIFF.

PORTAKABIN: A prefabricated office unit made by the company of the same name. Frequently found on building sites, these box-like constructions provide a convenient and instant haven from the elements, being warm, cozy, draftproof, and ultimately portable. These units have the added advantage of being able to be linked together into PORTAKABIN Central, or even stacked, one on top of the other, into PORTAKABIN Heights. Pronunciation is crucial to the desirability or otherwise of these boxes. For years, as a child, I thought they were called pour-takka-bins and thus were something to haul one's trash around inside, although why one would wish to do such a thing was, for me, just one of the many mysteries of grown-up life. In fact, I realized later, they are called porta (as in *portable*) kabins (as in *cabin*). There. See? Clear as mud.

PUKKA: Belonging to, or sounding like one comes from an aristocratic family who can trace their ancestors all the way back to the Middle Ages. A PUKKA accent sounds as if its owner is attempting to speak while holding a small plum in his or her mouth. Think Queen (the British regent, not the rock band). Remember how the British royal family speak? *You* (yes, *you*) can easily fake a PUKKA accent by sprinkling your conversation with some of the following:

"Oak-ay-yahh" for *yes*.

"I say" for *duhh*.

"Hee-ah, hee-ah" for *yes* x 2.

"Hoo . . . rahh" for *yes* x 3.

"Ebb-sull-yute-lay nurt" for *no way*.

Pronounced *PUCK-uh*.

WIBBLERS: This refers to that unfortunate sector of dragon-kind who have allowed their gross appetites free rein. Wolfing down princesses, knights, cupcakes, fries and mayonnaise, and lashings of sweet brown fizzy drinks, dragons who once had taut and muscular bodies are now wibbly-wobbly sacks-o'-flab. Hence the need for dragon diets, dragon gyms, and, regrettably, the magazine known as *Weight WIBBLERS Anonymous*, whose masthead reads *"If you wibble round your bum, then you sure need to swim and run,"* to which the only reply has to be *"If swimming is so good for keeping you slim, then explain whales!"*

WRINKLY ORIENTATED: Generated by, or on the subject of WRINKLIES. A WRINKLY is anyone who has crossed the invisible divide separating the years 25 and 26. Some may disagree and state categorically that WRINKLY-dom begins after 30; some thump their frail and antique fists and maintain that 40 is the threshold of decrepitude. Myself, I prefer to acknowledge that I am, indeed, a WRINKLY, but should I ever wish to reduce the pleated and folded nature of my WRINKLY skin, I could consume fries by the bucketload and within a short time, I'd metamorphose from WRINKLY to WIBBLER.

About the Author

Debi Gliori admits that she can't tone down her "gross and disgusting" nature, and her many fans love her for it. She also confesses a certain similarity between the passionate, colorful Strega-Borgias and her own family. She is the author of *Pure Dead Magic*, *Pure Dead Wicked*, *Pure Dead Brilliant*, *Pure Dead Trouble*, and *Pure Dead Batty* and has written and illustrated numerous picture books.

Ms. Gliori lives in Scotland and has at least five children and one golden retriever.